# KILLER INSTINCT

A SNAKE JONES MYSTERY

# KILLER INSTINCT

## MARILYN VICTOR AND MICHAEL ALLAN MALLORY

**FIVE STAR**
*A part of Gale, Cengage Learning*

GALE
CENGAGE Learning™

Detroit • New York • San Francisco • New Haven, Conn • Waterville, Maine • London

## GALE
CENGAGE Learning

**LIBRARY OF CONGRESS CATALOGING-IN-PUBLICATION DATA**

Victor, Marilyn.
    Killer instinct : a Snake Jones mystery / Marilyn Victor and Michael Allan Mallory. — 1st ed.
        p. cm.
    ISBN-13: 978-1-59414-894-1
    ISBN-10: 1-59414-894-5
    1. Zoologists—Fiction. 2. Women biologists—Fiction. 3. Environmentalists—Fiction. 4. Wolves—Control—Fiction. 5. Animal welfare—Fiction. 6. Superior National Forest (Minn.)—Fiction. 7. Minnesota—Fiction. I. Mallory, Michael Allan. II. Title.
    PS3622.I286K55 2010
    813'.6—dc22                                    2010036699

First Edition. First Printing: December 2010.
Published in 2010 in conjunction with Tekno Books and Ed Gorman.

Printed in the United States of America
1 2 3 4 5 6 7 14 13 12 11 10

# DEDICATION

To Alice Duncan, our wonderful editor, who offers nothing but encouragement and good suggestions. To the real Snake Jones for letting us borrow her name and putting her fictional self into harm's way. To Ella Pearson, our biggest fan. And to the memory of Steve Irwin and to all Wildlife Warriors everywhere.

# ACKNOWLEDGMENTS

The Minnesota Wolf Institute does not exist. Although the MWI was inspired by the International Wolf Center (IWC) in Ely, Minnesota, the events depicted in this story are fictional and have no connection to the IWC. The authors wish to thank the staff and administrators of the IWC for information that helped in the research for this book. Special thanks to Lori Schmidt, Wolf Curator, for answering questions and for her dedication to her mission. While trying to honor the spirit of the IWC, the authors have taken some liberties for dramatic purposes. Any opinions expressed in the following pages are not necessarily those of the staff of the IWC.

For more information about the mission of the International Wolf Center, or to make a donation, please check out their website at www.wolf.org.

Thanks to Dan Stark, Wolf Management Specialist for the Minnesota Department of Natural Resources; John Erb, DNR Wolf Biologist; and Mary Manning, DNR Conservation Officer for their invaluable information.

Appreciation to Jenny Barnett, Director of Wildlife Conservation at the Binder Park Zoo for her wolf escape story, which provided inspiration for parts of this novel.

And finally, many thanks to Jimmy Pichner of the Minnesota Zoo for his knowledge of firearms and his entertaining wolf stories.

## Acknowledgments

Any factual errors are entirely the responsibility of the authors.

# CHAPTER 1

I wanted to strangle the old man—if he didn't kill me first.

"The only good wolf is a dead wolf," he said, his nose pointed at me like a bayonet. "Shoot 'em all, every last one of 'em."

The sun was barely peeking over the tips of Superior National Forest and already I had riled up one of the locals. The only thing on my mind had been keeping my sleep-deprived eyes open long enough to pay Signe Amunson for a coffee and bran muffin, when the old geezer bulldozed into our conversation.

He hobbled closer, displaying an overcrowded mouth of yellow teeth. "Nothin' but varmints. Worthless murdering scavengers. We got rid of them in the old country. We should do it here, too!"

"Excuse me?"

"You heard me."

The old man's flannel shirt hung like limp laundry on a wire hanger, as if he had once been a more robust man. Stooped and worn, life in the North Country had obviously been hard on him. I should have felt some pity, or at least a little respect for my elders. Instead, I wanted to mount his grizzly old head on the wall with the rest of the hunting trophies hanging in Last Chance Outfitters.

Thankfully, the store had few shoppers this early and no one else to witness the steam geysering out my ears. I had been listening to this man's diatribe for the last ten minutes and was about to blow. For the moment, I struggled to hold on to my

9

temper and politely ignored the old codger's spittle sprinkling my jacket. With the Minnesota Valley Zoo logo stitched into the pocket, anything I said in anger might tarnish the reputation of the zoo.

He jabbed at me with a chicken bone of a finger. "You're cryin' boo-hoo because a few damned wolves got shot. Hell, whoever killed 'em ought to get a medal."

"Ivar Bjorklund." Signe rebuked him in a voice that could freeze molten lava. It drew a raised eyebrow from the other. "This young lady is a guest in our town—and a customer in my store—so I'll thank you not to harass her."

"Harass her? What about me? Them devils been harassing me for months!" His rheumy eyes bristled at me from beneath wiry, stark white eyebrows, as if I were personally responsible for his troubles.

"I'm sorry," I said, "I don't understand. Are you saying you're having trouble with wolves?"

Okay . . .

I'm not at my best before my first cup of coffee, and two nights of tossing and turning on Gina's lumpy couch hadn't made me any friendlier. Last night had been particularly hard, knowing this morning I'd be part of the team investigating the suspicious deaths of four wolves found in the woods just outside Wolf Lake. Still, I managed to count to ten. And took several deep breaths. It was past time to disarm the old fart. I deal with the uninformed, opinionated public all the time, so I knew how to be diplomatic.

I flashed him my sweetest, suck-up-to-the-donating-zoo-patrons smile and, with the same tone of voice I used when addressing children that don't know any better, introduced myself.

"I don't believe we've met. I'm Lavender Jones." I wasn't about to give this grumpy old coot any more ammunition by telling him everyone called me Snake. Snake? What the hell kind of name is that for a girl?

Bjorklund eyed my extended hand as if it were covered in hippopotamus poo. "I bet you're one of them damned SOS tree huggers, aren't you? We don't need any more of you goodie-two-boots up here. I heard what you said to Signe. You're here for them dead wolves those students found. You care more about them mangy four-legged varmints than honest, hard-working taxpayers. Whoever killed them wolves should've saved some ammo for the likes of you!"

"Ivar Bjorklund, that's enough!" Signe's hand slammed down on the wooden counter behind me, rattling the coins in her ancient cash register. The menace in her eye was as sharp as the hunting knives in the display rack next to her.

I squared my shoulders. A good cause was every bit as eye opening as a jolt of a double latte. I'd had a little too much of this old man's ignorant rhetoric this morning and was more than willing to let him have it with both barrels—

"Mr. Bjorklund." Gina jumped out from an aisle of Quetico backpacks she'd been lurking behind. No doubt enjoying my discomfort.

A small woman with long auburn hair, she placed her shapely frame between Bjorklund and me, where she stood her ground like a bull terrier up against an ornery steer. "You know who I am? Gina Brown from the wolf institute." Her commanding voice belied the sweet softness of her face.

I tried to move around her, but she put a hand out to stop me. This is the way it had been in college: me putting my foot in my mouth and Gina coming to the rescue. Her timing was better these days. This time she stopped me before I could taste shoe leather.

"I know who you are, Flicka," the old man answered, eyes narrowing into watery slits.

"Then you know if you've got a problem with the wolves, you

talk to me. Don't take it out on my friend. She's doesn't work at the institute."

Confused, Bjorklund jerked a thumb at my khaki jacket.

Gina shook her head. "That's not one of our uniforms. She works for the zoo down in Apple Valley. She's here to film *Zoofari.*" When the blank stare came, Gina added, "The wildlife series? Sunday night? Channel three?" She indicated my arm patch, hoping the visual aid would jog a response.

Ivar Bjorklund snorted. "From the Cities? Ain't that just wonderful." Meaning, of course, it wasn't. "Last thing we need is some fancy-ass six-one-two-er sticking her nose in our business."

"Enough!" Signe barreled around the counter, her ample breasts jutting out like a pair of targeted torpedoes. Easily she had fifty pounds on him and was just as tall. "This is my store and I won't let you treat a customer like that. I thought you had better manners Ivar Magnus Bjorklund." She planted her hands on her sturdy hips. "Lily would be ashamed of you."

At the mention of Lily, the old man wilted. I'd seen basset hounds with happier faces.

Gina tugged on my arm and yanked me into an aisle filled with Gore-Tex gear. "You got yourself in the middle of a firestorm that time."

"I could have handled it."

Gina snorted. "Yeah, like a rattlesnake. You were poised for the kill."

I didn't argue the point. Maybe it was just as well. I wasn't just representing the zoo but also *Zoofari*. Bad publicity would reflect on the show. And that mattered too much. Jeff and I had put a second mortgage on our home and sold off other assets to make the little zoo series our own. Which was why I was in Wolf Lake, scouting locations for our next episode. Headlines that read *Snake Jones Attacks Senior Citizen* wouldn't have gone far toward signing up the ever-important sponsors we needed. Although they might have gotten me a stint on *The Jerry Springer Show.*

"What was that crack about six-one-two-ers?" I asked, sneaking another peek at Bjorklund, who was getting a harsh dressing-down from Signe.

"Remember when Minneapolis and St. Paul were still under the six-one-two area code? Calling you a six-one-two-er is an old Wolf Lake slam." Her sly smile left me with the impression she was guilty of using the slur herself.

I smiled back thinly, willing myself to relax and take my internal warning system off full battle stations alert. It was kind of funny. I had wanted some local color. Just got a bit more than I had bargained for. I prided myself on being a pleasant, easy person to be with, not some crazy woman out to slap up angry old geezers.

"What was that about SOS?" I asked.

She lifted her shoulders. "Some eco-cranks leaving notes on people's doors. Call themselves Stewards of Superior." She offered me a sympathetic sigh. "You must have sucky karma. The crankiest guy in St. Louis County, and you find him. It's not usually this exciting around here, y'know."

I did know. As the gateway to the Boundary Waters Canoe Area Wilderness, Wolf Lake, Minnesota, was one of the crown jewels in the national park system. Dad used to rent a cabin on Burntside Lake, just northwest of town, for a week each July. With no hot running water or indoor plumbing, it hadn't been Mom's favorite vacation spot. So it was Dad's week with the kids while she stayed home to sanitize the house in peace and quiet. Like all tourist economies, Wolf Lake catered to its visitors. Signe's Last Chance Outfitters offered camping supplies, clothing, fishing gear, maps, and souvenirs to the curious and the ill prepared. Amid the birch wood wainscoting, rustic pine floorboards, and bodiless animal trophies mounted overhead, she had installed a convenient little grocery and coffee bar. These touches, coupled by her Mother Earth personality, made Signe's a sought-after comfort zone.

Peering into the glass case that protected life's greatest temptations, I gave into the comfort of a peanut butter candy bar. Bran muffin be damned, I decided. After enduring the abuse of Wolf Lake's most unlikable senior citizen, a little chocolate and peanut butter was just what the doctor ordered.

A hand touched my elbow, and I turned to face two old relics smiling at me from a small table at the fringe of the coffee bar. The two men had slipped in just as Bjorklund was finishing his diatribe. They turned toward me in unison, wilting flowers in twin pots angling for the sun.

"Don't let that old sour puss scare you off," Gus said in a raspy voice, more folds and creases etching his face than a Galapagos tortoise, except the tortoise had more hair.

"You bet," his companion agreed. Mooney winked suggestively. "We don't get enough cuties like you in here."

Gus gave a friendly display of teeth—what was left of them. "If you're not busy this evening, honey, I've got no plans."

Mooney chortled. "You don't have plans every evening!"

The two old retirees practically lived at Last Chance Outfitters, spending the better part of their day at the small table, playing the world's slowest game of checkers, and offering their opinions to anyone who'd listen. I'd spoken to them a few times since first making Signe's acquaintance.

"Sorry boys." Gina started guiding me away. "We need to get going. Peter's waiting."

Mooney perked up. "Peter Bunyan?"

"That's right."

"Say, ask him how his big brother Paul's doing. His *big* brother Paul."

"Yeah," Gus added, barely able to contain himself. "Ask him if he's still got that big blue ox."

The two old men chuckled at each other, as though sharing the in-joke of the century.

Gina rolled her eyes. "It wasn't funny the first twenty times, guys." Yet she still winked at them affectionately.

As we made for the exit, I glanced back to see Signe leaning over the counter, her hand gripped tightly around Ivar Bjork-lund's wrist. I couldn't hear what she was saying, but there was a minacious look on her face.

"How long does it take to pick up a couple cups of coffee?" Peter Bunyan jibed as I slid in next to him on the bench seat of his pickup. I handed him a steaming cup of joe.

"Ivar Bjorklund," was all Gina said as she pushed me closer to Peter and slammed the door shut.

Peter nodded with understanding and cranked the engine.

Outside Signe's, a carpenter dropped a pile of lumber next to the rickety timber stairs that led up to the store. He took a deep drag on his cigarette and blew smoke rings over his head as Bjorklund stepped into the open air, nearly taking a tumble over the loose logs. The cranky old Swede turned, snarled something I couldn't make out, and jabbed the bony chicken finger at the other man.

"That's Cole Novak," Gina explained with a nod toward the scruffy man who raised a one finger salute at the old goat's back. "There's no love lost between those two."

Bjorklund spat on the ground, then climbed the metal stairs into a bright yellow mini school bus. His Nordic features were austere and uncompromising behind the wheel, like the red iron ore rocks that had once been the boon to mining towns like Wolf Lake. As we pulled onto Sheridan Avenue, I twisted in my seat for a last glimpse. I couldn't see Bjorklund's face, only the morning sun glinting off the window glass as the bus passed beneath the pine bough insignia of Last Chance Outfitters.

I thought about the old man. His fury, so quick to spark, must rage from deep fires. I was curious and felt sorry for him at the same time. It was preferable to dwelling on the unpleasant task ahead of us. Four wild gray wolves were dead. Their carcasses found in Superior National Forest. Our job was to find out what and who had killed them.

# CHAPTER 2

"Nothing on GPS." Gina frowned at the handheld device.

The Department of Natural Resources truck sat on a side road off Highway 1, the crisp September air heavy with the scent of pine trees. On mornings like this frost nipped at your ankles before the sun climbed high, a chilly reminder that the forest and its creatures would soon prepare for winter as only felt in the North Woods.

Gina stood in the bed of the Dodge Ram 2500. Her knees pressed against the rear window, a Yagi antenna now in one hand, a receiver in the other, trying to catch a signal from a radio collar. If she did, it would make finding the dead wolves a whole lot easier. After a few seconds, she shook her head. "Nothing on GPS or VHF. Either those bad boys weren't collared or the collars stopped working." She set down the equipment and jumped out of the truck.

Peter slipped on a pair of mirrored aviator shades. "Or maybe someone disabled the collars."

"Wouldn't the collars send out some kind of signal after the wolves stopped moving?" I asked, feeling the odd duck here. Peter was a conservation officer for the DNR. Gina, my old college friend, worked as a wolf biologist at the Minnesota Wolf Institute. Most of my waking hours were spent on the Minnesota Valley Zoo's tropics and Australian trails. Sun bears and kangaroos were more my style, so I was excited to immerse myself in *Canis lupus,* creature of legend and mythology.

17

"They probably are," Gina said. "Problem is, we don't have the resources to check the signals on a daily basis. The last time I did any aerial tracking was two weeks ago. A lot can happen in two weeks."

"That sucks." I knew about tight budgets and priorities. It was how Jeff and I ended up owning *Zoofari*. Originally the brainstorm of the Minnesota Valley Zoo, a lack of funding had forced them to cut the program, giving Jeff and me the opportunity to mortgage our lives to keep *Zoofari* going. Only now that they were no longer responsible for the series, the zoo wasn't as eager to give us time off to film it, and vacation time was quickly dwindling.

Peter leaned against the hood of his pickup with an inquisitive smile. "You look preoccupied, Snake."

"Do I?"

"It's Ivar," Gina said. "He chewed on her quite a bit back at Signe's."

Peter scratched his jaw. "He does have a short fuse these days. He still hasn't adjusted to being without Lily."

"That's his wife?" I asked.

Gina nodded.

"I gather she passed away."

"Poor Lily died six months ago. Some kind of cancer."

"Oh, Gina, that's so recent. No wonder the old guy was in a foul mood."

"I s'pose. Ivar and Lily were together nearly forty years. Their only son died during Desert Storm. Then Lily got sick. Being alone has been tough on him."

"He's mad at the world and everyone in it," Peter said in honeyed tones that could've guaranteed a career in broadcast radio, a voice capable of making you believe anything. Fortyish, with a Dudley Do-Right chin and a lumberjack's sturdy physique, Conservation Officer Peter Bunyan wore a persistent half-smile that gave you the uncanny feeling he knew your secrets and might tell if you didn't cooperate. Quiet authority radiated from him. In his easy posture. His confident demeanor. The uniform helped. He looked very official in the khaki shirt with the DNR shield arm patch. Dark green shoulder bars and pocket flaps heightened the sense of authority. So did the sidearm.

With an impatient glance at us, Gina opened the truck door. "We should get moving."

Too bad. The cool morning air and sun felt good. But we had a job to do, so we climbed into the green pickup and rumbled on. Highway 1 out of Wolf Lake hadn't changed much since I was a kid. It had been hacked out of the dense wilderness in the early 1920s as a logging road. Beautifully scenic, it had no breakdown lane. The trees ran up to the edge of the curving, twisting roadway like crazed fans at a rock concert rushing up to the stage. At nearly four million acres, Superior National Forest was the largest boreal forest in America, boasting over a thousand pristine lakes and streams surrounded by dense tracks of coniferous and deciduous forest.

As we picked up speed, the ride grew more dangerous. Points along the highway twisted and turned as treacherously as an Olympic bobsled run.

"Why is Mr. Bjorklund so down on wolves?" I asked after we'd put on a few miles.

Peter took his eyes off the road for a moment to turn my way. "The short answer is economics. Ivar runs a small sheep farm down in Red Iron. He's lost a couple of sheep to predation recently. He blames the wolves. The Feds will still compensate him, but it isn't enough. He's been driving a school bus to make ends meet."

That earned a modicum of compassion for the old man. Out here in the middle of the boreal forest, without family, the loss of a close loved one, particularly a spouse, could be more than life changing; it could be catastrophic. And then to have to worry about finances on top of it. There was something terribly wrong with the world when a man his age, who had worked hard all of his life, had to take a second job to survive.

"Was it?" I asked. "Wolves, I mean."

"More likely coyotes," Peter answered. "Or a feral dog. Not that you'll convince Ivar of that."

"Yeah, he hates wolves. Do many people up here feel the way he does?"

"Not as many as in the old days."

Gina grunted in agreement. "It's been more than forty years since an Iron Range politician dragged frozen wolf carcasses onto the steps of the state capital. In those days hating wolves was good politics."

"I'm afraid she's right," Peter acknowledged. "Maybe it was because Minnesota still had wolves. All the other states back then, except Alaska, had exterminated their populations."

Peter had touched a nerve. Gina swiveled around, her brown eyes large. "Thank God the late sixties changed that. The environmental movement made people think of nature differently, more holistically. Attitudes began to change." She exhaled with a measure of satisfaction. "People up here in the Arrowhead region love living in the wilderness. Most of them also love the creatures that live here with them."

"Most," agreed Peter, "but not all."

A crease darkened her brow. "There's a holdover from when the gray wolf was protected by the Feds. Earlier this year the management of the wolf population was turned over to the State."

"Other folks, like farmers and ranchers, are concerned for their livelihoods."

Gina snorted and turned away to gaze out her open window,

oddly silent, as though she were holding back. Sitting beside her, I could feel nervous tension oozing from her. And when she looped a wayward strand of hair behind her ear, I caught a slight tremble in her hand. This couldn't be easy for her. Tracking the local wolf packs was part of her job. It occurred to me, as I'm sure it had occurred to Gina, that it was possible she knew the very wolves we were searching for today. That upped the stakes.

The truck slowed and turned off Highway 1 onto the belly of Black Fir Road, a lonely stretch of gravel that snaked on for miles.

"Watch the road, ladies," Peter's soothing voice advised. "Since we can't count on the radio collars, we'll have to do this the old-fashioned way. That marker should show up in the next five miles."

Good thinking on the part of those bicyclists, I thought. They'd had the presence of mind to mark the location after stumbling across the wolf carcasses. After a long day trip, the two college students had stopped to relieve themselves in the woods, nearly tripping over the remains in the underbrush. Deciding they couldn't ignore this, the two young men stripped an aspen branch and jammed it into the side of the road, then pedaled back to Wolf Lake to report their find.

Yes, good thinking. However, spotting one skinny stick against the backdrop of the forest was like, well, finding a stick in the forest.

A yellow cloud swirled up on the road ahead. The dust devil raced toward us.

Peter cracked a smile. "Lyle Almquist." He uttered the name as though no less a personage than Elvis Presley had emerged from the woods. "Lyle lives out here. We're driving through Red Iron Township. Population eighty-three. Don't strain your eyes looking for a town. The houses are scattered in the forest. Folks out here like their privacy."

The yellow cloud loomed larger. Peter angled the truck closer to the right shoulder where tree branches whipped perilously close to Gina's window.

"Hey, watch it." She shied back.

"Sorry," Peter sang out, enjoying the moment. "Gotta give Lyle a wide berth. He's getting up there in years and likes the center of the road."

Lovely.

Not exactly a confidence builder. My eyes fixed on the oncoming missile, expecting it to veer away once the driver got close. He didn't. The rusty, dented white truck clanked by us at full speed, hell bent for somewhere. All I saw of the driver was a beefy flannel-covered arm that waved as it passed. The rear of the pickup was a blur of wooden posts, pulleys, rusty chains and two heavily scratched and banged-up fifty-five-gallon drums that shimmied like fat fleas on a hot griddle.

Peter steered us back to our full lane, his square chin lifting as he glanced into the rearview mirror. "Lyle would be a good guy to talk to. He knows this area and may have seen something. Lived here his whole life. Worked the iron ore mines when he was young. Now he's a leather crafter. Signe and some of the other merchants sell his trinkets."

"Crafts," Gina corrected, rolling her eyes. "Trinkets sound so cheap. There's nothing cheap about Lyle's work. Snake, his tooled leather belts are works of art. And his deerskin jackets! Gorgeous."

If Gina's rebuke had bothered Peter, I couldn't tell. He smiled back unfazed. "My point was that Lyle may drive like the devil, but he's good with his hands. A bit long in the tooth, but he keeps his eyes open."

"On that note, guys," Gina said, "we should be watching the road. That marker should be coming up soon."

The trees rushed by with a relentless sameness, offering no landmarks, no point of reference. I began to wonder if we'd already missed the marker.

Then—

"Wait! Over there." I pointed, squinting through the sun's glare on the windshield. "See them?"

"See what?" Peter scanned the road.

"Ravens. Up in that tree. Hear them?"

A flock of the large black birds perched in the upper branches of a sprawling oak, dark specks against a lush green backdrop. More of the birds soared into view to roost on the tree as their raucous cawing filtered over the engine of the truck.

Gina angled her head out the window for a better look. "That's it. I can see the marker. Good work, Snake." She fell back into her seat, a stricken expression on her face. "She's a great observer. Didn't I tell you?" Her praise was mitigated by the dread of what was to come.

"Wolf birds." Peter nodded approvingly. "You know a thing or two about wolves after all."

I was gratified I'd impressed him. Fortunately, I had spent the last two days at the wolf institute, surrounded by people dedicated to the study of this remarkable animal. I was bound to absorb something. Ravens are known as wolf birds because they often fly after wolf packs. Being opportunistic birds, they've been known to alert wolves to possible prey, getting a share of the spoils as their reward. My guess was these ravens were still with the wolves they had followed, scavenging them as they would have any other kill.

The birds scattered as the pickup pulled onto the shoulder. They circled above in a dark spiral, a few alighting on the high branches of the oak where they stared at us with indignant black eyes. The three of us stepped carefully through the thicket of trees, searching the ground clutter for signs.

It would be easy to get lost in these woods. Raw wilderness extended as far as the eye could see. My hiking boots forged through the scrub grass and I ducked under a fir branch. It was a daunting place of ankle-eating ruts and shadowy hollows surrounded by legions of silent timber grenadiers, where darkness could swoop down with a heart-catching suddenness.

A pang of dread fisted around my heart at the bleak prospect of what lay ahead. After a few false turns, a flutter of black wings behind a wild blueberry bush drew our attention.

"That's it," Peter said darkly.

The grip on my heart tightened.

"Oh—" Gina stopped dead in her tracks.

There were four carcasses in all. Tossed in a loose pile, pockmarked by small bloodied rips where the ravens had picked at the bodies. Without the ripping jaws of the wolves to do their work for them, the birds had struggled to tear open the flesh.

Gina and I stood by quietly as Peter knelt to examine the remains. At the sound of a raspy-throated *Hraaak! Hraaak!* I gazed upward and smiled at a great blue heron soaring overhead, a welcome distraction, given the solemnity of the moment. After it flew behind me, I sidled over to a gap in the trees for a better view of the wonderful specimen. Blue-gray wings laconically flapped a quarter mile away toward a hill, which rose above the endless tree canopy like an island amid a green ocean. Two birch trees shot up from the hill top, leaning toward each other like a big white X. The heron came to rest upon one of the upper branches, where it became a dark speck against the forest.

I turned back to Peter as he stirred. "Looks like they were shot. I see the entry points." Raking the nearby ground with his eyes, he stood up, walked around the area briefly before coming back to where we stood. "The carcasses were dumped here. They were killed somewhere else."

"Ya think?" Gina mocked with surprising acrimony. "I doubt four wolves dropped dead on top of each other on their own."

Peter's gaze was steady, patient. "That has nothing to do with it. There's not enough blood. No shell casings."

"And too many trees," I added. "How could anyone shoot four live wolves with this much cover?"

Peter Bunyan smiled his funny half-smile.

"What?" I said after a moment.

"Gina was right about you, Snake. You notice things."

Normally, I'd glow at a compliment like that. Not this time. The senseless waste of wildlife saddened me. Sickened my sense of morality. Tears stung at the corners of my eyes and I tried to think of something else. Jeff. His ten thousand–watt smile. A fight I had had with my brother. I'd seen senseless killings before, but would never become desensitized to them.

"Who would do this?" I asked, the words catching in my throat.

"Who wouldn't?" Gina said bitterly, her eyes glued to the gruesome mound of wolf flesh. "Ever since the Feds took them off the Endangered Species List, there have been people just itchin' for open season."

"That's not fair, Gina." Peter came to stand beside her, watching her closely.

"Isn't it? Those were collared animals." Gina's petite frame stiffened as her gaze hardened. "Part of the Red Iron Pack. The one at the bottom was the dominant male. The one with the white tipped tail—I put the radio collar on him myself."

The collars were now conspicuously missing from the dead animals. I put a hand on her shoulder to acknowledge her pain. She shrugged it off. The senseless carnage was awful, but so much worse when you had personally worked with the animals. Gina had been tracking this pack for months.

"It's crap like this that makes me ashamed to be a member of the human race." Gina swung around and stomped off into the dark shelter of a stand of jack pines.

Peter signaled for me to follow him. "Give her a moment." We walked back to the DNR truck together. "Let's get the tarps. I want a necropsy done on these guys as soon as possible."

In the trees behind us, alone with the dead animals, Gina Brown vented to the forest, the full fury of her rage unleashed. She blasted the tree canopy with the f-bomb several times, sending the ravens off in a cacophony of squawks and beating wings.

"You gutless son of a bitch!" she screamed. "You worthless piece of shit! I won't let you get away with this!"

Peter and I exchanged looks. Even he seemed concerned. This wasn't the Gina Brown I remembered from college. That Gina had been able to take life's punches on the chin without losing a smile. The woman raging in the woods was a smoldering stick of dynamite. It wasn't just the dead wolves, I began to realize; something else was going on. The way she sniped at Peter suggested a history between them. But I couldn't ask. Not now.

Opening the glove box, he handed me a pair of work gloves and we pulled the tarps out of the back of the pickup.

A crunch of boots on dry ground announced Gina's return. She marched back toward us, hands clenched at her side. "I'm going to find who did this," she told us. "I'll hunt them down the same way they hunted those poor wolves."

Peter and I locked eyes.

# CHAPTER 3

"The woman's psychotic!"

"That's a bit extreme," I said, settling into the oversized armchair. I knew this could be a long phone conversation. I would have preferred to be in the kitchen helping Gina, closer to the delectable aromas of garlic and Italian spices, than discussing our mother with my kid sister.

"Schizoid, then." Cricket's voice whined at me from Gina's cell phone.

"Manipulative, maybe—"

"Overbearing. Interfering! You have to agree with interfering."

"I'll go with interfering."

"The woman needs a hobby—"

"You are her hobby!"

Silence.

I pictured my sister pacing back and forth across my kitchen, snatching up a potato chip each time she got within arm's reach of the counter. Cricket was a changeling. Unlike my brother and I, who were both tall, large-boned and cursed with unmanageable thick brown hair, our baby sister was elfin petite, blond and spilling over with nervous energy.

"Cricket?" I said at the prolonged silence "Are you there?"

"Yeah. I'm just thinking over what you said. You're right, Snake. I am Mom's hobby. How depressing."

My little sister had been one of those change-of-life babies.

Ten years younger than me, Mom had held on to her more tightly than a sloth to a tree. I'd always suspected it was because Dad was now gone and my mother felt she could undo some of his influence. Like her name. Gentian Clark is the name on my sister's birth certificate, continuing Mother Clark's floral name pattern for her girls. Dad bestowed the nickname on to Gen and she became Cricket, much to Mom's chagrin. After a lifetime of watching the younger Clark girl bend to her mother's wishes, it amused me to see Cricket only now starting to rebel against the woman.

"She's driving me nuts!" Cricket's voice spiked and I pulled my ear away from the phone. I slouched down in the comfy chair. This was going to be good.

"What's her latest outrage?" I hated to ask, but felt that familiar big sister obligation pulling words out of my mouth.

"A blind date—"

"Another one? What happened to the last guy Mom set you up with?"

"You mean overdriven-successful-emotionally-unavailable guy? Or was it I-don't-read-books-they're-too-much-of-a-commitment guy?"

I snorted into the phone, enjoying the irony. I've wrestled crocodiles in Australia, rounded up feral pigs in Tasmania and rooted for poisonous snakes in the sagebrush of the Arizona desert, yet my little sister regularly and fearlessly went on blind dates set up by our mother. And people call me brave!

"Three days at your house has been a vacation." Cricket munched on another potato chip. "With you and Jeff traveling so much, I should probably just move in. You've got that extra room over the barn. I can keep an eye on things when you're gone."

Bad idea. Not that I was against my little sister living with me. The flaw was that Mother would blame me for masterminding the plan. Not that Cricket would care. I'd be the one catching the heat. I just wasn't in the mood to go into that with her.

A banging pan in the direction of the kitchen paved my escape. "Cricket, I gotta go."

"I'll even pay rent!"

"Gina needs help in the kitchen." I was already shuffling across the hardwood floor to the kitchen, motioning to Gina to bang the pans some more.

"I sense chickening out here," Cricket accused. "You're not afraid of getting on Mom's bad side, are you?"

"Yes! Gotta run. Goodbye."

"Little sister?" Gina asked, her back to me as she mixed a pot of marinara sauce on the stove. For the past hour, the detectable aroma of garlic and Italian spices had wafted from the kitchen. My stomach was growling.

"Thanks for letting me use your cell phone. Mine couldn't pick up a signal."

"It happens. You seem a little down. Bad news?"

"No, just feel a little guilty hanging up on her. Sometimes Cricket doesn't understand the meaning of the word no."

"Gee. I wonder where she got that from?"

I cringed. "Please tell me I was never that bad."

Gina nodded toward the bookshelf against the living room wall. "Remember when that picture was taken?"

The bookshelf was an assembly of bricks and pine boards stacked one atop the other. A very homemade utilitarian structure. Very Gina Brown. I picked up the five by seven frame. Four delirious, scruffy and very hungry girls grinned out from the photo. Gina and I sat in the middle, arms dangling around each other's neck. It was our first year at college and we looked it. My hair was cropped short back then. I'd learned how much electricity a hair dryer used, so the hair had been sacrificed to save the planet. Gina had lost the baby fat since then. She was even more of a looker now.

She wandered over, wiping her hands on a dishtowel and wearing an air of domestic contentment. It pleased me to see the rigors of the day behind her, the dead wolves pushed to the back of her mind, at least temporarily. The yoga session she'd talked me through had helped ease her tension, while the meditation soothed scuffed emotions. Once again she seemed the Gina I'd known from our days at Northland College.

"Remember that trip was your idea." Gina gave me The Look, implying it had been all my fault. "You whined, begged, cajoled and threatened until we got so sick of listening to you, we finally said yes."

I tilted my head back and laughed. Up to that point, all my previous nature encounters had involved a cozy cabin in a well-stocked resort. "No showers, no electricity, bad food, no motor vehicles for a week. Just the four of us camping and canoeing."

"And you forgot the toilet paper."

"And we had to use leaves." I had been about the same age Cricket was now. Thinking of it that way, I knew we had been way too young and ill prepared for that trip. Four young city girls, exerting their independence in the Boundary Waters of northern Minnesota.

"My butt was sore for a week." Gina scratched the rear of her sweatpants as she shuffled back to the kitchen to tend the pasta.

So happy were we to see civilization after seven days in the wilderness, we headed straight for the Pizza Hut in Wolf Lake and ordered more food than we could have scarfed down in a week. Our hot young waiter had taken the photo in exchange for Gina's phone number.

Gina motioned me toward the round dining table and refilled my wine glass. "Dinner is served."

Considering she used to think McDonald's was a gourmet meal, I was surprised cooking a marinara sauce from scratch

"Who are these people?"

"Nobody knows. Those things"—her hand fluttered at the paper as though it were contaminated—"started showing up about six months ago."

While annoying and intimidating, I found it difficult to see the posting of the flyer as anything more than a rag-tag group of environmentalists trying to raise the awareness of people. Misguided and not very effective, but relatively harmless.

Gina saw it otherwise. My lack of outrage only stoked her fires. "These guys are like the KKK! They hide behind their anonymity so they don't have to answer to anyone!" She balled her hands into angry fists that seemed to grab the air by its lapels. "Fanatics who work in secret have no one to hold them accountable. They can go ape shit without paying the price. When groups believe their own dogma without question, believe they're the guardians of morality and that they're the only defenders of truth or goodness, that's when things get scary. You know what comes after that, don't you?"

I took a step back from the venom in her voice. "What?"

Her eyes narrowed and her voice darkened. "They turn violent."

*They turn violent.*

Those words would later swoop back down on me as being strangely prophetic.

# CHAPTER 4

The Dodge Ram bumped along the loose gravel road. The dense green landscape of aspen, black fir, elm and white-cedar dipped and rolled with the undulations of Black Fir Road. If another vehicle had been a hundred feet ahead or behind us, we couldn't tell.

"My theory," explained Peter Bunyan as he gripped the wheel, "is that with millions of acres of forest at his disposal, our wolf shooter didn't have to travel far to dump the remains. So why would he?"

I saw his point. "Anyplace would do. Trees, shrubs, under-growth, it's all pretty much the same."

"Right. No point driving fifty miles to dump the carcasses when you've got the same woods nearby. Which means our shooter is probably a local, someone who lives within five or ten miles of the dump location."

"That covers a lot of people."

"Except"—Peter smiled at me—"an old chum of yours lives just two miles west of the dump area. Ivar Bjorklund."

"So that's where we're going."

"I thought that'd interest you, Snake."

How convenient that Bjorklund lived so close to where we'd collected the wolf remains. That and his ornery attitude from the day before made the old coot my number one suspect, unfair as that seemed.

I was flattered Peter had invited me along, considering it

should have been Gina, with me shadowing them. However, at the last minute she begged off. Too much going on at the wolf institute today and, she admitted, she was still too upset over yesterday. She'd worked closely with the Red Iron pack. Seeing those carcasses stacked like cord wood had been too much for her. Gina had insisted I go with Peter, and he was too much of a gentleman to uninvite me. In one sense, I wish he had. I had a *Zoofari* segment yet to organize. When Jeff and the crew arrived in Wolf Lake in a few days they'd want to start shooting footage and get back home.

I probably should have turned Peter down.

Truth was I didn't want to be with Gina all day. Not today. It shamed me to realize it. I loved reconnecting with her after so many years, but her volcanic outburst in the forest yesterday and her rant last night at finding the SOS flyer made me uneasy. Something was wrong with her. The feisty yet sweet young woman I'd known a decade ago seemed like a Jekyll and Hyde, one minute spouting New Age aphorisms of finding nirvana in the North Woods, then charging around the next like a wounded Tasmanian devil.

I needed time away from her. Besides, accompanying the DNR CO made me feel like I was helping. Make no mistake, I wanted to catch the creep who'd shot those wolves as much as anybody.

The pickup turned off Black Fir Road onto a dirt driveway. The name on the rusty mailbox said Bjorklund. I inhaled sharply.

"You up for this?"

"Sure," I said.

Peter called my bluff. "I'm not convinced," he said, and chuckled.

"I'll be okay."

At the end of the driveway sat a squat, neglected rambler-style house. Faded lemon siding and two hues of peeling blue trim boards spoke of better times. Off to the side a rotting wood frame suggested a garden, yet rather than flowers or vegetables, this garden yielded stones. Large and plentiful. Apparently, it had been a good year for rocks. In front of the property sat two vehicles, one a mud-splattered Chevy Blazer and the other a white Grand Prix.

I sat up, turning to Peter. "We're looking for someone who drives a truck or has a trailer."

"What makes you say that?"

"It's a safe bet the shooter didn't haul four bloody wolf carcasses in the back seat of his BMW."

Peter chuckled. "The only problem with your suggestion is our location. You know how many people in the Iron Range drive a pickup, SUV or have a trailer hitch?"

"A lot of them, I suppose."

"The same goes for the rifle. The necropsy and ballistics reports came back this morning. The wolves were shot with .30-06 slugs, probably from a fast-action rifle. Pump or lever. Although," he reconsidered, "I wouldn't rule out a bolt-action rifle."

I took his word for it. What I know about guns you could write on the back of a fly's wing. On the other hand, you could write what I know about flies on both sides of a gunstock.

"Could they have been trapped and shot at close range?" I had read about some of the trapping methods in Trudeau's book last night. Steel jaws were preferred. Then the animal was dispatched with a bullet to the head—if he hadn't chewed his leg off and escaped.

"The bullet wounds say otherwise."

That at least was a relief. If they had been shot in the wild, I liked to think that they had at least had a chance to run.

He shook his head. "I'm making this more complicated than

it has to be. You were right. Those four wolves were probably shot in an open area. Maybe even a rendezvous site."

"Wouldn't the first shot have scattered the animals?"

"Not really. They'd want to know what direction the danger's coming from in order to know where it's safe to run to. For a few seconds they'd hesitate as the bullets flew."

Peter killed the engine and eyed the new, sparkling white Grand Prix that mocked the aging Blazer. "What's Forrest Hansen doing here this time of day?" Cocking his head toward me, he explained, "Hansen lives just down the road. Our next stop. Guess this saves us a trip." Though Peter didn't seem all that happy about it.

Two men appeared around the corner of one of the faded red barns, a large, classical structure with a badly patched roof. One was the stooping figure of Ivar Bjorklund. I assumed the younger man by his side was Forrest Hansen. As soon as they saw us, their conversation came to an abrupt stop.

They barely gave Peter Bunyan a glance as we slid out of the truck. Instead, both men fixated on me. I tried not to fidget, once more questioning my motives for coming. Had they sensed I was excess baggage? A fraud? It couldn't have been my stunning good looks. My husband tells me I'm gorgeous. But then he thinks his favorite crocodile is a beauty, too. And right now I would have preferred fending off the predatory gaze of a hungry croc to the glare the two men directed at me.

Peter slipped off his sunglasses and slid them into his jacket pocket. He oozed quiet authority in his uniform, a fact he seemed to emphasize, resting his hand on his sidearm. "Ivar. Forrest." He gave them each a curt nod before introducing me. "Ivar, you've already met Snake Jones."

The old Swede narrowed his eyes suspiciously. "Didn't call herself that yesterday. Said her name was Lilac or something."

I brushed my ponytail off the back of my collar and smoothed out my jacket, hoping I, too, could wear an air of authority. "Lavender's my given name. My friends call me Snake." And you could be my friend, too, you old grump. Just don't go all cranky on me.

I offered my hand as a token. This time Bjorklund accepted it, more out of habit than actual courtesy I suspected. Or it could have been Peter's presence that encouraged him to be civil. He stuffed the piece of paper he had been holding into his shirt pocket and offered me a slab of a hand: dry, callused, and devoid of heat, like gripping a chunk of tundra turf. I expected it to crumble in my hand. His lips barely twitched, an attempt at a smile, although I'd want that verified by a panel of judges before I put myself out on a limb.

In contrast, Forrest Hansen was quite personable. A little too personable, I soon discovered.

"Nice to meet you," he drawled as though this were a life-changing moment. Mine.

Shorter than Bjorklund by a head, Hansen was close to my height: five foot six. Massive, muscled arms sprouted from a boulder-sized chest, giving the impression his head was swiveling between his shoulders without the benefit of a neck. Pumped up and ready to pop, he was a man involved in a serious love affair with heavy weights. And himself, if the tightly stretched black Spandex pullover was any indication.

"Forrest's a manager at Lohmann-Tate Paper Mill," Peter offered as I began thinking that no common laborer possessed the nicely manicured cuticles and smooth hands that were gripping mine in a double love fest. He wasn't letting go, either.

"Is there a mill in Wolf Lake?" I asked, smiling through gritted teeth as I snatched back my hand.

"I commute to Hibbing. Snake, huh?" He tilted his head back to give me the once-over. "How'd a pretty girl like you get a name like Snake?'

Oh please! Like I'd never heard that one before. Even Jimmy Dupinski had better pick-up lines back in the seventh grade. I let the comment pass. I had to play nice with the natives. His eyes sized me up like I was a prize filly at the state fair. Not even the pretense of subtlety. It creeped me out. Forrest Hansen's ego was as overly developed as his inflated biceps.

Ivar Bjorklund's physique was another story, more of a walking clothes rack than a man. He seemed in danger of withering away before my very eyes. Pale blue eyes flicked in my direction like an accusation. "This about them dead wolves? That why you brung her?"

Peter inclined his head, his square dimpled chin brushing the top of his collar. "We're investigating the shooting."

"Figured it wasn't about my livestock."

"That's not fair, Ivar. It hasn't been five weeks since I was here listening to your complaint. You submitted the compensation forms. It takes time—"

"Forget it." The other cut him off sharply. "Just makin' conversation, Peter. No need to get your shorts bunched in a knot. You wanna talk about dead wolves, fine. But I got work to do."

Without another word he swung about and tramped back toward the smaller of the two barns. At first glimpse, he appeared only slightly more durable than a house of cards. Yet he was still a big man, long-limbed, walking with a purposeful stride. If Hansen was an industrial complex, Bjorklund was a slum. The body of the old Swede was the ghost of a once vigorous man, a victim of time, sickness, or maybe the downhill slide after losing a loved one.

The second barn smelled of livestock and pine. It was a workshop, staging and storage area with large corrals and bins on the floor. Ropes, bailing wire and wooden hand tools hung neatly from an oak wall rack. If Bjorklund's house had been given over to neglect, his tools had not. They were worn but well cared for.

Peter, thumbs hooked in his belt, stood next to Hansen. "Surprised to see you here on a work day, Forrest."

A pair of heavily muscled shoulders gave an exaggerated shrug. "I'm taking a half day off to help Ivar with some chores. His hired help only comes twice a week and I wanted to bounce some ideas off him for a project at the mill."

Given Bjorklund's delicate physique, I wasn't sure you could bounce a nickel off the man without knocking him down.

A humorless smirk spread across the old man's face at Hansen's remark. "Worked at the paper mill for thirty-eight years. Until the accident." Bjorklund raised his left hand to display several crooked fingers. "Corrugating machine. Put me on long-term disability."

I shuddered at the thought of catching fingers in any kind of machine. A machine that corrugated sounded especially vicious. By now the two men had taken up positions at a large square table frame, a roll of chicken wire partially stretched across its top. Hansen flattened the wire in place while Bjorklund hammered it down. That's when I spied a pelt of fleece hanging from a hook behind them. I walked over to touch the lustrous, silky wool.

"Icelandic," Bjorklund grunted, still concentrating on his hammering.

"You raise Icelandic sheep?" I'd been to Iceland. For my earth studies group in college I'd spent three weeks on a sheep farm there. I had fallen in love with the rugged, pristine landscapes, glaciers and all. Which was saying a lot from a girl who hated the cold.

I let out a sigh of contentment as I brushed the luxurious pelt against my cheek. Peter quirked a curious eyebrow at me. I smiled back. "Icelandic sheep produce some of the most prized wools in the world. They're one of the oldest, purest breeds. Direct descendents of the sheep the early Vikings brought with them when they settled Iceland. They've never been cross-bred—at least in Iceland. They're the same as they were eleven hundred years ago." I sank my fingers into the tantalizingly soft wool.

Ivar Bjorklund regarded me with new eyes. *"Det var som tusan!"* Well, I'll be damned!

It was an expression I remembered from the sprightly old Swedish couple living across the alley when I grew up. It gave me a sense of power repeating it in front of my mother, the only time I could get away with swearing in our house. The fact that she was proud I was learning the language of her grandparents doubled the pleasure for me.

The corner of Bjorklund's mouth twitched. Not a smile. You could never call it a smile. More a tacit acknowledgment that I was okay, that I knew my stuff. Regarding me with a kind of benign tolerance, he indicated the table. "Come November is the second shearing. I'm making the place ready before it gets cold."

It was a fleece sorting table. Dirt and second cuts would fall through the screen openings to the barn floor as the wool was processed over it.

Peter took a step forward. "Can we get back to the wolves?" It wasn't a question. "They were killed five to six days ago. Their carcasses were found a few miles down the road. Did either of you hear gunshots or notice anything unusual during the last week?"

The two men exchanged a glance.

"I heard no shots," replied Bjorklund, dangling the hammer at his side.

"See a truck with something covered in the back?"

"No—well, except for that Cole Novak fella. The one fixin'

up Signe's steps," he added for my benefit. "He drove by in one 'a them SUVs with something sticking out the back. It was wrapped in canvas, I think."

Cole Novak. The carpenter I'd seen Bjorklund chewing out as we left Last Chance Outfitters yesterday.

Peter was interested. "Novak had something in his SUV? Could you tell what it was?"

"You don't listen very well, do you? I said it was covered up." Bjorklund hammered a staple through the wire with a decisive blow.

Peter shifted. "How about you, Forrest?"

Hansen sucked in a deep chest-inflating breath that was clearly meant for me. He was posing. Puffed up like a male sage grouse strutting his stuff for a would-be mate. I half-wondered if he was going to do the twitchy little dance that went with it.

"Haven't seen a thing, Bunyan." Hansen shot me a surreptitious leer. I smiled back thinly, though not for the reason he was thinking.

The conservation officer bit his lower lip while deliberating his next question. He proceeded with caution. "You know I have to ask this, guys. Either of you know who might've done this? Anyone been bragging about shooting at wolves?"

Hansen snorted. "Killing a wolf ain't no crime in my book."

"C'mon, Forrest . . ."

"Some of us don't care if you ever catch the guy. The way I see it, he did us a favor."

"Amen to that!" seconded Bjorklund with a vicious pound of his hammer.

"Guys, I'm just doing my job."

"Isn't it also your job to find the wolves responsible for killing Ivar's ewes?"

Peter's jaw muscles tightened. "I told you last time I don't think a wolf is your marauder; it's likely a stray coyote or a lynx.

Ivar, you filed for compensation—"

"Like I've tried to tell you before," Bjorklund said sourly. "They ain't stopping."

"Which is why last time I was here, I offered to get an Agri agent out to set traps and you said no."

"Traps won't stop 'em. Them wolves are too smart. I tell you what will work is if I start shooting the varmints."

"And you can do that."

"Since when?" Taken aback, the old man glanced at Hansen, who eyed the conservation officer with suspicion.

"I told you last time, Ivar. You have the right to protect your livestock under Minnesota law. You're allowed to shoot a wolf if it strays on your property and poses an immediate threat to your animals."

Bjorklund rested both hands on the sorting table and leaned forward, searching the face of the other. "What about the Feds? Won't they have something to say?"

"Not since the gray wolf was removed from federal protection. Now their management falls under the DNR's jurisdiction. I told you that, Ivar, not more than five months ago. Things may change again if the wolf is put back on the threatened list, but for now it's our responsibility."

A mixture of shock and surprise washed across both men's faces.

"So it's okay if I shoot a wolf on my property?" Bjorklund repeated.

"Yes," Peter said. "I'd rather you first attempted to scare it off, but if it's stalking one of your animals or about to attack, you can shoot to kill. However, you'll need to save the carcass and call the DNR."

Bjorklund and Hansen seemed surprised by Peter's information and darned pleased. Too pleased, if you asked me.

Peter stirred. He gestured toward the door. "I've always been up front with you, Ivar. I came here on other business, but I don't want you to feel like your problems aren't getting the attention they deserve. Let's go out and take another look at the most recent kill site. Maybe Snake'll see something I missed."

Bjorklund studied me skeptically but, after a moment's hesitation, he softened. He set down his hammer and led the way. He shuffled past the barns to the pasture beyond. Sheep with long, shaggy coats of cream, caramel, silver and milk chocolate dotted the open field. My steps lengthened, hurrying to the fence to get closer to his flock. I was careful to keep my hands off the triad of thin electrical wires that ran above the top rung of the fencing.

A ram approached the fence and stuck his nose through the slats, sniffing my outstretched hand. "They're gorgeous animals, Mr. Bjorklund."

The old Swede actually cracked a full smile this time, showcasing a mouth of yellow teeth. "That's Thorbjörn," he said, opening the gate and welcoming us through. "It means—"

"—Thor's bear. My grandfather's name was Thor Bjornson." I'd spent hours learning the meaning of my Swedish ancestors names from him. I could well imagine this shaggy animal standing by the side of the Norse god. Those thick curling horns would have been capable of creating quite a bit of thunder on their own.

We headed to an area where the small fenced-in pasture ran to the edge of the forest. I turned at the sound of a distant barking. At the far end of the field an energetic border collie disengaged from a group of sheep to run toward us at full stride, head down. The dog skidded to a stop next to Bjorklund, who stroked his head with open affection.

"Good boy, Oskar," he said.

Oskar barked twice and beat a quick tattoo on the ground with his tail. Then he rolled over to have his belly rubbed. He must've thought he was a good boy, too.

The woods beyond the fence loomed dark and tangled. Rough shrubs and tamaracks mixed with quaking aspens to form a shadowy thicket from which any creature could emerge without warning. Bjorklund regarded the timberline with unease before shifting his attention to the patch of ground at his feet. His mouth formed a severe line. "This is it."

Peter squatted to inspect the ground. "You've cleared away the blood and soil. Good."

"Lily loved that ewe," Bjorklund said with sweet nostalgia. "Tova. Peace of Thor. It was the first Icelandic we bought. All these sheep, they were her idea. Gave them all good Scandinavian names. And she knew the meaning of every last one of them."

He scanned the ground, head down, hiding the extra shine in his eyes. A pang of sympathy stabbed at my heart. I began to understand his anger at the wolves. They had taken more than his livestock; they had taken one of the few tangible threads still connecting him to his wife.

"Any other attacks?" Peter asked.

"No."

"Your sheep been acting up at all?"

Bjorklund jerked his thumb to the pasture. "Icelandics don't have the same herd instincts as other sheep. But they've been keeping their distance from this side of the fence, congregating near that tree." He pointed to where a group of eight animals clustered under the skirt of a large hemlock, munching at the grass. "They started doing that a couple weeks ago after the last attack. I don't dare leave Oskar out when I'm not around. He'd let a wolf tear him apart before he'd leave those sheep."

Peter acknowledged his concern with a slight nod. "The paw prints still here?"

"Yeah, they're there. Ain't had rain in awhile."

I'm a pretty fair tracker, not because I work with animals or any other professional training, but simply because it was something I enjoyed. Even as a kid I was always trying to pick out animal tracks wherever I went. I couldn't see these prints. Not at first. Finally, after focusing where Peter was scanning the ground, I began to see the nearly eroded markings in the patchy grass and hard earth. The partial oval pattern with four toe and claw points grew clearer. With a conservation officer standing in front of me I didn't feel it my place to speak.

"Like I said last time, Ivar. One animal. One paw print. Wolves usually hunt in packs."

The old Swede was unconvinced. "Could've been a lone wolf."

"Possibly. But it's an old print. Months old. And no other wolf signs. I think he was a traveler. Which is why I suspect some other animal is after your sheep."

"Hmmph!" Bjorklund grunted back. "But you can't be absolutely positive it ain't a wolf?"

"No . . . I can't."

Bjorklund shot Forrest Hansen a meaningful look. "Guess it's up to me to take care of things, then."

I didn't like the sound of that. Neither did Peter, judging by the way he stood up. "Ivar, be careful you stay within the law."

"What the hell's that supposed to mean?" Forrest Hansen glared back.

"It means you can't bait them to come on your property, you can't go off on an expedition to hunt them. The wolves still have protections under Minnesota law. If they're not on your property, leave them alone."

Hansen shook his head. "We're talking about a man defending his livelihood," he said with heat. "What if the wolf kills a sheep and trots off Ivar's property before he gets off a shot? Can Ivar chase after him? I bet not! The laws are set by Feds or lawmakers who're in the back pocket of the tree huggers. Don't hurt the animals!" Hansen mocked in a singsong voice. "Don't cut down the trees!" Hansen stood defiantly, aching for the discussion to come to blows.

Peter moistened his lips and drew in a long, calming breath. "All I'm doing is telling you what you can do and what you can't," he said, making sure Hansen appreciated the distinction.

"Don't give me that, Peter. You're protecting your wolves. It's only a matter of time before they attack again. It's their nature. Before long we'll be like they are in Idaho. There'll be no game here either."

I'd had about enough of this bonehead's opinions. I took a deep breath, repeating one of Gina's calming chants to myself.

"Critics said the same thing about reintroducing wolves back in Yellowstone, said the elk herds would suffer. Guess what? It didn't happen. In fact, the whole ecosystem improved after the wolves returned."

Hansen wasn't buying it. "The wolves kill too many animals. That leaves less game for sportsmen."

"So, you're a hunter, right?" I asked, not waiting for an answer, my voice level as I gave him the once-over. "And judging by all those muscles, you're pretty good at it."

The old Swede chuckled behind me. "Forrest took blue ribbons at the last two county fairs and was a sharpshooter in the Army."

"Really?" I feigned admiration. "Then you must kill every deer you shoot."

Another chuckle, which annoyed Hansen.

"No?"

"He didn't get squat last year."

"Near froze my ass off in that damned stand," Forrest grumbled.

"Gee, how's that possible? You with a high-powered rifle and the white-tailed deer population at record levels."

Muscle Boy eyed me suspiciously. "It's not that easy to hit a deer from a distance, particularly if it's moving."

I folded my arms across my chest and smiled. "Then you've got something in common with wolves. They're only successful bringing down their prey one in ten times. Which means most of the time they go hungry. And it's dangerous work. Since they primarily hunt large ungulates—deer, elk, moose—a powerful hoof to the head or sharp antler to the body could kill or maim."

Hansen waved me off. "You aren't going to change my mind. Wolves are predators. They don't belong in the woods with people. Look at our moose population. It's gone down."

"You can blame that one on climate change," Peter piped in. "Too many warm winters and hot summers. Not wolf predation."

Hansen glowered at us, fists closed at his side. At least my outburst had accomplished one thing; he was no longer flirting with me. "More government propaganda. Part of the Fed's plan to take away our guns. Get rid of the game animals, and sportsmen no longer need firearms."

My jaw dropped so far I thought it would bounce off the ground. I was speechless.

Peter didn't even bother concealing his amusement. "Kill all the game animals to get rid of your guns? I don't remember getting the memo on that one."

Hansen smoldered. He didn't like being mocked.

"Enough." Bjorklund put out a restraining hand when his friend made an aggressive move. "Forrest, shut up. You're starting to sound like that idiot Novak." The old man appealed to Peter. "All I care about are my sheep."

"I know, Ivar. Losing an animal is a hardship. I am trying to help. We need a measured response to these attacks."

"Pah!" Hansen spat. "More double talk."

"Forrest. Let it be. Peter's not the bad guy here."

Problem was, Hansen didn't want to let it be. His whole demeanor was like an attack dog straining at the leash.

"Forrest . . ." Bjorklund repeated, more forcibly this time.

The fire slowly subsided in Hansen's eyes but did not extinguish. His chest rose and fell with forced breaths. The clear message was that he had backed down only because of his friend.

Peter surveyed the sheep grazing in the pasture and offered Bjorklund an olive branch. "Look, I still think it's a coyote harassing your flock. I'm doing all I can to find him. Remember what I said. You can use your rifle to protect your livestock. Just be careful, okay?"

The sheep farmer nodded. He sent Oskar off to the far end of the pasture then turned toward Peter, mollified.

Harmony was restored. Or a semblance of it.

It didn't last.

We'd started back to the barns when I remembered something. I stopped in my tracks and the words blurted out. "Mr. Bjorklund, what kind of rifle do you own? Is it a .30-06?"

# CHAPTER 5

"Just in time for poop patrol!"

Debbie Wong's cheerful smile greeted me as she emerged from the wolf lab. I took the plastic bucket and aluminum tongs she offered.

She must've seen me coming. Picking up animal scat is not one of my favorite activities. However, Debbie made it sound like a grand day out. In this case, I had actually been looking forward to the task as part of the full MWI experience. After all, I'd hurried up to Wolf Lake on Friday just to make sure I was there for the weekly wolf feeding. In order to simulate the feast or famine of life in the wild, the wolves at the institute were only fed once every seven days. Along with other visitors sitting in the observation area, I'd been excited to watch one of Debbie's assistants roll out a wheelbarrow loaded with a road-kill deer, and dump it on the ground scant yards from the viewing window. Then the wolves were released from holding. They ran to their supper and began a methodical ripping and tearing of flesh. Having watched them devour the deer carcass, it seemed only fitting I return to help clean up the aftermath.

Debbie opened the tall gate to the chain-link fence and we entered the main enclosure. The wolf curator took special care to make sure the gate was secured after her. In the adjacent holding area, behind the fencing, four gray wolves paced anxiously, curious and concerned about the visitors in their enclosure. With them was Claudette, one of the wolf care staff, there to watch the animals and ensure their well-being, and our safety as well.

Three other staff members and long-term volunteers roamed the enclosure with us, each armed with a white bucket and metal tongs, eyes to the ground. In the wooded area just up the hill I glimpsed other staffers.

"How'd it go with Ivar?" Debbie inquired pleasantly, indicating a furry coil in the grass near my hiking boots.

I snatched up the scat and turned the tongs to examine my prize before dropping it in my bucket. Wolves chew through fur, skin, bone and sinew. They eat every part of their prey, the waste by-product of which resembled a furry dried sausage. No smell at all. When you don't get to eat regularly, you'd better have an efficient digestive system.

"I could live without another encounter with Ivar Bjorklund," I confessed.

It had not ended well at the sheep farmer's. Whatever rapport Peter had gained with the old man was crushed after my query about his weapons arsenal. With a Nordic curse, Bjorklund had tromped across the yard and into his house, anger giving him a spurt of surprising agility. When he returned with a rifle moments later, he rammed it into my chest. He then strongly suggested Peter and I get off his property. I felt like a fool. I'd needlessly upset the old man. I didn't want to tell Debbie how annoyed Peter had been with me.

I frowned at the crab grass. I'd have to apologize to Peter next time I saw him.

"Ivar's all right," Debbie said, misinterpreting my reaction. "A bit crusty, but that's just his way. He's going through a rough patch right now. Did you talk to anyone else about those dead wolves?" Her black eyes rested on me with keen interest.

"No, got sidetracked. We were on our way to talk to a Moua Vang, one of Bjorklund's neighbors, when Peter got a call on his truck radio. A driver reported seeing a moose caught in a wire fence on Highway 1."

"Oh, my."

"We were near the area, about fifteen minutes away."

"Is the moose okay?"

"Yeah. It was a young male. Got his antlers tangled up in an old piece of wire fence while he was grazing. Poor guy was spooked, but Peter calmed him down long enough for me to cut through the wire. Good thing he had those wire cutters in the back of his truck."

"And you guys made it out in one piece?"

"Barely! The moose kept jabbing his antlers at us while we tried to get him free."

Debbie clapped her hands together in delight. "Gina must've enjoyed that. She loves moose."

I didn't hide my surprise. "Gina wasn't with us. I thought she was here. She bowed out this morning, said she had too many things to get done at work."

"I haven't seen her all day."

I shook my head.

Debbie smiled knowingly and shrugged. The motion brushed her straight black hair against her shoulders and made the point more emphatically.

Gina had lied to me.

For an instant I didn't know how to react. I simply stood there with a puzzled expression that mirrored my confusion.

Around us, staffers walked with eyes to the ground in search of "diamonds in the rough." It reminded me of hunting for Easter eggs at my grandfather's farm, a comparison my mother would have found disgusting. I nearly commented on this when—

"Snake, I heard you were back!"

As if on cue, Gina waved from the tall metal gate. She closed it behind her with a decisive clang and strode across the grassy landscape.

"Gina!" Debbie welcomed in a dry tone. "We were just talking about you." She winked at me.

"Looks like Rufus's been at the saplings again." Gina grinned with affection. A dozen yards from us, two workmen were setting a small aspen into a hole near the man-made pond, the last of three young trees. Rufus had been the runt of the pups three years ago and now was a favorite. "He thinks the trees are big chew toys."

"So what have you been doing all day?" I asked, bending down to pick up another chunk of wolf scat.

She hesitated for a moment as if reluctant to tell me. "Ah, I was tracking."

I frowned. "Tracking what?"

She shrugged as if it was of no consequence. "I got a call from Scotty just after you left this morning."

"Scotty? The pilot?"

"Yes'm."

"You went aerial tracking without me?" Annoyance burned my cheeks. "Wasn't the plan to do this later so we could film it for *Zoofari*?" Shaggy, our cameraman, had talked about nothing else since we first decided to come up here. As he'd put it, he was stoked.

She was unabashed. "Sorry, Snake. I don't control the flight schedule. Remember I said it's kinda irregular? It depends on when Scotty can get the Cessna. A slot opened up today, so we jumped at the chance to take some readings."

True, she had said the plane, owned by the U.S. Geological Survey, was used for other duties besides aerial telemetry.

"I did try calling your cell, but all I got was your voice mail."

"Par for the course," I sighed. "I've had nothing but trouble getting a signal since I got to Wolf Lake."

I was still stewing. Not because I'd missed her call, but because she'd been the one who had insisted I go with Peter this morning without her, insisted her work at the wolf institute couldn't be put off. As a result I'd missed a fabulous opportunity to track wolves from the air.

I glared at Gina, who averted her eyes.

This wouldn't do, I realized. Maybe I was being too sensitive. Gina had a job to do without tripping over me everywhere. Her explanation had been plausible. Just let it go. After mucking things up with Peter earlier, I wasn't in a mood for more discord. I needed to make nice.

It was Gina who changed the subject. "How did it go with Peter this morning?"

"Okay. We didn't make any headway with Bjorklund. Didn't get any new info on those dead wolves."

Gina frowned. "Damn."

Debbie touched her gently on the arm. "I haven't seen you since yesterday. We were all sorry to hear those four wolves were from the Red Iron pack. You've been tracking them for a long time."

Tireless runners, gray wolves can cover up to fifty miles a day at a steady lope, which had left employees at the institute hoping the dead animals had been strangers passing through the area. Knowing they'd been members of a local pack had added to the sorrow felt by the staff.

"Whoa, ladies, looks like a somber party over there!"

The hyper enthusiastic voice came from the other end of the pond where Danny Hoffman straddled a landscape log with one foot and a small boulder with the other. He was in the act of emptying a plastic yellow bucket. A stream of water and minnows poured into the pond.

"Hope I'm not intruding." Danny approached with caution, his expressive face searching us out. He had the slim build of an eighteen-year-old in a middle-aged man's body, a stud in his left ear and a glint in his eye that came from being an entertainer.

"No, you're not," Debbie answered.

"Some pretty glum faces over here. Thought I'd commiserate with you ladies. Um, exactly what is it we're not happy about?"

Debbie explained about the wolf carcasses.

"I heard about it this morning. Anything new?"

"Not much," I answered. "Except we know someone shot the wolves with a .30-06 last week, according to the necropsy."

"That sucks, man. Why do people have to be such frickin' shitheads?"

It was one of the eternal questions of the Cosmos, for which I and every philosopher in western civilization had no answer. Before the topic of the dark nature of human kind dragged us further into the gloom, I shamelessly changed the subject.

"How're the minnows working out?"

Danny's enthusiasm popped up like a jack-in-the-box. "Way cool! We can't keep the pond stocked."

A very pleased Debbie Wong agreed. "It's the most successful enrichment we've added this year. The minnows bring out the hunting instinct in the wolves. Aila's learned to dunk her head to catch them."

"Rufus's been watching her," Danny added. "He's tried the head dunk, but he's also figured out how to use his big ol' paws to scoop them up."

I smiled back. Danny Hoffman was better than TV. In the few days I'd been at the facility, his stories had kept me laughing. The top button of his shirt was open. Something I'd never noticed before caught my attention.

"Danny, what's that on your neck?"

"It's a tattoo."

I leaned forward. "I'd asked for a refund. It's smudged."

"Oh, it's just a stick-on. My band played a gig last weekend.

Had to look the part. I am lead guitarist and singer."

"Stick-on? Isn't that kind of—pardon the expression—wimpy for a rocker? Why not a real tattoo?"

He balked. "Are you nuts? Those things hurt!"

I shook my head and smiled. "Artistic compromise, Danny?"

"You got it. Music is my passion. So're my guitars. Love my Fender Stratocaster. Didja know Jimi Hendrix closed Woodstock with a 'sixty-eight Strat? But music doesn't pay the bills. A death's head tattoo isn't good for the day job. And I like working here."

Gina smiled broadly. "Danny's being modest. Working here isn't a fill-in job for him. He's totally devoted to the animals. If we ever need a substitute to cover a shift when someone's sick, we can always count on Dan-O."

"What's so hard doing what you love, man? Wolves are way cool." His eyes shined on me, the new person in the group. "They're ten times smarter than the smartest dog and can eat up to thirty pounds of meat after a kill. And did you know they have webbed feet? Yeah, baby!" He arched his back and played an air guitar riff. After which Danny collected himself and lost his badass smirk. He leaned closer to Gina. "You gonna get those bastards, right?"

Her smile turned icy. "Count on it, Dan-O."

# CHAPTER 6

Then the howling started from the holding area. The wolves were agitated, particularly Lakota, who paced behind the fence, gazing into the main enclosure. He uttered several short barks then howled. Another series of guttural barks followed, which ended in a sustained howl. This served as a rallying cry to the three other wolves, who trotted over to join him. Soon all lifted their heads and crooned their mournful, haunting cry toward the heavens.

Debbie glanced at me wryly. "That's bark howling, Snake. If you ever hear that in the woods, you know you've really annoyed a wolf. Lakota's not happy. Too many strangers in his territory. It's bothering him more today than usual. Danny, would you tell the others to wrap things up? I'd like to get the wolves out of holding. I'll have Claudette get the meatballs ready."

As a bribe for going into holding, the wolves knew raw hamburger meatballs awaited them when they returned. To make it more interesting for them and the visitors watching from behind the glass, the juicy morsels were hidden within the acre-and-a-half enclosure. The wolves would have to hunt for their treats. They loved it. And the visitors loved watching them scamper to sniff out boulders, logs and trees.

"What's the matter, Lakota?" Debbie strode to the holding fence in long, purposeful strides. She walked everywhere with a sense she was on a mission. She never sauntered or strolled; she cruised. If you didn't keep pace with her, she'd pass you by.

Only in our case we didn't follow. With agitated animals, the fewer of us near them the better. Gina and I observed from a distance. Debbie knelt by the chain-link fence.

"She'd normally go in with them," Gina said. "But with the public watching, she doesn't want to be seen with the wolves jumping on her."

"Why's that?"

"People'd think they're dogs. It sends the wrong message to the public. Makes them think they're pets. Those are still wild animals. They trust Debbie because she raised them from pups."

The four gray wolves jockeyed for her attention. Lakota, the leader, seemed the most comforted at seeing Debbie. Her fingers got drenched from the lick fest from his snout squeezed through the chain links. Rufus, the beta wolf, muscled in a second later but was kept at bay by a short, stern growl from Lakota. Even though Rufus was the largest member of the pack, weighing over 110 pounds, he deferred. I was reminded how, after humans and other primates, wolves have the closest knit social structure of all animals.

Rufus flipped over on his back in a show of submission, still angling toward Debbie.

Gina laughed. "What a clown! He's four years old and still behaves like an adolescent at times."

"He's pushy, isn't he?"

"Yeah, Rufus keeps challenging Lakota for the top position. He'll win some day. Lakota's getting old. That's why you saw Debbie speak to Lakota first. It reinforces his position in the pack. She tries to talk to each wolf in order of its status. It helps keep the peace. If she'd spoken to Cheyenne first, Lakota might've felt threatened."

I nodded. Cheyenne was my favorite. The Omega wolf. The lowest ranking member, the animal most picked on. Lakota's brother. He was the gentlest of the lot and the least afraid of people, often coming up to the windows to observe the visitors as they observed him. A sweet animal. Last, but certainly not least, was Aila. Rufus's sister and Lakota's consort. Aila was the hunter. Though smallest in size, she was the most likely to pounce on prey that entered the enclosure, be it a stray bird, squirrel, or rodent.

I smiled at Gina. "Lakota shows such confidence and calm. He's so regal. You can tell he's the alpha male."

"Yeah, he does rally his pack. He's a great father, too. Funny how he's the most skittish around strangers. By the way, we don't call them 'alpha' anymore. Debbie says the preferred term now is to say he's the dominant wolf. Too much baggage associated with alpha."

"That'll take me some time to get used to."

"Me too," she admitted.

I peered through the observation windows behind me. The patrons eagerly watched Debbie with her wolves. Though I'm sure they were getting impatient for a closer view of the canids.

Gina motioned for me to follow. "Let's help the workmen get their tools out of here."

"Hey, speaking of tools. You promised to show me your new software tool, that new tracking program."

"Now's as good a time as any. Let's get the gate for these guys and we can go to the wolf lab."

The Minnesota Wolf Institute is located on the fringe of the city along Highway 169, where it juts out of the forest like a grand chalet, complete with sloping rooflines, bracketed eaves and exposed rafters. The 22,000-square-foot facility houses exhibit halls, offices, classrooms and laboratories within an architecture that exalts in exposed beams and trusses, wood-paneled walls and vaulted wood ceilings—with the notable exception of the wolf lab. In what seems clever improvisation, the wolf lab occupies space originally designed for a large double garage. Its décor is no-frills white. Containers, equipment, papers and supplies jammed together in cluttered harmony. It reminded me of my office at the zoo. The animals and patrons got first-class treatment. Staff made do.

A desktop PC sat atop a battered old wooden desk wedged between a bookcase and a rack of electronic equipment. Gina flopped down in the chair and I took a seat behind her. While she logged on, I glanced around and saw familiar containers of topical antibiotics, peroxide, zinc oxide, Cosequin and Durlactin. From the latter two I assumed one of the wolves in the retired pack enclosure suffered from joint problems. The older wolves had their own enclosure, off exhibit, where they could spend the remainder of their lives quietly away from the eyes of the public.

The metallic side door creaked open. In stepped Peter Bunyan, looking ready to arrest someone. Like me. His manner was somber, professional. My heart did a back flip. Had I screwed things up so badly?

"Ladies."

"Hey Peter." Gina tossed him a cordial smile, oblivious to my distress.

"Peter." I nodded pleasantly, hoping to thaw the ice. What I really wanted was to find a hole and crawl into it. He had been all business during the moose rescue and then spent most of the ride on the way back to Wolf Lake talking on his radio. There had been no opportunity for apologies. Seeing him again so soon was awkward and he wasn't helping, seeming all official in his uniform, his manner more unreadable than usual. All I knew was my cheeks burned.

"You came at a good time." Gina motioned at the computer screen. "I was about to show Snake the new tracking software. You've asked about it."

"That's why I came," he said. He pulled over a folding chair and dropped into it.

Normally, I'm pretty good at reading body language and vibes from people. Only this time my guilt got in the way. Peter wasn't exactly standoffish, but he wasn't behaving like my pal either. Were we pretending nothing had happened earlier? If so, that wasn't going to cut it for me. Not with him sitting two feet away.

"I screwed up, Peter!" I blurted. "I should never have asked Mr. Bjorklund for his gun. I should've kept my mouth shut. I shouldn't even have tagged along with you."

For a count of five the conservation officer regarded me with a steady, thoughtful gaze before the half-smile spread across his lips like a slow sunrise. "You did mess things up, Snake," he said with a detached calm devoid of blame. "I was a little ticked off at first. But, well, it was Ivar. Everything upsets him. Whether the question about his firearms came from you or me, he still would've taken offense."

"You're being generous."

"Oh, I'm not letting you off the hook—"

I averted my gaze. My cheeks flushed.

"—but no real harm was done. And maybe some good. However, next time you might let me ask the pointed questions."

I nodded back vigorously, secretly pleased to hear him say "next time." Did that mean there would be a next time? I hoped so. I was still eager to help with the investigation. I was also annoyed at myself. I hated making mistakes. We all make them. It's just I hated letting people down, hated them knowing things went wrong because of something I did. Jeff says it's because I have such high expectations of myself.

Gina's interest was piqued. "What'd I miss? Sounds juicy!"

Peter deferred to me. I quickly explained how my question about Bjorklund's rifle got us thrown off his property.

Gina leaned back, entirely satisfied. "That's my girl! Glad I'm not the only one around here whose mouth gets her in trouble."

With the mood lightened, Gina went on. "You'll both get a kick out of the tracking software. It's amazing. It's based on that map." She waved to a large map of the Upper Midwest tacked on the adjacent wall, pockmarked with tiny holes and colored pins. "Each pin represents a signal from a radio-collared wolf."

Her expert fingers did a fandango across the computer keyboard. A drop-down menu appeared on the LCD screen. With a few mouse clicks, the map on the wall was now electronically displayed before us. The jumble of colored dots was indecipherable. Most of the arrowhead region of Minnesota was covered, flowing into Canada and western Wisconsin.

"These markers are all loaded into a central database that—"

Gina halted as the side door banged open and Debbie strode in, her attention focused on removing a piece of straw from her sleeve. "Hey, Gina, have you seen the Bio-Spot? The flies are chewing at Aila's ears again—oops!" Glancing up, she realized they weren't alone. "Sorry."

"It's okay. I'm showing off RTAD."

"Great." Debbie sat on the edge of the table opposite me. "It's experimental software we're testing for the DNR and U.S. Geological Survey, part of the reason Gina's working here."

"Yeah, it's way cool."

Debbie beamed like a proud parent. "RTAD stands for Radio Telemetry Archive Database. It lets us manipulate the data from different perspectives. We can see migration patterns, examine wolf territories, perform on-the-fly analysis."

"I'll say." Gina grew animated. "It opens up a whole new world. For instance, we're working on the hypothesis that the four Red Iron pack wolves were killed within a ten-mile radius of where the bicyclists found their carcasses. The computer can remove the clutter of the other data points." Three mouse clicks later, she sat back. "There."

Nearly all the red dots had vanished from the on-screen map, which left twenty or so points overlaid by a geographical grid. "The grid," Gina explained, "can be narrowed."

The significance of this wasn't lost on me. "Will the grid pinpoint to a specific address?" I leaned closer to the screen. "If the last markers for the pack can be linked to a certain property, we might be able to narrow the focus to one, maybe two, neighborhoods."

"Exactly," agreed Debbie.

Peter rubbed his hands together. "Let's see."

With a flourish, Gina drew her mouse in an ellipsis around Wolf Lake. The image zoomed in and I was startled to see distinct landscape features. "Don't get too excited," she said. "Remember telemetry readings aren't always regular. Depends on funding." Her soft brown eyes rested on us, hoping we understood. "Wolf tracking is low on the USGS totem pole. The DNR doesn't have a lot of cash devoted to it, either. We can't get the airplane every week and there are problems with the GPS readings, too. It means gaps in the data. Even so, this should be helpful . . ."

Peter nodded toward the display. "What are we seeing here?"

"This is the Red Iron pack's wanderings in the last eight months. I've restricted it to a perimeter of ten miles around Wolf Lake." Gina radiated confidence. She was in her element. Although she loved fieldwork—being outside and working with animals—where she really shined was taking raw data and crunching it into something meaningful. At Northland College, Gina had suffered through the required physics class for her major. Bored, struggling to keep up, it wasn't until she found a way to apply what she learned that she began to excel. For her final exam she calculated the force of impact of an attacking mountain lion, and explained the physics of how a wolf could take down prey ten times its size. It was from Gina Brown I learned the value of taking theoretical knowledge and applying it to practical purposes.

I waved at the LCD display. "I don't quite follow. I see a mass of woodland and water. Can you get in closer?"

"No sooner said than done." A move of the mouse wheel, and the targeted section filled the viewing area. A light blue overlay came into view representing roads, highways, landmarks and towns. "There's Black Fir Road. Here, I'll highlight it in yellow. And here's where the wolf carcasses were found." A bright red X appeared in contact with the snaking yellow line.

Peter noticed a pattern on the display. "The wolves often crossed Black Fir Road in this area."

"Remember," Gina cautioned, "these are snapshots in time, not continuous data. Many of the readings are at least a week apart, sometimes two or three. Only three pack members wore radio collars. It'd be a mistake to assume they always traveled together. Animals do disburse from time to time. Unfortunately, the data doesn't come with sound effects."

Debbie explained, "One of reasons wolves howl is to find the other members of the pack."

"I think the reason the wolves crossed Black Fir Road there is because it's unpopulated. Farther south leads to less dense forests and more deer."

Peter's mouth formed a furtive line. "Let's cut to the chase. Snake made a good point. Does your data show the Red Iron pack moving on to the property of anyone along Black Fir Road?"

"No. They avoided any of the settled areas. The data from the past eight months shows a fairly consistent routine."

"I guess that's good news."

Debbie considered the conservation officer curiously. "You don't sound like it's good news."

"It's like this, Deb. If we could prove the wolves had repeatedly visited someplace like Ivar Bjorklund's, then we'd have a pretty good idea why the wolves were killed and who shot them. This data says it's unlikely they went near Ivar's place, which leaves things up in the air."

"You still can't rule Ivar out," Gina protested. "He's the closest to the carcass site. And he's got motive."

"I'm not ruling anyone out," Peter said with forced calm as his color rose. "But be aware that Ivar's not the closest person to the carcass site. His neighbor, Moua Vang, is actually closer by a few hundred feet."

"Where's the last signal?" I asked, trying to divert Gina.

With fast-acting fingers, Gina removed all but the last six readings on the monitor.

"You're now looking at the last ten weeks."

Much less clutter now. "Which is the last reading?"

"This one." She indicated a marker well away from Black Fir.

My heart sank. "When was that taken?"

"Nine days ago."

It still didn't make sense to me, but something I'd seen in the clutter before had caught my eye. "Go back five months. Put all the data up."

"Did you see something, Snake?"

"Not sure. There seems to be a clustering of dots in a couple of areas. Too bad you can't animate these markers in sequence."

"Who says I can't?" Gina entered a command string that brought up a dialogue box from which she chose four radio buttons. "How's that?" She turned to me for approval.

I felt a rush of excitement. "Is this a continuous loop?" The dots moved along in paths, ovals, a few in random patterns.

"Yes," Gina replied.

It was clear now. In all the meandering dot patterns, two dots barely moved at all at the beginning and near the end of the loop.

"Freeze." Debbie Wong's hand reached out to the screen. "I see it now! Those two points show the least movement."

Both markers were near Black Fir Road. My skin tingled. Had we gotten it?

Gina beamed at us. "I say we have a winner. Those two locations show up twice."

The wolf curator agreed. "One's probably a den, the other a rendezvous site."

"How can you tell?"

Debbie turned toward me. "Spring is when wolves have pups. In those early weeks, when the pack goes out to hunt, the pups stay behind in the den. One member of the pack always remains to baby-sit. This wolf is likely that guardian. These additional readings are from that time. Now it's September and the pups are old enough to join the rest of the pack at the kill or rendezvous sites. That's why this one animal, a beta wolf, moves away from this area in the more recent signals."

"So you're saying this marker—" I stretched forward to touch the dot on the left side of the screen "—is the rendezvous site because the marker isn't there consistently. But this other one is the den because the beta wolf is staying behind to protect the pups."

"Yes, basically."

"And that tells us what?"

Peter stirred, the leather in his gun belt creaking. "Both these markers are close to Black Fir Road. My bet's the wolves were shot at one of these locations. Far easier to kill them in a regular gathering place than if they're on the move."

Darth Vader's theme song began to play from the vicinity of Debbie's hip. "It's the school. I have to take this, guys." She gave us an apologetic smile and moved to the corner of the wolf lab to answer the call.

"Okay . . ." My brain still wrestled with this information. Something bugged me about the shooter's logic. "Why not leave the wolves where they were shot—in the woods?"

Nobody could answer that.

I stretched forward again, tapping the marker closest to Black Fir Road. "This is all forest, right?"

"Both markers are," Gina confirmed.

My hand found comfort at the base of my neck, fingers twirling my ponytail. "I don't get it. Why move the carcasses?"

"Someone making a political statement?" Gina suggested. "They wanted them found so they had bragging rights and could get their anti-wolf cause some attention."

"But no one has claimed responsibility."

"Not yet."

Peter cleared his throat. "If someone wanted to make some kind of statement, he could've dumped them on a busy road or at the entrance of the wolf institute. Those carcasses weren't meant to be found."

My hands gestured emptily. "It's something else. We're just not seeing it. What if someone is—"

"—hiding something," Gina jumped in. "Something at one of those marker sites!"

Peter Bunyan hauled his six-foot frame out of the chair. "Only one way to find out. Let's check out those two sites. You've got the GPS coordinates. And there's still two hours of daylight. You coming, Deb?"

" 'Fraid not." She pulled her jacket off a plastic tub on the floor. "Wish I could, guys, but I gotta go. The bus never showed up after school. I have to pick up the kids."

"The school bus?" Peter was surprised. "That's Ivar. He's been driving that bus for over a year. He's never late."

Debbie touched Peter's shoulder. "He's an old man with health problems. Maybe he fell asleep or had a medical issue. If I find out differently, I'll call your cell."

The long shadows stretched across Black Fir Road as the sun skimmed along the top of the pines. All I hoped for was to locate one of the marker positions and see if it told us anything. Odds were the wolves had been killed elsewhere.

"This may get us nothing," Peter said, as though reading my mind, preparing us for disappointment. His pickup bounced over a rut in the road. "No guarantees we'll find any pot of gold at the end of this rainbow, assuming we can find the place."

Gina waved her handheld GPS device. "Oh, we'll find the site if this baby's working properly."

He cracked a smile. "Gina loves her technology."

"It's not your grandfather's DNR anymore, Peter."

I nodded. "Too bad Debbie got called away. We could have used another pair of eyes."

"Yeah," Peter agreed. "When we're finished, I'll swing by Ivar's place, make sure he's all right."

A glint of sunlight winked at us from the forest.

"What was that?" He squinted into the trees.

"Not yet, Peter." Gina's eyes stayed glued to her GPS.

Peter stopped the truck. He yanked it in reverse, backed up fifty feet, then stopped. He peered through the foliage. "That break in the trees, where the brush is overgrown, that's an old driveway. Belongs to an old abandoned lot. The dirt driveway was put in, but no one ever built anything on the property. The sun's flashing off something back there."

"We're not there yet." Gina waved the GPS.

"Nothing should be back there . . ."

Peter sucked on his lower lip thoughtfully. After a moment's hesitation, he put his pickup in drive. He turned onto the narrow driveway, slowly piloting past the stand of evergreens until the dirt path opened up. Surrounded by leafy trees, some just starting to show the promise of vivid reds and golds, we turned a bend, the source of the sun sparkle becoming clear: a small yellow school bus. Parked along the overgrown roadway, its folding doors stood wide open.

A tingle of dread danced up my scalp.

"What the hell?" Peter puzzled, as we drew nearer. "Why would Ivar bring the bus back here?"

"Engine trouble?" I suggested half-heartedly, suspecting whatever the reason, it wouldn't be so benign.

The three of us leaned forward in the cab, straining to see. Peter pulled up behind the bus and killed the engine. He quickly slipped out of the truck, Gina and me close on his heels.

A flock of geese honked overhead, their V formation pointing in the same direction as the empty bus. The dry ground crunched beneath our feet as we walked past the mini bus toward an open area of wild grass between the trees.

Up ahead, a crow took to the air as it saw us. Faded blue fabric lay crumpled on the ground where it had stood.

"Oh!" Gina gasped and turned away, retching.

I squinted ahead, already knowing what I'd see. The faded colors became a flannel shirt and washed-out jeans.

Peter sprinted forward and knelt beside the prone body. One aged, liver-marked hand was dug into the grass, the other, stretched past the head as if reaching, clutched a small sprig of leaves with determination. A blossom of red stained the blue plaid of the flannel.

"It's Ivar." With a hard swallow, Peter slowly rose to his feet. "He's dead. He's been shot."

# CHAPTER 7

Darkness had come on silent wolf paws to consume the waning daylight. Now headlights from three vehicles illuminated the crime scene: Peter's truck and two Wolf Lake police cruisers.

"Shot once in the chest." Police Chief Tom Manske, who knelt by the body, raised his head. His complexion took on a ghastly pallor under the stark halogen light. "My guess from a high-velocity rifle, going by the blood on his chest and what I can see of the wound."

"So the killer stared Ivar in the face when he shot him," offered a young officer who stood nearby.

"Yeah." Manske rose to his full height, grunting from the effort.

"Death wasn't instantaneous, though," I said. "Mr. Bjorklund lived for another minute or two."

Manske regarded me, his mouth set with disapproval. Like why was I talking? It made me feel as if I had been watching a play in a theater and had just blurted out a line for one of the actors on stage. He answered my question, though, but directed it to Peter, as if I wasn't even there. A lawman thing, I suppose. "Looks to me death wasn't immediate."

"That's about twelve feet." Peter frowned at bloodied marks in the grass. Gone was the amicable conservation officer I'd ridden with. He looked hard as nails now, focused on what needed doing.

Manske shook his head. "Blood there . . . there . . . and there.

It appears Ivar was shot by the driveway and collapsed. He must've revived long enough to crawl here, leaving the blood smears in the grass. The killer was gone by then, or would've finished the job."

Peter squinted toward the forest, now a dark void beyond the little clearing. "Where d'you think he was going?"

"Trying to get away? Doesn't make much sense, does it? He could've gone to the bus. The keys are still in the ignition."

"Maybe he knew he couldn't make it that far. Knew he only had moments."

The two men shook their heads.

I wanted to say something else, but the police chief intimidated me. He made me feel as if I was contaminating his crime scene by just being there, even though I was standing on the driveway, keeping my distance. The ghostly light didn't help. Still, the chief was just a mean-looking son of a bitch. Stern eyes, pockmarked face, bristle mustache over a severe mouth. If I'd seen his photo in a police lineup without the uniform, I'd have picked Tom Manske for a serial killer.

"You calling in the BCA, Tom?" Officer Lomax asked.

"Yeah. This is too messy for us. I'll make the call when I get back to the station. You realize, Don, you'll have to spend the night here. I'll relieve you in the morning."

"Sure." Officer Lomax took it in stride. In fact, he even seemed excited at the prospect. I wondered if this was his first murder.

Manske gave a sharp nod. "Tell you what. When we're done, you grab some dinner and come back. I'll hang out here till you return."

As they made arrangements, I turned to see how Gina was doing. She'd moved away from the crime scene, leaning against the DNR pickup, toying with a piece of bark. Initially, I put her grim silence down to the shock of finding the body. It was an eerie feeling for me to see Bjorklund's lifeless body face down in the scrub grass; I'd spoken to him only hours before. How much worse for Gina, who'd known him. As far as I knew, she'd never seen violent death up close before—not in a human being. She seemed lost. The clues were there: somber expression, compressed lips, hooded eyes and sagging shoulders, all signs she'd shuttered herself close. Peter's concern toward her confirmed my suspicion.

"What have we here?" said Manske, diverting my attention. Squatting beside the dead man, he picked up a crumpled, blood-smeared piece of paper. "It was under the body. Didn't see it before."

Something flew over my head. A bat chasing a meal. The insects were out, attracted by the headlights.

As if handling an ancient artifact, Chief Manske delicately unfolded the sheet, careful not to rip it. Then he held it to the light. Even from my vantage point I recognized the green paper and big bold letters. The same message Gina had found tacked to her kitchen door. Stewards of Superior had had Ivar Bjorklund in their sights.

Peter reached for the paper. His voice turned crisp. "Maybe Ivar's killer didn't leave right away. Maybe he enjoyed tormenting him, watching him die."

"You thinking it's one of them SOS creeps?"

"It was no secret how Ivar felt about wolves. He hated them. Everyone knew it. He was a person of interest in my investigation."

"Sounds like your main suspect. Was he?"

Peter shrugged. "One of them. The four wolf carcasses were found near his property."

"The newspaper did a story on them this morning, so word would've gotten out. All it takes is for a few radical members of a group to ratchet things up and you get a mess like this."

"But murder? I don't know, Tom. This is way beyond anything the SOS has done before."

"Just thinking out loud. To some warped mind, Ivar got what was coming to him. All right, Don, let's wrap things up—"

"Wait. There's something else!" The words tumbled out before I knew it. All eyes swiveled toward me. "Sorry. I don't mean to be a pain, but what about his hand?"

"What about his hand?"

"What's in it?" I answered.

"It's a twig."

"Actually, it's an elm twig with leaves. Don't you think that's odd?"

"Not really. The man's crawling on the ground on his belly. He's liable to grab anything. He pulled that seedling right out by its roots."

"From where I'm standing, it's more than that. It's like he's stretching out; reaching for that sprig of leaves. It might mean something."

"Like what?" Manske asked. Though his expression was stern, his voice was patient, interested.

"I dunno," I answered lamely.

"Maybe," Peter suggested, "he grabbed the twig to write something in the dirt."

"Except there's no dirt. Just grass and wildflowers. The dirt's on the road."

Peter agreed. "Good point. I suppose he realized he couldn't make it very far."

Manske seized on this. "That'd explain why he didn't go for the school bus or try to get help. He knew he had only seconds."

I pointed at the evidence on the ground; the flattened vegetation, the blood. "Mr. Bjorklund dragged himself past a maple leaf, a broken aspen branch and several oak twigs. With his dying strength, he deliberately went for the elm twig with its three leaves. Why?"

For the first time the police chief appeared to take me seriously. Slowly, thoughtfully, he began to nod, as if beginning to understand the importance of this curiosity.

"I can't tell you what it means," I added in frustration, "but it seems like Mr. Bjorklund's trying to tell us something."

Again he nodded, only the sound of the crickets filling the void in conversation.

Manske scratched the side of his neck. "Maybe it does mean something. We'll keep that in mind."

I offered a furtive smile of gratitude.

Officer Lomax squinted at his watch and was about to comment when—

"I told you not to touch anything!" Peter, who'd gone over to check on Gina, shook his head in disbelief. "For crying out loud, that's evidence."

"Huh? Oh, sorry."

"Do you realize you've contaminated it just by touching it?"

"Wha—? Oh!" Startled, she fumbled with her hands and dropped the piece of bark to the ground.

I jogged over to the school bus to see what was happening. Peter could barely contain his anger. "Too late now. Where'd you find it?"

Flustered and repentant, Gina backed away. "I—I found it on the ground. Under the radiator. I didn't think it was anything important—"

"This is a crime scene. You've got to be more careful. We don't know if they're other fingerprints on this. But now it's covered in yours!"

She pressed her lips tightly together, lowering her head, hangdog.

Pulling out a handkerchief, Peter knelt and carefully picked up the object from the road, where it had nearly vanished in the darkness.

"What is it?" asked Manske, trotting over, Officer Lomax two steps behind him.

What I'd thought was a piece of bark turned out to be some kind of hand tool. It had a cylindrical wooden handle embedded with a tapered metal shaft. It was small. Small enough to fit in the palm of your hand.

"It's an old v-gouge." Peter held it up in the harsh light. "The kind woodworkers use for fine detail."

Manske leaned forward. His bushy eyebrows knitted as he squinted. "It's not dirty or tarnished. It hasn't been here long. Somebody dropped this here recently." He stared at Peter with significance.

"The lab folks might get something useful off this," Peter agreed. "Do you have something to put this in, Chief?"

"I have some paper bags in my trunk."

Manske and Officer Lomax made for the former's cruiser. Peter paused mid-step and turned to Gina, who was still visibly shaken, her arms wrapped around herself. Her head was bowed, as though she couldn't bear to look into Peter's eyes.

"I'm sorry," she muttered, her gaze fixed to the ground.

He closed his eyes and exhaled a purging breath. She couldn't see it, but his manner eased. The honeyed voice returned. "I know you are. Please be more careful. Sorry I yelled." Without another word, he took off after the other two, leaving Gina and me alone in the shadows by the school bus.

"You okay?" I asked.

"I screwed up."

"Guess it was your turn," I said in a lighter tone, invoking the memory of my earlier faux pas that day.

A glimmer of a smile creased her lips before darker moods chased it away.

What a difference a day makes. Yesterday morning I'd encountered Ivar Bjorklund, an outspoken wolf-hater, while today I'd seen him as a determined old man struggling against the cruel winds of Fate. With the loss of his beloved Lily, the energy to fight off the world had been leaching out of him. Yet he'd survived. I admired that. He hadn't deserved to die like this, and I said as much to Gina.

Her eyes flicked up. "Awfully forgiving of you, Snake, considering how he ripped into you the other day."

"He was a spiteful old man. He still didn't deserve to be murdered."

Gina regarded me quietly, her face a clouded mask of indifference. It didn't mean she felt nothing, only that she'd stuffed her feelings into a deep closet and locked the door. She'd never been the crying kind. Not in public. Not if she could help it. She certainly wouldn't let loose her tears in front of anyone, me included. That, at least, hadn't changed.

I wish it had.

# CHAPTER 8

The Angel of Doom hovered near the threshold of Last Chance Outfitters, poised to deliver bad tidings, if she had to. Her grim countenance stared back at me from the window: five foot six, thirty-five, with straight dark brown hair tied back to reveal a not unattractive face. The ghostly specter was clad in a khaki shirt and blue jeans and a light cloth jacket that was just sufficient to keep her warm on a cool morning. Thoughtful and apprehensive pond scum-green eyes looked back at me from the glass.

Mine.

Gina and I got home late after a morale-boosting dinner at the Dairy Queen on Sheridan. An Oreo Blizzard seemed essential to our well-being. It wasn't until I settled down for the night on Gina's couch that I considered Signe Amunson. She'd known Ivar Bjorklund for most of her life. Though it was none of my business, I didn't want her to find out about his death through town gossip or a news item in the *Wolf Lake Echo*.

So there I was bright and early on her doorstep.

The Angel of Doom was a role I'd taken on before. The first time was in tenth grade when Mom was unable to break the news to Cricket about her gerbil, Houdini. He was on the loose again, escaped from his habitat, perhaps even dead. For my mother, a loose rodent was far worse, for it meant the little rat-faced escape artist could show up at any time. Anywhere. The mere idea that one day she might be confronted by Houdini from behind the shower curtain while she was buck-naked totally freaked her out.

Or worse—

She'd step on his decomposing corpse with her bare feet. No, Mom was much too keyed up imagining the worst possible outcome to tend to her third child's grief, so it fell upon number one daughter to inform Sis about the great escape. Cricket took the news far better than Mom. And for the record, we never did find Houdini. Or his remains.

Turns out I could have saved my breath. Cole Novak stood in the parking lot, already setting up his saw horses.

"She knows," he announced, his eyes on his work, not on me.

"About Mr. Bjorklund?"

"Oh, yeah."

A fine film of sawdust lightened his dark, flyaway hair and flecked his wire-rimmed spectacles, while small chips of wood clung to a two-day growth of whiskers. Novak had a face that looked as if it had seen too much of the world and was not favorably impressed. A lighted cigarette dangled from his lips, defying the laws of gravity. Whenever he spoke, it jumped and wiggled like the baton of a band conductor.

The cigarette curtsied at his lips. "News travels fast in a small town, especially when it ain't good."

This was the man Ivar Bjorklund had seen drive by around the time of the wolf shootings and claimed there was something covered up in the back of Novak's SUV. Probably nothing more ominous than a stack of two-by-fours, covered with a tarp. Still . . .

"How's she taking it?" I asked.

The cigarette shrugged. His eyes peered at me over the top of his glasses. "She's a good Swede." A jet of smoke spiraled from the corner of his mouth for emphasis and I took a step back, trying to stay upwind of him. He didn't have to say more. That stoic Norse/Swede genealogy ran in my family, too, leaving some of us no choice but to face the world with a facade of indifference.

It was early and Signe's place was deserted. All except for the woman herself, who stood by the cash register, counting coins before the start of her business day. She glanced up and smiled as she always did when I came in, making me wonder if Novak knew what he was talking about. Signe was the picture of rugged immigrant stock, the sort you pictured walking behind a plough pulled by a team of oxen on the windblown prairie.

"You okay?" I ventured, searching her face.

Signe seemed puzzled. "Why wouldn't I be?"

"Ivar—"

"You've come to comfort me." She smiled at the kindness. "Snake, aren't you sweet? I'm okay. Really."

"I wanted to be sure."

She nodded her understanding, then turned her back to fiddle with something behind the counter. "It's sad about Ivar. The poor man's been through so much. What with Lily and all." She spoke of him as if he were still alive, as if she had been told of some new tragedy in his life, rather than his death. "The cancer ate away her stomach, you know. The poor thing was an invalid for the last two years of her life."

She moved around the counter avoiding my gaze. She straightened a stack of leather mouse pads, each embossed with a finely detailed image of a deer, elk, or moose. Then she went to an aisle display, adjusting packages of fishing lures that didn't need adjusting.

"Gina said he was dedicated to Lily."

"He was. Some told Ivar he should've put her in a nursing home. There's a nice fancy place in Tower where he could visit Lily whenever he wanted. Wouldn't hear of it. Not while he was alive, he said. He'd take care of her. And he did. He did everything for her with never a complaint. Even when his own health began to fail, he kept at it. I think he used himself up caring for her." Signe's eyes flicked up to me with surprising intensity. Awareness dawned in them, a sense of unfairness. Even more. "Lily died and Ivar started to really go downhill—"

Signe stopped abruptly, catching herself before she fell down a slippery slope of emotions. She sagged into the chair Mooney would occupy within an hour, her forearms resting on the checkerboard. The realization of Bjorklund's death seemed to have finally hit her.

"I hear he was murdered."

I nodded, finding my voice caught in my throat.

"Dear Lord," she breathed.

I lowered myself into the chair next to her. Gus wouldn't mind. In fact, he'd probably revel in it when he found out.

"Did he suffer?"

I shuffled my feet, searching for the right words. Except there weren't any. "I can't say."

She clung to my words, so eager for comfort. I saw it in her careworn eyes. She bowed her head and mumbled a prayer. My hand rested on hers. A furtive smile touched her lips as her fingers firmly clasped mine.

"Signe," I asked softly, "do you have any idea who could've done this?"

She shook her head, which sent her tumbleweed of white hair rolling from side to side.

"No one with a grudge?"

"I don't know, Snake. Ivar rubbed people the wrong way. Far as I know, nobody took it personally. Not enough to kill him."

"Can you be sure of that?"

"No," she admitted, troubled. Then inhaled sharply and eyed me philosophically. "I may not be the world's greatest business woman, but one thing I'm fairly good at is seeing into the hearts of people. Which isn't to say I'm infallible, you understand. It's just that I know a lot of the people in Wolf Lake. They're good folks. I can't believe anyone would want Ivar dead."

And yet the man had been violently murdered.

Signe must have had a pipeline into my heart just then because she squeezed my hand and leaned in closer. "You don't understand. Despite the way he came across, Ivar was one of the kindest, most good-hearted men I ever knew. A lot of people in this town remember him that way."

I must have looked gobsmacked.

"I'm serious," she said. The intensity of her gaze burned the back of my retinas. "One winter when I was a young girl, my brother Gunnar went sledding with Ivar. Both were seventeen. This is really dipping into the past, let me tell you." She gave a little laugh. "Being boys, they had to try the steepest hill. Gunnar shot down this big slope by Miller's farm and smacked into a buried rock. It launched his sled in the air like a rocket, right into the side of a big ol' oak tree. The sled broke into three pieces, Gunnar's leg into two."

"Geez!" I winced.

"He couldn't walk. The pain was unbearable. And it was twenty degrees below zero—and this was no windchill. It was the air temperature! Gunnar was freezing and Ivar was afraid to leave him to get help. So Ivar hoisted my brother across his shoulders and trudged the two miles back to our house through two feet of snow. That was the sort of man Ivar Bjorklund was!"

And so very long ago, I nearly pointed out but didn't, not wanting to ruin the moment. She was basking in the memory, admiration and affection radiating from her like the warmth of a campfire on a cold autumn night. She needed the comfort of that image. Who was I to take it away from her?

For me it was hard to reconcile the vibrant young Ivar of her story to the worn-out old man I'd met days before. The tall, rail-thin sheep farmer seemed barely able to hoist a lamb to his shoulders, let alone another man. Yet he'd had plenty of strength for heavy hammer blows while fixing the shearing table. Strong enough to gun down four wolves and carry off their remains?

My gaze rested on the mounted deer head on the wall opposite. The glassy eyes stared back at me, at issue with my reservations on the matter. I had to agree. Right or wrong, I couldn't shake the notion that Bjorklund's death was somehow tied up with the dead wolves.

"It was close," Signe continued, eyes glistening. "The doctor said another twenty minutes in the cold and my brother would've lost his toes and fingers to frostbite. Ivar saved him, Snake."

"Mr. Bjorklund—" I felt compelled to address him as Mister Bjorklund in her presence. She had that affect on you, projecting an aura of proper respect and good manners. "Mr. Bjorklund lived alone, just him and his dog?"

"Yah. Thank the Lord he has Oskar for company. Had." Her brow furrowed at the mistake. "And those sheep. How he and Lily doted on them."

"They're pretty impressive," I said, remembering the ram Thorbjörn and the rest of the gorgeous Icelandics.

Folding her arms under her imposing bosom, Signe regarded me like a favorite aunt. "I just hope Ivar didn't get snippy with you again. There's no call for that. I'm afraid without Lily he had no one to help him with the social graces."

"Except you."

The suggestion visibly startled her. "I guess. Never thought of it that way . . ." She grew fond of the idea, as though it satisfied some personal need.

"Mr. Bjorklund treated me fine. It was the other guy who creeped me out."

"Other guy?"

"Forrest Hansen."

Signe made a face. "Ivar's mentioned him. Hansen's been to the store once." This last uttered in a hollow, antiseptic tone that did not cover the man with bouquets. "Can't say why, exactly, but he rubbed me the wrong way."

"He just wanted to rub me."

"Pardon?"

I told her about Mr. Muscles' poses and not-so-veiled flirtations, then his wolf rantings. "It's all a government plot to take away his guns, he said."

She shook her head in disbelief. "Doesn't surprise me one bit. From my one meeting with him, he struck me as a very odd duck. I know Ivar used to work for him. And they're neighbors. Still seems an odd friendship, if you ask me."

The door swung open with a loud tinkle of the bell. A customer. Signe quickly gathered herself, applying a cheerful face with which she greeted her visitor as though he were her new best friend.

The open door had let in the full roar of a circular saw as it ripped through lumber. Cole Novak, a flash of memory reminded, once worked at the paper mill with Hansen. Perhaps he had insight. I knew he'd have an opinion. Insight, though, was preferred.

Novak offered a phlegmatic smirk as I trotted down the half-finished steps. "Good luck finding the killer."

"The police are handling the investigation—"

"I was talking about the wolves."

I stopped and turned. "Any ideas who might've shot them?" In light of last night's murder, my question seemed a cold thing to utter. I let the feeling pass, deciding to take advantage of the opening.

The cigarette shifted to the other side of his mouth. Novak stared at me over the top of his glasses. "Some people don't want the government sticking its nose in their business. I'm one of them. Particularly the federal government."

Okay, I wasn't sure where this curve ball had come from. First Forrest Hansen, now Novak. I seemed to have hit the anti-government jackpot with these two. I struggled to keep my opinions to myself. "The Feds aren't involved in the wolf kill investigation. It's local. The DNR."

"Yeah, for now. But wolves were protected by the Feds not that long ago. Some folks up here never got over that. Just as some didn't like their land being taken away to make up the Boundary Waters Canoe Area Wilderness."

"Aren't we talking about two different things?"

"Nah, it's still a bloated bureaucracy getting on the backs of the little guy."

"You're against big government."

"Big. Small. Hell, I'm against them all. The liberals, conservatives. Give any of them half a chance, they'll screw things up. Meanwhile the people in the middle never get in power, not enough of them. But you know if they do, they'll screw it up, too." His eyes lingered on me, as if to ensure I understood the import of this homespun truth.

It was evident the man could talk forever on the subject, so I tried another tactic. Most men can't resist a little flattery. "You do nice work."

"Not hard stuff. Just some treads and risers."

"And new posts and floorboards for the porch." I leaned back, gesturing at a spot above the door. "And the new sign."

The new sign for Last Chance Outfitters popped with three dark green pine boughs clustered against lettering painted like logs.

"You've done a very professional job," I added.

He stepped back to admire his work. "Not half bad, if I say so myself. The sign wasn't part of the original work order, but

Signe added it after I told her the old sign was too beat up and a fresh coat of paint wouldn't last long. Without blinking an eye, she said to build a new one. I can always count on Signe for work, particularly when I need it most." A jet of smoke puffed out for emphasis. I took a step back, trying to stay upwind.

"That's nice of her."

"Better than nice." Novak leaned in, his eyes narrowing behind sawdust-flecked spectacles. "Six years ago I was fired from the mill. Finding work was hard. Signe knew I was handy with tools and did some woodworking, so she gave me odd jobs here and at her house, and told her customers. Kept me afloat. She offered me work when others wouldn't even talk to me. Signe Amunson's a great lady."

The circular saw roared to life, showering wood dust and the wonderful scent of cedar into the crisp morning air, then stopped as the end plank dropped to the asphalt.

"Hope you find the SOB who shot those wolves," he added, turning the board on the sawhorse. "Wolves are okay. They're just trying to make a living in a hostile world. People just won't let them be." It seemed Cole Novak was talking as much about himself as the wolves. "The problem," he added as an afterthought, "isn't the wildlife. It's people. People are greedy. They always want more. They can't share. Get rid of the people and the world would be a much better place to live in."

I let the comment pass.

"The mill you worked at. Was that the Lohmann-Tate Paper Mill in Hibbing?"

"None other." He bent down to unplug his saw from an orange extension cord.

"Did you know Forrest Hansen? He's a manager there."

Novak paused as a young couple came up the steps and entered Signe's, his gaze searing into me. His words, when they came, seemed to be dredged up from a deep and stagnant well. "I know Hansen. Very well. He's the lying son of a bitch who fired me."

Whatever else he said was lost by the blare of a horn and screeching tires. Gina's pickup slammed to a halt in the parking lot. Distress had drained the color from her face.

"Snake! Get over to the wolf institute now! The wolves have escaped!"

"*What?* How's that possible?"

"Somebody cut the fence!"

# CHAPTER 9

My worst dreams, the ones that jolt me out of a sound sleep in a dazed panic, are of animal escapes. Of a high-powered rifle shoved into my hands and being on the front line to stop the anticipated carnage. Aware the charging tiger must be stopped before it kills innocent people, I agonize over the fate of the animal. I have to think of the safety of our patrons first, knowing it wasn't the tiger's fault he got loose. Some person was to blame: the person who goaded it, the architect who designed a faulty enclosure, the contractor who didn't follow specs, or the keeper who forgot to lock a door. Regardless, it's always the animal that pays the ultimate price.

Thankfully, most escapes aren't that dramatic. The raccoons that busy themselves with unlocking their exhibit door and having playtime in a zookeeper's office. The flamingo that manages to catch a breeze in Kansas and disappears over the enclosure fence. A year later, he's seen bumming around with a wild flamingo in a Louisiana bayou.

Big or small, animal escapes are traumatic for care staff.

The good news was the wolf institute wasn't yet open, which meant the staff didn't have to deal with the public and a crisis at the same time. Not for another hour and a half, at least.

I'd ridden with Gina so she could fill me in on the details. "Some friggin' a-hole sliced up the perimeter fence last night," she'd said, eyes ablaze. "He put raw meat on the ground on the other side of the opening to lure the wolves outside."

Unlike zoos, which routinely take many animals off exhibit in the evening for their feed and the night, the wolves at the MWI lived within their enclosure and were moved into holding only when necessary.

"If we're lucky, the animals won't wander far," she said as we pulled into the parking lot. "This is the only home they've known. They've got plenty to eat. They're happy here." She sighed. "Though no one's told them that. This is why we practice escape drills during the year, so everyone knows what they should do and where they should be. When Debbie called this morning with a code Epsilon, we scrambled."

We barely slid into our parking stall before jumping out of Gina's pickup. In through the rear entrance, we rushed along the corridor to the classroom that had been converted to the escape command center. It was now vacated, though not long ago, judging by the askew folding chairs and empty coffee cups in the wastebasket. A map of the Wolf Lake area was taped to the front wall, marked up in sectors with a black magic marker. Next to it, on white poster paper, hung a hand drawn map of the MWI with highlighted areas in red and orange.

"I'm here, Marlene," Gina announced, breathless.

A young woman in her twenties, arranging stacks of paper on one of the tables, cast a perfunctory eye in my direction. "Debbie wants you outside the rear perimeter fence. She's there with the rest of the wolf care team."

"Thanks!" Gina said, halfway out the door. We hurried back the way we'd come, banged shut the door and fumbled with the lock on the enclosure gate. Once inside, we sprinted through the enclosure up the sloping hill to the wooded back acres.

The breach wasn't hard to find. A gaping hole the size of a dog house stared at us from the tall chain-link fence, its jagged ends peeled away like some monster exit wound. The exhibit wolves now had all of Superior National Forest as their playground.

We crawled through the opening on hands and knees, the grass still cool and moist from the dew. Gina stood and wiped her hands on the flanks of her jeans. In one easy motion she reached back and gathered her long auburn hair into a ponytail and secured it with a rubber band. She was ready for action. Raw determination had chased off any semblance of sweetness in her delicate features.

"Snake, I'm going out to search. You have to stay here."

"Sure."

"It's important you do. It's all part of the escape plan. I'll explain later. You can help Peter." Without another word, she bolted into the woods and out of sight.

I spun around. About thirty yards from me stood the DNR CO. I ambled over. "This is all part of the plan," I repeated after the amenities were exchanged

"Pretty much." He gazed out into the wooded landscape. "People are scattered at key stations with radios and binoculars." He tapped the set of field glasses dangling around his neck.

I shoved my hands into the pockets of my cloth jacket. "Wish I was out there with them doing something."

"We are doing something: providing an anchor point. Besides, if the wolves are still close by we don't want to send in a crowd. Could spook 'em. Then they'd run deeper into the forest."

"Who's out there?"

"Debbie, Claudette, Danny, and now Gina."

"The primary wolf caregivers."

"Right. The only humans the pack trusts." Peter turned philosophical. "Wolves are tricky. They've got one of the most tightly knit social structures in the world. They're intensely loyal and caring to other members of their pack, including humans. Yet if you don't get introduced to a wolf pup before it's four months old, you're out of luck. He'll never trust you. He won't bond with you. He'll tolerate you, but he'll never trust you."

Now I got it. If Peter, or I, or anyone other than the four searchers out there came across the escapees, we risked scattering them. Though we might manage to herd the animals in the right direction, they could also easily run circles around us and take off for parts unknown. We'd never get them to come to us when we called. It was the people the wolves had bonded with who had the best chance of bringing them home. That's what Debbie and the others desperately hoped.

Peter methodically scanned the forest back and forth like a lighthouse beacon.

"Will this work?" I asked.

"Odds are good. Usually when Debbie calls them, the wolves come running. If they see her, they'll come to her. And if it doesn't work, I've got this." He tapped his work boot against a large wire cage on the ground. A Tru-Catch humane trap.

"Are we setting it up?"

"Not yet. If Debbie and the others can gather the pack and herd them toward the opening, we won't need it."

"How many of those things d'you have? If Debbie can't round up the pack you'll need more."

"Already being done. Traps are being set up along the perimeter as we speak. This one and the other one over there are a little too close to the opening to set up right now. We want to wait awhile."

And that's what we did. Wait. It was murder not to run out and join the others in the search. Peter and I had our post, though, and were contributing to the hunt. We wanted to do more. A raven cawed in a treetop, breaking the silence. The sound of movement seized our attention. A squirrel jumped for a spindly branch and caught it in a spectacular aerial display. No wolves, though.

I exhaled. "This sucks."

"It does."

In the distance I heard a faint call: "Lakota . . . Lakota, where are you, boy?"

Then a flutter of color. Movement. I grabbed Peter's arm. "You see that?"

"Yes!" he said excitedly. "It's them!"

Seconds later, Debbie Wong appeared a hundred yards away. I could barely make her out between the trees and foliage; she trotted at an easy, measured pace. And she wasn't alone.

"How many?" I asked impatiently, craning my neck.

"Three. Only three."

In time Debbie approached us, three wolves loping near her, excited, cavorting, as though the last few hours were all a wonderful game. A short young woman with big hair and an electric smile brought up the rear. With her short legs, Claudette struggled to keep up but didn't seem to mind; she was grinning from ear to ear.

So was I. I wished Jeff and the *Zoofari* crew was here to film this. What a thrilling episode it'd be. One Animal Planet would love to get their hands on. It might even get me off the hook with Billie. My director was sure to give me a cussing after she realized how much time I'd been spending searching for a wolf killer rather than scouting film locations.

As she got close, Debbie's extended palm told us not to move. I understood. Any movement on our part could distract the wolves away from Debbie to us. And that could cause problems. Animals view the world differently from human beings. Humans tend to see what we want to see, usually only noticing the big picture. Animals focus on details. Movement. What's different? Is that dangerous? For them it's a matter of survival.

"Lakota! Inside," Debbie coaxed, kneeling by the fence opening, her voice full of encouragement. Lakota did not comply.

Instead, the pack leader lovingly licked her face then reared up on his hind legs to nuzzle her head. Gently but firmly she pressed him down. When he did it again, she pressed him down harder. "No!"

"She's showing dominance," Peter said softly. "She can't let Lakota or any other of the wolves jump on her, even in play. Their play tests the social hierarchy."

Aila slipped in to nip at Cheyenne and placed a forepaw on Debbie's back. Lakota's ears flipped back and his lips curled to expose sharp teeth. He growled. "No. Behave," Debbie admonished. She went on all fours and crawled back through the opening into the enclosure. The wolves followed. Claudette, who had remained outside to usher the animals forward, brought up the rear. Only after all were on the other side of the fence did Debbie stroke and talk affectionately to the wolves as they capered around her.

"Claudette. Keep them in the enclosure but guard the opening."

The petite woman with the cascades of curly black hair nodded, eyeing the rip in the fence with trepidation. "You want me to block it with something?"

"Yeah, your body. We'll keep it open for a while. I'm going back out for Rufus. My hope is Lakota will start making noise and Rufus will respond to the call. We want to leave a way for him to get back in."

Claudette nodded. "Got it."

"And if Rufus sees the others inside the enclosure, he may want to join them. That's why I don't want them in holding right now." Debbie heaved a mammoth sigh. "This is where we wing it. I'm counting on you, Claudette. Can you keep them inside the fence?"

"Yes."

"If you see Rufus, call him to you. Give me thirty minutes.

After that I'll come back and we'll seal up the opening."

Looking slightly overwhelmed, Claudette gave a quick nod and turned to her charges. Lakota and his two pack mates trotted around their enclosure, sniffing new smells and re-familiarizing themselves with their home.

"Good work, Deb!" Peter Bunyan beamed as we approached the fence opening.

She lurched to her feet after crawling back through. "I was lucky. I found Cheyenne. He led me to Lakota and Aila, who were checking out something under an old log."

"What about Rufus?" I asked.

"No one's seen him." Debbie cast worried eyes toward the woods. "I gotta get back out there." She unclipped the hand-held radio from her belt. It squawked into life. "Danny. Gina. Lakota, Aila and Cheyenne are back inside the enclosure. Keep searching for another thirty minutes, then we'll lock things down. Got that? Three-zero minutes. Then report back to the command center. Out." She lowered her radio and tossed us a furtive smile. "Man! It's not even ten A.M. and I'm exhausted! I'm having second thoughts about that opening. If Claudette needs help, will you and Snake make sure the wolves don't get out? And Peter, I'm thinking it wouldn't hurt to set up your traps now. Thanks guys!" Debbie Wong took off at a dead run. Long legs propelled her deeper into the woods, her straight black hair bouncing with each urgent stride.

"I hope she finds him," I murmured, almost like a prayer.

"Yeah," Peter grunted, not sounding optimistic.

My eyes slid over to the fence. "Who would do something like this?"

"Whoever did it came prepared. Used a bolt cutter. Made short work of it."

"But why?"

Peter motioned for me to follow. We walked back across the

carpet of dead leaves to the first trap. "Chief Manske was here earlier assessing the damage. He told me something interesting. The ballistics report came back on Ivar Bjorklund. The rifle that killed him is the same one that killed the Red Iron wolves."

My eyes got big. "So there is a connection between the two killings. Does Manske think the same guy cut the fence?"

"No, he doesn't."

"He doesn't? What d'you think?"

I held one side of the Tru-Catch trap as Peter raised the door, which squealed into place. "Me, I think this little fence-cutting incident is a little too convenient for the murderer. It distracts the police, me, and the MWI staff who're helping me."

"So you think it's the same guy?"

"I didn't say that. But the timing bothers me. In all the years the wolf institute's been open, this is the only time the place has been vandalized."

"The timing does stink—and so does that!" I waved my hand in front of my nose, giving the evil eye toward the plastic container he just opened. The rank odor of raw and old meat assaulted my nostrils.

"That's road kill beaver. It's mixed in with raw hamburger. Our bait." Peter took a handful, wadded it into a ball and loaded the back door trigger mechanism.

"Okay," I pressed, "you won't go on the record. What's your unofficial opinion, Officer Bunyan?"

"Off the record? Yeah, I think it's the same guy. Not a shred of proof, only suspicion." More bait was placed on the ground a foot from the trap entrance, and some a few yards farther out.

We made our way to the second trap, some hundred yards away. While I tried to focus on the task at hand, my thoughts swarmed like a cloud of gnats. "Peter, what if Manske's right and the guy who cut open the fence has nothing to do with the killings?"

"Then that would suck." Peter squatted before the trap, raising its wire mesh door. "In the old days we had more probable suspects. The anti-wolf crowd was very vocal then. Some even militant. Things are different now. Even the farmers and ranchers affected by wolf predation aren't rabidly opposed to wolves—"

"Except for Bjorklund and Hansen."

"My point is even those guys wouldn't resort to this kind of vandalism."

"Yeah." I snorted. "They'd be more likely to shoot 'em than let them roam free!"

"There's that," Peter agreed. He gestured for the bait container. "What concerns me is the fanatic fringe, someone out there who burns with righteous indignation and feels justified in breaking the law if it serves his cause."

"Like the Stewards of Superior?"

"Not so much them." He baited the trap and stood up, regarding me somberly. "It doesn't matter who. Sometimes there isn't much difference between one extremist and another. Their tactics are often the same. Whether ultra-religious, ultra-conservative, ultra-liberal, fanatic animal hater or animal lover— all extremists have only one mindset. To get back at you. And the worst of them do it with violence."

He turned away as if his own words disgusted him. We walked back silently together toward the perimeter fence. The morning sun glinted above the treetops. In that transitional time between summer and autumn, the cool morning air warmed quickly.

"So why a conservation officer?" I finally asked, our boots crunching on the forest leaf litter.

He managed a wan, ironic smile. "I almost became a wildlife biologist. A wolf biologist, in fact. But I felt pulled in another direction."

"You must like helping the underdog."

"Actually, that's not far from the truth. My grandfather was a bounty hunter back in the nineteen-thirties. Back then a wolf pelt would fetch thirty-five dollars. My first hunting lesson with the old man was in the seventies when I was a teenager. He took me to a den of wolf pups, so young they didn't even have their eyes open yet. When I said I didn't want to shoot them he got all over me. Called me names. He finally badgered me into pulling the trigger . . ." Peter's voice trailed away, hollow. He slipped on his aviator sunglasses.

He didn't elaborate. He didn't have to. I'd read the history, seen the photos of strings of wolf pelts dangling like laundry on a clothesline. I'm not against hunting. It's what predators do, and we are predators. Responsible hunters I have no problem with. Most hunters support habitat conservation programs like Ducks Unlimited. What tears me up is cruelty for the sheer joy of it. Club them to death, set them on fire, garrote their puppies. Humankind's hatred of wolves went far beyond the intolerance to a pest. Yet the same people who hate the wolf would likely sacrifice a kidney for their own dog. How could you love dogs and hate wolves? The answer, I suspected, is that the wolf was simply too successful a competitor for its own good, exterminated from nearly every country because it was too intelligent, too good at hunting the same prey as us. Humans have never been good at sharing resources.

After some silent reflection, he smiled thinly. "That's when I decided to go into law enforcement."

"Those deaths must have haunted you."

"It wasn't only that. I'd heard stories from conservation officers I'd met in school. Stories like the guy who swerved off the highway to deliberately run over a Canada goose. 'It's only a goose,' he said after he was pulled over."

"Only a goose," I repeated, my gut churning.

"Or there's the one about the guy who killed a deer at a local golf course because he'd just got a new rifle and wanted to shoot something. Anything." Peter shook his head in disbelief. "Guys like that mess it up for everyone else. Someone has to stop them. And that was me, Snake."

"Peter, if you were a superhero," I teased, "you'd be the Punisher."

"Who's that?"

"A man who seeks retribution for law breakers. My brother loved those comic books. The Punisher goes too far and kills the bad guys. You wouldn't be so violent." I smiled slyly, tossing him a sidelong glance.

He gave an awkward little smile back and averted his gaze.

I checked my watch. Fifteen minutes had passed. "It's not looking good."

He scratched his unshaven chin stubble, no doubt the result of having rushed out of the house first thing this morning. "If Rufus doesn't come back, let's hope his survival instincts are good. He's never had to hunt for a meal."

Hope shined in my eyes. "Maybe that's a good thing? After a few weeks of being hungry he might come back to the place he knows there's food."

"If we're lucky. It's the wilderness out there and he's on his own. He could get run over. Might meet up with a bear. If he approaches another pack, he'd be lucky if they drove him off. They might kill him."

A sickening feeling twisted my insides. "That's not all. The guy who killed the wolves is still out there. I just hope Rufus doesn't cross paths with him."

Peter grunted softly in agreement.

Far away we heard Gina calling Rufus, followed by a silence broken only by the rustling of high tree branches and a few birds. Peter turned to face me directly, slipping off his aviator shades. "Snake, you know Gina fairly well."

"Not so well these days."

"You were best friends in college."

"Sure, we did everything together. At least, until I transferred to Friends University in Wichita. That was over fifteen years ago, Peter."

"But you've kept in touch."

"We did for a while before she dropped off the edge of the world. It was only four months ago when I found out she worked at the wolf institute."

"When did you lose contact?"

All these questions about Gina. It pinged my emotional radar. There'd been the tension I'd noticed between Peter and Gina. A romance gone bad? Working with someone you had feelings for could be hellish, particularly if you still held those feelings and the other person didn't. That might account for Gina's bitchfest the other day around Peter. I'd even teased her about how she seemed really chummy with the rugged DNR officer. At the mere suggestion of a romantic liaison between them, she stiffened up like a rabbit spying an approaching badger. Without actually saying so, her body language made it clear that particular subject was off limits. Very unlike the old Gina. No subject was taboo to that carefree girl.

"Nine years ago," I replied. "That was the last time I'd spoken to Gina until recently. She just stopped returning my calls. After a while I gave up." And it hurt. Close friends one day, next day you're not. And you don't know why.

Peter pressed his lips together pensively, his thoughts turning inward as if doing his own numeric calculations. Afterward, he let out a shallow breath, his shoulders relaxed and he slipped on his shades. I'd given him the wrong answer, I could tell, and the defenses were going back up. He rested his hands on his leather belt, which creaked under the weight.

"Gina's been through a lot since then," he said. "Life's

thrown her some curves. Some bad ones. She bounces back most of the time. You know that."

He assumed I knew a lot more than I did.

"Her one fault," I offered in hopes he'd volunteer more, "has always been her temper. She's never been afraid to speak her mind."

"She doesn't hold back, that's for sure. Even so, she does bottle up some emotions. A little too much, if you ask me."

"Like what?"

"Her real feelings on some touchy subjects," he said in a way that didn't really answer the question. Before I could prod him on, Peter turned at movement in the forest, a raven that had swooped down to pick at some morsel on the ground. "We grew up together in Bemidji. Her brother was one of my best friends."

"Irresistible Ian," I grinned. A wild rock star mop of hair and sparkling eyes that could melt a heart two blocks away. All the girls had been crazy over Ian Brown. Including *moi*. If I'd been a few years older, I would have made a play for him myself. Over Gina Brown's overprotective body, that is. She really adored her older brother and watched out for him as if she had been the older sibling.

"What's Ian up to these days? Gina was really vague when I asked her."

Peter blanched slightly. He recovered with an unconvincing nonchalance. "He lives in Tower. He's got his own life now. We don't see much of each other anymore. Kinda like what happened between you and Gina."

There was more to it than that. Some undercurrent I couldn't follow. I was about to dig deeper when—

Peter stabbed out a finger. "Rufus!"

# Chapter 10

A flash of fur sent my heart jumping. A gray streak moved between trees and shrubs too far away to clearly see. But it was larger than a dog. Before I could draw my next breath, a large gray wolf trotted into view and stopped a hundred feet before us.

Danny Hoffman panted into sight moments later. "Rufus!! Hold up. It's me, boy!"

Rufus knew. It was why he had whirled around and was waiting for Danny to get just close enough before he took off again. Rufus was playing.

Peter and I spread out, widening our arms, hoping if Rufus came in our direction we'd steer him toward the perimeter fence or one of the traps. After running a wide circle, Rufus trotted into a small clearing and stopped. He sniffed the air. Danny approached cautiously, gently calling his name. Step by step he inched closer. Rufus lowered his snout to the ground so he could get a better sniff at the approaching human, tail gently wagging.

"It's me, Rufus. You know me."

A dry branch snapped under Danny's foot like a rifle shot. Rufus froze, ears flipping back. Danny moved and Rufus tore off like a bullet for the underbrush, jumping over a fallen log in one bound, and was gone.

Danny Hoffman swore and dropped to his knees in frustration. Debbie jogged out from behind a stand of birch trees to give encouragement to him. Danny gave a curt nod, clambered to his feet and trotted after Rufus. The wolf curator watched Danny fade off and spoke into her radio before trudging back to join us. After a deep breath, she plopped onto the grass. The chain-link fence rattled when her back slumped against it.

"Rufus's gone." She sighed. "It's time I get on with things. Gina and Danny'll stay out there for a while. What a disaster!" The back of her head banged against the fence. She jammed her eyes shut to close off the world.

Peter and I stood in front of her. He removed his sunglasses, concern and tenderness in his gaze.

"I've got so much to do." Debbie picked at a straw on her jeans. "I've got to let the administrator know what's happened, put phase two in motion, review the press statement, contact the media—what else? I know there's something I'm forgetting." She gave a half-hearted shrug. "I don't need this!" She called to the sky. "We've never had an escape. What kills me is people aren't going to pay attention to the fact that some outsider did this. All they'll hear is that wolves got out of their enclosure and we'll be blamed."

"You did your best," I said, feeling the need to offer some words of comfort, inadequate as they were.

She nodded and forced a smile, rallying her optimism. "At least we got three of them back. Though I'm sure I'll be second-guessed for not using tranquilizer darts." Debbie turned to me. "Snake, do you get that at the zoo? People who don't know how tranquilizers work?"

"Yeah. They've seen too many movies. They think tranquilizer darts are these feathery little things that prick the animal's hide and knock 'em out immediately."

In reality, they're big syringes full of drugs. Tranquilizer guns detonate an explosive charge to inject the drugs when it strikes the animal. It's no little sting; this is a painful wallop that can cause serious injuries.

"I don't want to have to dart Rufus if I can avoid it. Not when there's a chance of rounding him up without harming him."

I nodded back. "I saw a wolverine's leg bone shattered from a tranquilizer dart. It nearly lost its leg. On top of that, the drugs failed to knock him out and he kept trying to run on it, which caused more damage."

"Exactly!"

Large mammals—a bear or rhino—could take the impact of the dart in stride, whereas a bobcat, lynx, or even a wolf might suffer serious damage.

"And there's the delay," Peter put in. "You've got a fifteen- to twenty-minute lag before the drug sedates the animal. You made the right call, Deb."

"Yeah . . ."

"Even if you'd managed to fire a T-dart into Rufus and the detonation didn't cripple him, you'd have one terrified animal, in pain, running for his life for the next twenty minutes. Into Superior National Forest. You'd never find him!"

"And I'd have a sedated wolf alone, vulnerable to predators. Thanks, Peter." Debbie offered a wan smile. "I needed to hear that." With quiet determination she hauled herself up and appraised the hole in the fence. "I'd really like to leave that open. He might come back. Escaped captive animals often do. They'll roam around for a while, then return to their enclosures the same way they got out. I'd like to leave it open for Rufus. But I can't. I can't keep the others in holding indefinitely."

"I suppose not," Peter agreed.

"I know!" Debbie snapped her fingers. "I'll get the spare roll of fencing. Could you guys bring the far trap inside the enclosure? We'll put it a few feet inside the opening and use the spare fencing to seal off the gaps. That way if Rufus wanders back and is looking for the hole in the fence, he'll find it. The trap should get him and our little addition will keep Lakota and his mates from getting out."

"Sounds like a plan!" I said, antsy to help.

She brushed aside her black bangs. Satisfaction that she'd done the best she could temporarily chased away the weight of her troubles.

We returned with the wire mesh trap, barely pushing it through the jagged opening in the chain-link fence.

"Debbie," I asked. "What else can we do?"

A grateful smile came my way. "Thanks for offering. Once we're done here, I've got a job for you and Gina."


"What a crappy day!" Gina slammed the door to her pickup. The two of us walked toward the main entrance of the wolf institute on legs as heavy and stiff as concrete. It was near closing time. A long, frustrating day.

We caught up with Debbie in the escape command center. She was going over a task list with several volunteers when she caught sight of us. "You guys look beat."

I flopped into a Samsonite chair. "We must've put in ten to twelve miles on foot this afternoon."

"More than that!" Gina grumbled. "Snake and I covered all of sector three." She nodded toward the map. "No signs of Rufus. No one we saw had seen a wandering wolf. We spoke to a lot of people, gave out phone numbers and did the PR thing."

"At least you missed the media frenzy. We had film crews from all the major channels here. Guess it must be a slow news week." Debbie offered us a weak smile. "Did people freak out when you told them there's a wolf on the loose?"

"Actually, no. The folks I spoke to were sympathetic. Helpful. Angry some shithead cut the fence open."

"But not afraid?"

"That a wolf's on the loose? Heck no. This is Wolf Lake. Seeing a wild wolf or moose or bear cross the highway or appear at the edge of town isn't a mind-blowing experience. It's no big deal."

Debbie relaxed a little. "I was hoping that would be the reaction, but you can never be sure. It'd be hard enough to find Rufus, let alone having to reassure people they're not in real danger."

"How're you holding up?" I asked.

She gave a dismissive shrug. "A mess. I'm running on adrenaline. I have to be Big Mamma to the staff and volunteers. All of them want to be out there scouring the woods for Rufus. But they have jobs to do here, too. We still have to keep the place open, take care of the animals. Just like normal. I know they'd rather be out there looking for him. It's frustrating for them."

"And you."

"And me," Debbie agreed.

"I suppose you'll be up all night."

"Yeah. No sleep for me tonight. After I take care of my kids, I'll be on the phone with the DNR. Plus I have to update the MWI board in Minneapolis on our status. And I'll come back for a few hours to relieve Danny. He volunteered to hang out in the back woods all night in case Rufus wanders back."

Gina bobbed her head. "I don't blame him. You feel like you're doing something. Maybe we should take a turn, Snake."

"Sure, but don't we have dinner plans?"

"Justin! Crap! I forgot. We're supposed to be at Justin Trudeau's in two hours," Gina said. "I wanted Snake to meet him. We could cancel. He'd understand."

"No, Gina. Go to Justin's. You and Snake've been out all day. You're both beat. You could use a good dinner and downtime. Besides, Justin lives in Sector Five. Ask him if he'll help us."

"Good idea!" The disappointments of the day vanished as a new purpose energized Gina.

We exited by the main entrance as the last of the patrons were let out. Waving at us from the adjoining gift shop, stood Danny Hoffman. "Hey, Gina, Snake. Tell me you guys have good news."

Gina shook her head. "Sorry, Dan-O. Wish I did."

"Bummer."

"You're gonna have a long night," I said, trying to lighten the moment. "Debbie said you're camping outside tonight."

"Yeah, I'm too wound up to sleep. My band's practicing this evening, but I told them I won't be there. Wouldn't be able to concentrate. They can blame it on artistic temperament." Danny cracked a wise-ass smile. "Hey, speaking of artists, Snake, I'd like you to meet Lyle Almquist."

From behind the gift counter, a large, heavyset man paused in the act of unpacking leather goods to watch us curiously from beneath a bushy set of white eyebrows. He stepped away from the glass display case to reveal a belly as impressive as the fifty-five-gallon drums I remembered shimmying in the back of his pickup. A plump, cheerful face smiled broadly behind a short-cropped beard the color of pure snow. Santa Claus. It was all I could think of.

Danny, skinny enough in contrast to have been one of Almquist's elves, gestured proudly toward me. "Lyle, this is the lady I was telling you about. Snake Jones from the Minnesota Valley Zoo."

He took my hand in a strong, smooth grasp. Nothing like the dry parchment touch of Ivar Bjorklund. Or the slimy two-handed vice grip of Forrest Hansen. Holy cow! I was shaking hands with Santa Claus. It was difficult for the little girl inside me to forget that pudgy face didn't belong to the Jolly One himself.

"Nice to meet you. Any luck finding your missing wolf?"

"No."

"I heard about the other ones, the dead wolves. Shame about that. I like wolves. That time of year, I suppose. Hunting season. Some of them hunters don't give a rat's ass what they shoot at. Then there's Ivar Bjorklund. Same thing. Somebody's careless with a gun—"

"It wasn't an accident, Lyle," Gina corrected. "That was intentional. Someone shot him and left him to die. He lived long enough to leave a message—or tried to."

Almquist was taken back. I guess the Wolf Lake rumor mill wasn't infallible.

"Didn't know that," he added darkly.

"You knew Mr. Bjorklund?" I asked.

"No. Not at all."

Danny shot him a curious look, and then moved out of the way as the gift store manager came back from refolding items on the t-shirt shelf. "Lyle's dropping off stuff for the gift shop," Danny explained. "His leather goods are only sold in a few select stores in town."

I nodded enthusiastically. "I've seen your work at Signe's. You're good."

"Good?" Danny took offense. "Lyle's a master."

He held up a soft leather jacket embossed with the portrait of a gray wolf. Gina had said Lyle was an artist but I wasn't prepared for the intricate detail he'd coaxed out of deer hide.

"It's gorgeous! Danny's right. You are a master."

"Told you. One of these days Lyle's gonna make me a custom jacket. Only mine'll have a portrait of Jimi Hendrix on the back."

Almquist's white eyebrows rose in confusion. "I thought you wanted that Springsteen fella."

Danny paused to reflect. "Yeah." Then shook his head. "I

don't know. Hard to make up my mind. It's a big commitment."

Almquist rolled his eyes and continued unpacking his box. He set a quantity of belts, wallets, slippers, mouse pads, vests and jackets on the counter for the tired store manager to process.

I remembered what Peter had said about Almquist being the guy to talk to if I wanted to know what was going on along Black Fir Road.

"Mr. Almquist?"

"Yes?" He turned toward me pleasantly.

"I believe you know Peter Bunyan. He's a conservation officer for the DNR."

"I know Peter."

"Gina and I are helping him with the investigation of the wolf kill. D'you have any ideas who might've shot the wolves? Maybe heard someone bragging about it. That kind of thing?"

A big, pudgy hand came up to stroke his silky white mustache. Almquist reflected. "Where were the carcasses found?"

"In the woods along Black Fir Road."

"You might talk to Moua Vang."

"I've heard that name before," I said to Gina. "Peter and I were on our way to talk to him when he got the call about the moose in distress. We never made it to Mr. Vang's."

That interested Gina. She tilted her head and regarded Almquist with interest. "You think Vang shot those wolves?"

"Whoa, not so fast! I said no such thing. I just said you might talk to the guy. I don't wanna get nobody in trouble."

"Then why did you mention him?" Gina pressed.

Almquist backed off. "All I meant was that Vang likes to shoot off his guns. I don't know what at. You'd have to ask him. I don't want to say any more."

"You don't have to," I said, not wanting to upset him further.

He paused to consider me. "I try to keep my nose clean. Others should do the same. I am sorry about those wolves getting killed. I'd like to get my hands on the guy myself."

"You and me both!" Gina echoed.

My fingers absently stroked the leather of the deerskin jacket on the counter. "It's so soft," I murmured, trying to distract my own misgivings about my old friend's itchy trigger finger.

"I tan some of my own hides. My process makes them a heckuva lot softer'n anything you'll find in most stores."

I had to agree, my fingers unable to resist the soft, buttery feel of the leather.

"Where do you get your skins?" I wondered out loud, thinking that one of his suppliers might know something about the slaughtered wolves.

"I used to hunt my own. Not anymore. Not worth the trouble."

"You no longer hunt?"

He gave a dismissive snort. "Don't hunt nothing these days other than my car keys. My hipbone's out of whack. My doctor says I'm about three years away from a total hip replacement. Getting around the woods is no picnic anymore." As if to illustrate, he stepped out from behind the counter with his empty cardboard box and hobbled toward the front doors. He moved quickly but with a lumbering gait. Before I could follow up with another question, the musical strains of "Tie Me Kangaroo Down, Sport" interrupted my thoughts. My cell phone.

My cell phone!

I was stunned. Had I found the one place in Wolf Lake where I could pick up a signal? I fumbled for my phone. "Hello?"

A rich Down Under baritone boomed into my ear. "How's my favorite green-eyed sheila?"

"Jeff! Say, how many other green-eyed sheilas do you know?"

"Only the cold-blooded kind, sweetheart: lizards and crocs.

None of 'em as gorgeous as you!" My husband's voice brought a smile to my weary face. His warmth and unabashed affection washed over me like a tropical surf. The stress of the day's events had made me forget how much I'd missed him, even though we'd only been apart a few days.

"It's great to hear your voice," I said, deciding not to tell him about the crisis at the wolf institute. There'd be plenty of time for that later. Or he'd be seeing it on the ten o'clock news. "What're you up to?"

"I was just going out for a bit of tucker with Billie and Shaggy and thought I'd better call the wife." Billie our director and Shaggy our cameraman were filming with Jeff in Duluth.

"Everything okay?" I asked, walking out of the gift shop so the manager could close things up. The phone crackled as I stepped by the door. For an instant, I thought I'd lost the signal when Jeff came back.

"We did a segment about non-native invasive species in Lake Superior. This biologist bloke showed us these sea lampreys that were killing the fish in droves. Ugly little buggers. Sounds like they've got them under control now."

"Did you finally get in the water?" I teased. This was Jeff's first time to Lake Superior. I remember him saying how he wanted to swim in the world's second largest freshwater lake.

"Dipped me toe in, that's all. Crikey! That water's bloody cold!"

I laughed. "Superior's always cold. It's too deep. You're used to those comfy tropical waters. Welcome to the great north."

"Wait till you see the great footage we took at the Duluth Zoo. We'll be leaving tomorrow, luv. If we can wrap up early, we should be up there by noon."

I stepped outside, the first stars still pale against a darkening sky. "Can't wait."

I watched Lyle Almquist's halting gait take him across the

parking lot to his beat-up white pickup truck. Not jolly Santa from this angle, I mused. Merely a tired, limping old man struggling to make a living.

"Did you get my message about . . ." Jeff's voice crackled into nothingness.

"Jeff?" I stepped back toward the doors, hoping to regain the signal.

". . . Animal Planet?"

"What?" He sounded like he was under water.

"Planet called . . . talk . . . a . . . series."

Then dead air.

Arrrgh!

I tried ringing him back, but there was no signal. Jeff had mentioned Animal Planet. What about them? Were they interested in our program?

"Snake, you okay?" Gina searched my face. "You look upset."

"I'm fine. Just production stuff." I dismissed her with a curt head shake. Truth was, I didn't want to jinx the deal by saying anything. And if I had misheard, I didn't want to get my hopes up. Last month we had sent some *Zoofari* tapes to a friend at Animal Planet. It was possible they wanted to see more, or they might even be interested in picking up the show, in which case I needed to get serious about why I was in Wolf Lake, which was not to be chasing down wolf hunters and murderers.

Danny joined us in the parking lot, digging in his tight-fitting pockets for keys. "He's lying, ya know."

"Who's lying?"

"Lyle." Danny gazed toward the departing white pickup rumbling down the driveway. "He knew Ivar. I saw them arguing in the parking lot of Zup's Market last week."

I shrugged, not really interested. My focus had to be on *Zoofari*, not who killed Ivar Bjorklund. That was for the police to figure out.

Gina wasn't buying it either. "Maybe Lyle's confused. So you saw Ivar arguing with Lyle. Hell, Ivar argued with everybody. Maybe Lyle cut him off at the intersection. You know how that old coot drives."

Danny shook his head. "It was more than that. Ivar was waving a piece of paper under Lyle's nose. He was riled up about something."

"He always was," said Gina without sympathy.

The tiny voice inside my head whispered suggestively: What if Ivar'd been waving a Stewards of Superior warning? Like the one found under his body.

# CHAPTER 11

Wild rice soup, sweet summer corn on the cob and sourdough pita bread cooked over an open fire, a simple meal that tasted like a feast. Staring into the campfire, I was glad Gina and I hadn't cancelled our dinner plans with Justin Trudeau. It was a much-needed ending to a stressful day. With the heat from the fire warming me from without and a hearty meal warming me from within, I felt myself loosening up for the first time all day.

Justin's home was a bit of theater in the woods. The single-story rustic house blended so well into the landscape, you could barely make it out in the dim evening light. The backyard integrated itself into the natural landscape like a thrust stage. Our fire claimed the center of the yard, surrounded by hand-hewn logs set in a hexagonal shape. Above us, the stars spread out against an endless curtain of cobalt sky.

It had been a long day. Awfully long. Bjorklund. The wolves. Rufus. It was too much in too small a space of time. With Peter's confirmation the same weapon had been used in the killing of man and wolves, we now had a connection. Like one of Jeff's brightly painted Australian boomerangs hanging in our home office, the thought kept coming back to me that Bjorklund's murder was some kind of payback.

It wasn't difficult to imagine some environmental extremist getting it into his head Ivar had killed those four wolves. The old Swede had made his opinions about them pretty clear at Signe's the other day. "Kill 'em all," he'd said. Any nut job wanting retribution for the deaths of those animals could've easily used that diatribe as an excuse to set the wheels in motion.

Peter Bunyan had been right about one thing: zealots of any type can be dangerous if they believe it's their God-given right to punish the wicked. It only takes one idiot to blacken the good deeds of other environmentalists. To make matters worse, an extremist group was already operating in northern Minnesota and had left their calling card under Bjorklund's body: the Stewards of Superior.

I didn't want to think about this right now. I only wanted peace. The heat from the flames seeped through my jacket and jeans, easing weary muscles into sublime relaxation. There were professionals working every angle, I was sure. They didn't need me. I needed to focus on getting another episode of *Zoofari* in the can and get back to the Minnesota Valley Zoo. Our new director, Butler Thomas, was not going to let Jeff and me take an indefinite leave of absence.

"Did you hear that?" Justin straightened up from the fire, turning his ear toward the forest. The flickering firelight cast undulating shadows under his jaw, lending his handsome Ojibwe features a ghostly aspect.

"What?" I asked.

"A wolf."

"I didn't hear . . ."

Then I did. Rising into my awareness like a whisper in the wind, a faint, mournful howl rose out of the darkness. It sent a thrill through me.

"Rufus?" Gina sprang up from where she had been sitting cross-legged, her hand up to her mouth, ready to make a return call to the lone wolf.

Justin put a hand out to stop her. "I've heard that call for the last four nights. It's not Rufus."

"Sounds far away," I said, giving Gina a gentle tug to sit back down beside me again.

"Could be. Hard to tell in this weather. The sound could carry five miles or more."

"Is he declaring his territory?" I asked.

"That's not a territorial howl. He's calling to his pack mates."

Pack mates that would never answer again? I wondered if the lone wolf was from the Red Iron pack. The cry came up again, fading seconds later like a disembodied spirit.

While Gina had been making an effort to keep the conversation going and was outwardly enjoying Justin's stories, she seemed preoccupied. Rufus's escape had knocked her flat, maybe even more than Bjorklund's murder. Or maybe all of the week's events were taking their toll. I recalled Peter's comments of the rough times she had gone through, feeling some guilt that I hadn't made more of an effort to stay in touch.

Justin stared out into the dark woods around us. He heaped another log onto the fire, poking at the tented logs with a long stick. Sparks and hot embers skittered out as flames writhed up in excitement. Stepping back to survey his work, Trudeau grunted with satisfaction.

The wolf called again.

"The Mongols believed they were descended from the wolf." Justin offered a meditative smile. "Genghis Khan and his people believed the wolf symbolized the attributes they most admired: superior intelligence, limitless endurance, wisdom. I like that. Much more benign than the medieval Catholic Church, which called the wolf the devil's dog, the incarnation of pure evil on Earth." He rose from his seat on the ground, grabbed the steaming cast iron pot from the fire and offered us some more soup.

Gina waved him off, patting her well-satisfied belly for emphasis.

"Snake?"

My hand held him at bay. "No thanks. I'm stuffed. Great dinner, Justin."

Now that I'd met him, it was easy to see why Gina had spoken so highly of Justin Trudeau. A great storyteller, he'd spent the last twenty minutes entertaining us with Native American wolf tales, information he was collecting for his next book. In his mid-forties, with long black hair and the lean, underfed build of a serious jogger, he had a gaze that penetrated beyond the backs of your eyeballs and into the depths of your being. His face spoke of having learned life's lessons the hard way, yet the deep creases at the edges of his eyes were not devoid of mirth. His face glowed in the orange firelight. His faded denim jacket hung open to reveal a black t-shirt emblazoned with the image of a single eagle feather.

Oh, and the voice. His soothing baritone comforted like hot chocolate on a frosty winter evening.

Setting down the metal pot, he lowered himself onto a log. "The wolf slaughter saddens me."

This last seemed like a personal loss, as if a family member had died. Brother wolf. If coyote was the trickster in Native American lore, wolf was the wise hunter.

"As does the death of Ivar," he added almost as an afterthought.

"What I can't understand is why," Gina said sharply. "Why was Ivar in that abandoned driveway? He was driving the school bus. He always took his responsibilities so seriously. He would never risk picking those kids up late."

"Meeting someone he knew?" I suggested.

"And that someone turned on him. Betrayed him."

"Who'd want to kill Ivar?" asked Justin. "That should be the first question. I didn't know him well, but he seemed harmless."

Harmless? Yeah, probably. Although he hadn't seemed that harmless when he had first slung his verbal darts at me. Later, I

met a much different Ivar at his farm. He had been a man trying to protect his sheep, missing a much-loved spouse and trying to make a life on his own in a world that wasn't all that
welcoming.

I turned to Justin. "Gina says you get around the woods. You
see things."

A wry glint animated Gina's face. "He's a phantom. Comes
and goes in the forest like the mist. Even the animals don't
always know he's there. That's how Justin gets those great
photos."

"Gina showed me your book. The pictures are nothing short
of astounding." The photos had left me feeling as if I had been
eavesdropping, a peeping Tom watching wolves being wolves,
totally unaware they were being watched.

Justin shrugged. "I guess."

"Don't be modest," Gina chided good-naturedly. "You're
made of marble. Or just your butt. I could never sit out in the
woods the way you do. Hours at a time. Not for a photograph."

"Not just a photograph. I take hundreds of shots, hoping for
one good picture," he explained. "You can't be in a hurry when
working with nature or animals. Both have a way of doing what
they want, when they want. It's like my current book. I spent
months trying to capture the perfect wolf lope." He held his
hands in front of him as if holding a camera and turned,
remembering that moment. "There's no mistaking the confident, easy stride of a gray wolf. Makes the most athletic dog appear clumsy by comparison. The narrow chest lets the wolf's
shoulders move more efficiently. He's born to run. I can't tell
you how many hundreds of shots it took to get the right one."
Trudeau leaned back a little, basking in the accomplishment.

"You're more patient than I'd be." I knew something of what
it took to capture wildlife on film. Even with a video camera,
getting the shot you wanted could be elusive.

"Stalking your prey—whether with a rifle or camera lens—requires stealth and persistence and being able to let the moment pass empty-handed. Fishermen do it all the time."

"And you."

"Believe me, it didn't come naturally." Justin made a sweeping gesture. "I didn't grow up in the woods. I was a city kid. Duluth. Some of my family was on the Rez. Not us. I never made it to the woods until my late teens. In fact, I spent fifteen years working as a structural engineer in Chicago before moving back to Minnesota. I didn't get into the nature thing until several years ago."

"Structural engineer? Beams and foundations?"

"Pretty much." He flashed a pragmatic smile. "I still take freelance assignments a few times a year. Enough to pay the bills so I can spend most weeks here or in the woods."

"Must be nice," I nodded, gazing up at the dark pines silhouetted against the indigo sky. Not everyone was fortunate enough to do what they loved. Being an animal keeper had been my lifelong dream. There was no other occupation I'd ever considered. Still, living out here, away from people and so close to the heartbeat of Mother Nature, was enticing.

Gina tossed a pebble into the fire. "Justin, did you know the Red Iron pack? Ever take photos of them?"

"No. Too close to home for me. I'm usually much farther north or east of Red Iron. Most of my stuff is near International Falls or Quetico."

"Oh."

"Gina's disappointed. She's hoping there'd be a mysterious figure lurking in one of your photographs."

Justin shifted on the log. He leaned closer, elbows resting on his thighs. "It's hunting season. For the next couple months I try to avoid lurking in the popular spots myself. Too many people taking pot shots at things. Don't want one of them to be me. Sounds like your investigation is off to a slow start."

"It's not my investigation," I corrected, maybe a little too ardently.

He sat up. "I thought you were helping Peter Bunyan."

"I tagged along. Don't know how much I was helping."

Gina bristled. "So you're giving up? Just like that?"

"I can't give up something I never started," I pointed out.

"You put your life on the line when your zoo director was killed. What's different about this?"

"It's not my turf. The Wolf Lake police and BCA can handle the murder investigation. And I'm sure Peter won't give up on finding who killed those wolves. Who needs me?"

Gina glowered at the fire, tossing in a dry twig. It crackled and sparked as it hit the flames. "You've changed. The Snake Clark I used to know would never've backed down from righting a wrong."

"Well, I'm Snake Jones now," I reminded her in jest. But her words resonated. Had I changed? I didn't remember myself as the crusader for justice at Northland College. That honor belonged to Gina. I was the follower, the amiable sidekick. How strange that now she turned to me for answers. Answers I didn't have. Answers I wasn't sure I could even find.

Justin refilled my wine glass. "I'm sure Peter wouldn't have asked you along if he hadn't thought you helpful."

"We talked to Ivar and his friend Forrest Hansen. I don't think I was much help." I remembered the old man's reaction when I asked about his gun. Not my most stellar moment.

"Forrest Hansen." Justin repeated the name with distaste. "Now there's a wolf in sheep's clothing."

"Oh? Now you've got my interest."

The dark eyes contemplated the fire before sliding over to address me. "He's not a pleasant man. Likes to show off. Impress people. In his way he belittles others."

An impatient Gina filled in the rest. "He's done time for assault and battery. Justin's nose will attest to that."

"He hit you?"

"More like beat him up."

"Gina," Justin admonished. "Don't exaggerate. Hansen doesn't like me. He was drunk and picked a fight. I wouldn't fight him. He knocked me down three times before his friends stopped him."

"And he went to jail for that?"

"No, the assault charge was long ago, when he was a teenager."

I pressed the small of my back into my log backrest. "Sounds like there's bad blood between you two."

"You could say that. Hansen blames me for the Fond du Lac tribe not selling him some land he wants to develop. Cost him a lot of money."

I thought of the lean, hungry-looking Justin standing up to Muscle-Boy. Peter and I had felt the lash of Hansen's anger in Bjorklund's pasture, all his anti-wolf sentiments spewing at us like poison. Only Ivar Bjorklund managed to rein him in.

Forrest Hansen. What was it about that name?

In the distance, the solitary wolf howled again. This time, the lone voice was met by a chorus of wails from another direction. Other wolves were in search of him.

Then it came to me. Bjorklund's dying act was to crawl back toward the trees to pluck a piece of the forest. Forest. Forrest Hansen?

Could that be the meaning of the elm twig clenched in the old Swede's fist?

# CHAPTER 12

Sleep did not come easily Wednesday night. Dreams of Ivar Bjorklund's ghost beating me with a tree branch and of finding Rufus dead on the side of the road kept me up half the night. That and Gina's lumpy couch. By morning, my stomach grumbled for fuel, but I had only coffee on my mind. The caffeinated kind. Not the herbal, organic made-from-sawdust brew Gina served. I needed the real deal, the kind served at Signe's Last Chance Outfitters.

"How's Gina doing?"

The contents of my environmentally friendly cup slopped over the lip as I took it from Signe's grasp. "Frazzled. She went in at the crack of dawn. I was awake long enough to say good-bye. I'm not a morning person."

A raspy voice called from the coffee bar. "You look tired." It was Gus. He and Mooney had just taken their seats behind the little table with the checkerboard. The two old-timers studied me with grandfatherly concern. "You getting enough rest, cutie?"

"Not last night." I slurped down several mouthfuls of go juice. Not very lady-like but it satisfied the monster in my belly.

Mooney, particularly frail looking, was barely able to shake a cautionary finger at me. "You shouldn't let that Gina keep you out late . . . unless she takes you to my place." He winked with a sly, toothy smile.

Gus elbowed him and chortled.

I laughed. "That wasn't it, guys. I couldn't sleep. Too much on my mind. Gina went in early for a big staff meeting. She's getting updated on the hunt for Rufus, our lost wolf."

Gus and Mooney waved at a customer who walked in. Ensconced behind their table, the Dukes of Decaf sipped coffee all day and greeted people as they entered, whether they knew them or not. It was part of their charm. Gus wore a brown cardigan sweater over a crisply pressed white shirt with a natty bow tie. Mooney sported a Ralph Lauren polo shirt. Both men wore dark cotton slacks and tennis shoes.

Signe Amunson pulled up the sleeves of her teal sweatshirt. "I saw Debbie Wong on the news last night. She was good. Very professional. She and Chief Manske were telling people to keep their eyes open for Rufus and to report any wolf sightings to the police."

"Oh, I missed that. I'm glad the word's getting out. The more eyes watching for Rufus, the better."

"Don't worry," Gus volunteered. "I'll keep a lookout for Rufus at the retirement home."

The wrinkles in Mooney's brow deepened. "How you gonna do that? You're here most of the day."

Gus was at a loss for words. I suppressed a smile.

Signe said, "I'm sure Gina's beside herself with worry."

"She is. They all are at the wolf institute. They're itching to get out and search. Danny Hoffman spent the night camped out behind the perimeter fence."

Mooney tugged at my sleeve. "I'd watch out for that Danny Hoffman. I hear he's involved in heavy metal."

Gus turned to Mooney with alarm. "Like mercury, chromium, and lead? That stuff's dangerous!"

"Actually guys, that's not what it means. Danny's in a heavy metal band. It's a kind of music."

"Music?" Confusion played in Mooney's face as he tried to puzzle it out.

Before I could explain, the front door burst open. In walked a laughing Cole Novak, hammer in hand, gesturing with the other outside. "Ya gotta see this!" he insisted to no one in particular, an unlit cigarette bobbing at the corner of his thin lips. "Some goofball tourist is in the middle of the street talking to a duck. He's squatting down like a duck, waving his arms like he wants to fly or mate with the damn thing." Everyone, including me, got a chuckle out of that. Some crowded around Novak at the front window. "Not from around here, I can tell you that much. A real tourist type, talkin' in some weird-ass accent like the bird's gonna understand him."

Weird-ass accent? I stopped laughing. "I think that goofball is my husband!" I hurried outside.

Jeff Jones, curator of the Australia Walkabout Trail at the Minnesota Valley Zoo, world class herpetologist, and star of *Zoofari*, was quacking and waddling like a giant, gangly duck. In the middle of Sheridan Avenue. Unfamiliar with the duck's credentials, I could only surmise from my vantage point that he seemed wholly unimpressed by the linguistic ability of my husband. The mallard shied away as Jeff approached, its emerald head bobbing as he went.

"C'mon little duck, go this way," Jeff coaxed in his broad Australian dialect. "No worries, mate. Your pal Jeff won't let you get run over. This way now. This way . . ."

Oblivious to the September chill, Jeff was clad in a khaki short-sleeved bush shirt, matching shorts, brown socks and hiking boots. His mop of sandy-colored hair fell into his sky-blue eyes as he stretched his arms out in a corralling gesture.

Whether persuaded by Jeff's ministrations or trying to keep his distance from this odd human, the mallard waddled post haste toward a grassy fringe with Jeff crab-walking in slow pursuit.

Yards away, Billie Bradshaw, *Zoofari*'s producer and director, leaned against the hood of her sedan, observing the proceedings with practiced patience. She had to. Working with Jeff required that. There was no telling when he'd go off on a tangent when an animal was involved. Whether diving into crocodile-infested waters or slithering up a tree in pursuit of a gecko, Jeff took advantage of the opportunities nature gave him.

A light breeze fluttered Billie's silver bangs to reveal a pair of caustic eyebrows. "Maybe we should be filming this wildlife encounter."

In reply, Arthur "Shaggy" Lutz, our cameraman, held up his hands to frame a shot with Jeff and the mallard. "Move over Jack Hanna! It's raw nature at its most dangerous. Can Jeff Jones survive the Man-Eating Duck of Wolf Lake?"

"The video'd sell a million copies," Billie mocked.

"Hey, maybe then we could afford a sound man! You wouldn't have to pull double duty."

"Triple duty," she corrected, but liked the suggestion.

They waved as I joined them. "What's going on?"

Billie nodded toward Sheridan Avenue. "That dumb duck was sitting in the middle of the street when we drove up. Jeff thought it might be lame. Of course, as soon as he gets close to it, the damned thing starts off through busy traffic! We had to stop cars and escort it to safety."

"It was pretty gnarly . . . I mean, we were worried about him," Shaggy remarked, correcting himself. He sounded abnormally stiff and proper.

I cocked my head to the side, really seeing him for the first time. "Shaggy, you shaved your goatee off."

"Arthur," he corrected, staring down at his loafers. "I'd prefer to be called Arthur, please."

That, too, was new. As were the neatly pressed chinos and button-down shirt.

"Look at you! All cleaned up." I grinned at him suspiciously. "So, Mr. Lutz, who's the girl?"

His color came up. "Trying to present myself more professionally. If I don't start taking myself seriously, no one else will."

"Arthur is teaching a video class," Jeff said over his shoulder, like an indulgent big brother, still ushering the bird out of harm's way. "He's a role model now."

Billie snorted. "Snake had it right the first time. It's always a woman."

I couldn't tell if Billie was amused or disgusted. She was old enough to be Shaggy's . . . er . . . Arthur's mother, but they had been working together closely over the last five years. She was comfortable with him. He complemented her style. A love interest for our cameraman could have her playing second fiddle.

I leaned to the side. "You kept the ponytail."

"There's only so far a guy will go to compromise for the Man!"

The duck squawked at us, as if annoyed our attention had been diverted from his plight. He maneuvered toward the street again and Jeff followed, offering encouragement to stay on the grass.

"Can't he fly?" I asked.

"Yes!" Arthur pointed toward the mallard, who winged his way skyward, perhaps fed up at the annoying human dogging him.

Satisfied the bird was safe, Jeff turned to me with a wide, welcoming grin. In two strides I was in his muscular arms. He planted a big wet one on my mouth and nearly squeezed me breathless. The world felt in good order again. It had been only four days since our parting, but I'd missed the guy. We had a lot to catch up on. Most important of which was the news about

Animal Planet, which my flaky cell reception had deprived me of hearing.

"How're you doin', luv?" Jeff beamed at me, radiating energy and good vibes, as incandescent as any lightbulb. "Been keeping out of trouble?"

I smiled back sweetly, ignoring the question. "You're early. I wasn't expecting you guys so soon."

"We finished at the Duluth Aquarium early this morning and drove straight up. Did you miss me?"

I felt his arm slip behind my waist and pull me closer. An audible sigh of contentment parted from my lips.

Billie, always the clock-watcher, cleared her throat. "We should check in at the Super 8, Jeff. We have a lot to go over for this afternoon."

"I've already spoken with Debbie," I said. "We're set. However, it might be a little crazy while we're there." I quickly recapped recent events regarding the wolf escape, Rufus, and the wolf slaughter.

"You've been busy!" Jeff was impressed.

Billie, on the other hand, lowered her chin and muttered something unintelligible to the asphalt. I'm sure she saw her shooting schedule crumble before her eyes.

"Debbie's still committed to our needs," I assured her. "We just have to be flexible. If sightings of Rufus come in, the wolf staff will need to deal with them."

"Wolf on the loose!" Arthur grinned. "I'm stoked!—I mean, I'm looking forward to getting some primo—um—first-class action shots of the drama."

I smiled at the well-groomed, neatly dressed cameraman, supportive of his efforts to improve himself, but secretly missing the erstwhile Shagster's bodacious banter. It'd take me a while to get used to buttoned-down Arthur.

The sound of passing traffic whooshed by.

"They're on pins and needles at the wolf institute," I said. "And there's another thing." I filled them in on the murder of Ivar Bjorklund.

All traces of humor evaporated from Jeff's face. That was one thing about America he was still adjusting to. Crime. Not that Australia is crime free. It's just that murders were rarer events in the remote areas where he'd lived and worked. He wasn't as inured to crime statistics as I was. Which may not speak well of me. Not that I take death lightly, it's just that some part of me had toughened long ago to this unpleasant aspect of life in America.

Billie Bradshaw, too jaded to offer anything other than a blanket indictment of the world, returned to the immediate topic of concern to her. "Do you think Debbie would let us film some of her staff meetings?"

"I know you, Billie. You want access to the escape command center."

Interest kindled in the steely eyes. "That sounds great. Showing the institute during a crisis would make a hell of a show. Even better if we can show them acting on a wolf sighting."

Jeff, bless him, wasn't thinking about the show. "Maybe there's something we can do to help."

Just what I'd hoped to hear. I was about to offer suggestions when Peter Bunyan's Dodge Ram pulled off Sheridan Avenue into Signe's parking lot. The DNR shield on the door stood out prominently as it swung open. Peter headed toward us.

Arthur eyed Peter's uniform with trepidation. "Whoa, did we do something wrong?"

"Relax. That's Officer Bunyan. Peter! Come meet the gang." I made the introductions.

"G'day, mate." Jeff pumped Peter's hand with the vigor of a politician out for votes. "I trust you've been taking good care of the missus."

"The missus can take care of herself, thank you very much," I said, giving him a playful poke in the ribs. "But Peter's been great. He knows some rendezvous locations for a wild wolf pack. I'm also trying to persuade him to get in front of the camera and do a spot for our wolf segment."

"Snake's been twisting my arm."

Billie appraised the other's handsome face and silky voice. "You'd be great. The camera will love you."

Peter shifted, uncomfortable at the thought of having a camera pointed at him. He turned to me. "I was driving by when I saw you. There's been a wolf sighting near Lyle Almquist's place."

"Rufus?" I asked, hopeful.

"Won't know till we check it out."

"We?"

"I thought you might want to come along. In fact, bring the crew if you like."

All eyes turned to Billie. Although Jeff and I owned the show and were the executive producers, day-to-day operations fell upon her. Ms. Bradshaw's brow knitted into a tight V under her bangs. She didn't like disruptions to her carefully laid-out plans. You'd think she'd be used to that by now, working with animals that seldom performed on schedule. Only she wasn't. We constantly had to retake shots when our nonhuman stars decided to relieve themselves on camera or were too cranky to work with. By nature Billie was a perfectionist who often had to grit her teeth to cope at what was thrown at her. Grumble and swear but keep going. That was her. Thankfully, Shaggy . . . rather, Arthur, was Mr. Go-with-the-Flow. Any more laid-back and he'd be stretched out in a casket. We could always count on him to get the million-dollar shot, which usually helped calm Billie's frayed nerves.

Billie folded her arms and pinned Jeff with a hard look.

"We're on a tight schedule. We've got to run over some of the setups for this afternoon at the wolf institute. I'm going to need you, Jeff. You're the one who wanted to get back to the Cities by Saturday."

Jeff nodded. "We've got those dingoes to ship off to the Kansas City Zoo on Monday. I need to prep them for the trip. I was even thinking about going along. Make sure they get settled in properly." Uncertainty clouded his face. "Not sure if we have the time to go with your friend, sweetheart."

"How about if I go?" I said. "It's not even nine-thirty. We aren't scheduled at the MWI until two. Why don't you guys check in at the motel, rest up from the drive, grab some lunch and I'll meet up with you by . . . noon?" I looked questioningly at Peter, who nodded back. "Good. We'll pow-wow when I get back."

Billie moved to the rear of her big sedan. She popped open the trunk. "Then take a camera with you, Snake. Arthur, can you get the spare out for her?" Her silvery hair fluttered in the warm breeze. She brought up a hand to shield her eyes against the sun. "If you see anything interesting, get it on film."

"Will do." I took the padded bag and went over to Jeff. I patted him affectionately on the cheek. "I'm really looking forward to spending time with you later. When I get back, I'll move my stuff from Gina's to the motel." I crinkled my nose.

He stroked the back of my head and gave my ponytail a love tug. "Later, sweetheart." He kissed me.

Peter put the camcorder bag in the bed of his pickup and I hopped in the cab. As he pulled away, I turned and waved again to my friends. My eyes drifted up to the sign above Last Chance Outfitters. The pine bough logo caught my attention. Three pine boughs. Ivar Bjorklund's dead hand had clutched onto a little branch with three elm leaves. Three leaves. Three pine boughs. It had to be a coincidence. Nothing more. Or maybe there hadn't been any pine trees near him. I scoured my memory and couldn't recall.

A cold chill ran through me as I realized Signe's name in Swedish meant "a sign." Could Bjorklund's dying message have referred to Signe's sign? Or her?

# CHAPTER 13

Evil Santa's workshop. That's what it felt like stepping into Lyle Almquist's garage studio. Strange, curious, and disturbing implements hung on rusty nails—wooden mallets, box cutters, skinning knives, and scrapers. Near one corner of the workspace stood a tanner's fleshing beam, comprised of a fence post propped against a sawhorse. On another shelf, a pair of rubber gloves waved over the side, goggles, waxed thread, dyes, paste wax and a kerosene tin listing behind them. Leaning against the old double garage doors was a wooden stretching frame, resembling some peculiar torture device as the deerskin within it was stretched tight to dry. The scent of new leather filled the air.

"I don't get many visitors." Almquist stared at us from under a pair of bushy white eyebrows. He paused in the act of threading a rawhide lace through a moccasin. "Something must be up to bring you here, Peter."

"Nothing to worry about, Lyle." Peter gave the older man a disarming smile and nodded toward me. "You've met Snake Jones."

"She's that animal expert from the Cities." He focused back on the moccasin, pulling tight the leather thread.

Animal expert.

I liked that. It was authoritative and vague at the same time. Put me on par with the conservation officer.

"One of your neighbors called. She thought she saw a wolf

crossing your backyard."

"Must be Jeanne. I've only got two neighbors. Both of 'em half a mile away."

"Yes, Jeanne Kreske. She was driving by and thought she saw a wolf-like animal run through your yard."

Almquist set down the moccasin. "You think it might be that missing wolf from the institute?"

"If we're lucky. Have you heard or seen anything?"

"I've been in the shop since the sun came up. I don't hear much when I'm workin' and, as you can see, there's only the one little window."

The half-open window let the only sunlight into the former garage. From outside the musical call of chickadees filtered in, which was in stark contrast to the deathly silence of animal hides inside. My more radical friends would have freaked out at the sight of all the deerskins and cowhides in the workshop. Not me. These animals hadn't been slaughtered for their skins; they'd been killed for food, their hides left over from the process. Now if I'd found a leopard skin on the wall, it would have been another matter. Santa had better watch out for me, as I'd be coming to town!

Almquist stepped away from the workbench, revealing a belly as impressive in girth as the barrels of solvents and chemicals on the floor behind him. "You wanna check my back property for your wolf, go ahead."

"Thanks, we'll do that. Say, Lyle, does Forrest Hansen still supply you with deerskins?"

Almquist's eyebrows were like a pair of hairy white caterpillars, slowly rolling up his forehead. "Yeah, I still get a few hides from Hansen. Now that fella on the frame was a road-kill deer, so don't go thinking he's illegally caught, Mr. DNR Officer. Saw him lying in a ditch last week off Highway 169." Almquist let out a hearty chuckle. Heck, the man even laughed like Santa

Claus, albeit a better-barbered version.

The sound of tires crunching on gravel silenced the birds. Peter looked out the window. He turned back to Almquist. "The smell of these skins doesn't attract varmints, does it? I could understand if you have to take a potshot at a stray coyote once in awhile."

Almquist bristled. "I know a coyote from a wolf, if that's what you're saying. I didn't shoot those wolves."

"I'm not saying you did, Lyle. I was talking about varmints in general."

Smooth, Peter was very smooth. The voice was like butter. He casually rested his right hand on his gun belt. The leather crafter considered him for a moment before returning to his moccasins.

The door squealed open on rusty hinges. Like a scene from an old Western, Chief Manske strode in like the town marshal surveying the ne'er-do-wells at the local saloon. He looked none too happy. "Well, no surprise," he intoned. "I didn't realize you two were part of my investigation. Peter. Mrs. Jones."

Peter straightened up, hoping to appease him. "Now don't get your nose out of joint, Tom. Snake and I are here on wolf institute business. We're not here about Ivar Bjorklund. A wolf was seen in the neighborhood. We're checking on the tip. It's within my jurisdiction."

Manske did a slow burn. His lips pressed together as his eyes shifted between Peter and me. "Fair enough. If you've got what you wanted, then I suggest you leave. I've got some questions I'd like to ask Mr. Almquist."

"They can stay," Almquist said, much to Manske's annoyance. "I've got nothing to say they can't hear. And I'd just as soon not repeat myself."

The police chief weighed his options and capitulated. "Fine. Have it your way. Mr. Almquist, do you own a gun?"

"You know damned well I do, Tom. An old Remington seven hundred. It was my dad's."

"Can I see it?"

"It's in the house. Let me fetch it." Almquist set down the unfinished moccasin, grumbling. "Don't know why you're bugging me about guns. It's like I told the lady last night. You ought to be talking to that Moua Vang character."

Manske shot me an irritated scowl. I smiled back pleasantly. "What about Moua Vang?" he grumbled at Almquist.

"All I know is what I see. Last week I was driving by his place and saw him taking pot shots at a bald eagle. Well, seems to me a man who shoots at one protected species isn't gonna give a damn about shootin' at another. If you're looking for your wolf shooter, I'd start with him."

Peter Bunyan shook his head. "Damn, I've spoken to Moua about shooting at eagles before."

Manske found that noteworthy. "So you know about this Vang?"

"Yeah."

"See," Almquist said with vindication, "I'm not shittin' you. I'm telling you, strange stuff goes on at his place at night. Fires and weird sounds. My niece tells me those Hmong people worship animals and spirits. Who knows what kind of strange voodoo goes on at his place?"

"Strange voodoo?" Manske repeated, somewhat disconcerted. Like there was any other kind.

"Hmong animal rituals. Magic. Hell! Maybe even animal sacrifices."

"And you've seen this with your own eyes?"

"Well . . . no. But people talk."

Manske held up his hand. "Skip Vang for the time being. Let's get back to Ivar."

"Don't know if I can help you any. I never talked to the man."

"Not at all?"

"No."

"What about last week?" I interjected. The opening had appeared and I dived for it, like jumping into a moving train; one hoped it was headed in the right direction. "You were seen arguing with Mr. Bjorklund in the parking lot of Zup's Market."

Chief Manske, glaring, seemed about to hush me into silence but deferred, more interested in hearing Almquist's answer than rebuking me.

The portly leather crafter never hesitated, chuckling with such enjoyment that his belly jiggled. "Strictly speaking, I don't think you can call it an argument, since Ivar was the one doing all the talking."

"Explain," Manske demanded.

"I was minding my own business, taking my groceries to my truck, when Ivar comes running across the parking lot, all worked up and demanding to talk. I barely got a word in edgewise. If I hadn't gotten into my truck and drove off, he'd still be out there ranting."

The police chief leaned in. "Why was he upset?"

"He had some bee up his butt about his wife and how I still owed him a refund for a pair of slippers that never got made—or some such thing."

"Was he right? Did you owe him money?"

"No, Tom. The slippers were only half made when she died. Ivar'd paid for them in advance. At the time he said he didn't want 'em no more. He didn't care about anything. Told me to do whatever I wanted. Well, when I got the opportunity, I sold them to someone else. Now, months later, he gets all bent out of shape about it!" The world was full of injustice, judging from Almquist's tone of voice. "I'd heard he was hot-headed, but never expected nothing like that."

"What about the paper?" I asked. "He was waving a piece of

paper at you."

Almquist frowned at me like I was a bothersome fly. I was an outsider. I'm sure he wondered where I got my information. It took him a moment to answer. "He had some numbers scribbled on the back of his water bill. It was some kind of tally with dates. What I owed him, he said. That kind of thing."

"You ever talk to him about it again?"

Almquist shook his head.

"What about this?" Manske dug his hand into his uniform pocket. "You work with tools, Lyle. You recognize this?" Almquist narrowed his gaze toward the plastic evidence bag dangling from Manske's fingers. "Well?"

"That's a v-gouge."

"Is that something you'd use?"

"Nah. That little guy's for cutting deep gouges. My work's too delicate for that. You want a carpenter or cabinet maker."

Manske gave a curt nod. "It was found near Ivar's body. Could he have dropped it?"

Lyle Almquist screwed his eyes toward the object, pressing his lips together in deep thought. "Maybe . . . didn't Ivar used to be a machinist? I don't think he would've used a gouge like that."

The chief slipped the bag back into his pocket. "Thanks for your help. We'll need to see that rifle of yours."

"Sure." The other chuckled through his snow-white beard. Jolly old Santa. "Nice you think an old fart like me still has it in him to shoot at them wolves." He halted his lumbering steps and considered Manske with new understanding. "Or do you think it was Ivar I was taking shots at?"

Manske didn't answer.

Minutes later the three of us left the workshop, the police chief cradling a scuffed-up Remington seven hundred in his arms. The door to the old garage closed behind us. We headed toward our cars. After I retrieved my video camera from the back of Peter's truck, the two of us would search Almquist's property for fresh wolf tracks.

"I can see this isn't the murder weapon," Manske said flatly. "Wrong caliber. Ivar was killed by a .30-06, same as the wolves. This rifle uses a .223 cartridge, the classic varmint-killer. Still, the tests may help us elminina—Mrs. Jones . . . ?"

I'd fallen a few paces behind, stopping at the rear of Almquist's pickup truck, a scratched, rusted, dented mess of banged-up barrels, chains, ropes, scattered toolboxes and whatnot. The truck was even more untidy than the workshop. But I had noticed something else.

"Isn't that animal fur?" I indicated the truck bed. I shot a hasty glance over my shoulder at the half-open garage window to make sure Almquist wasn't standing there.

Curious, Peter hastened over and leaned against the rear quarter panel to check out my discovery. "Yes, it is. Deer fur. What about it?"

The skin at the back of my neck tingled. "There's more of it. Over there. And there. From different animals. Shouldn't we get it analyzed? What if some of it came from a wolf? There's a lab in California that specializes in analysis of animal DNA for forensic purposes. If it proves a match with one of our dead wolves, then we've got our man."

"Snake," Peter said, at pains not to burst my bubble. "You know how much those tests cost? Almquist deals with animal skins. There could be fur from dozens of different species in that truck—from years of hauling them. The truck is ancient. I doubt the guy has ever cleaned out the bed, let alone washed it. Each sample would have to be looked at and tested. There just isn't money in the DNR budget for that."

"Besides," Tom Manske was quick to point out, "it'd only prove Almquist transported them. Not that he killed them—"

"But—"

"And we don't have probable cause to collect the evidence. I can pretty much guarantee you this rifle didn't kill either Ivar or your wolves. Nice try, though."

He flashed me a pity smile.

I burned. Not because Manske enjoyed putting me down, but because of how dumb it made me feel. They made it seem so easy on TV. Crime shows could run any lab test they wanted. Anytime. Anywhere. Whatever the cost. And get results back in record time. I felt like a rookie for having made the suggestion. I shut my mouth and slunk silently back to the truck, my ego bruised but not battered.

# Chapter 14

Dog tracks were what Peter and I found on Almquist's property. Fresh ones. But no wolf signs. The paw prints were unmistakable. It was a big dog, at least sixty pounds, but the prints were almost half the size of a wolf's forepaws. Rounder, too, and the tracks meandered. I was disappointed. I'd really hoped to bring Debbie, Gina and the others good news.

To our surprise, as we returned to Peter's truck we found Chief Manske resting in his car. He emerged from his vehicle when he saw us approach. "Done so soon?"

"It wasn't a wolf," Peter informed him as he stowed my camcorder bag. "I thought you'd be long gone by now, Tom."

"I thought I'd wait for you. Look, you and I both need to talk to Moua Vang. I've never met him, but you know the guy. Maybe we should combine forces on this one."

I blinked, unable to conceal my disbelief. Was this the same person who, only minutes ago, had complained that the DNR Conservation Officer and I were stepping on his delicate toes? Now he wanted us to ride with him? Maybe to keep an eye on us, I thought. Or maybe the man was a better opportunist than I gave him credit for. Peter Bunyan did know Vang. Why not use Peter to get to Vang? I would have.

The three of us climbed into the white police cruiser with the blue stripes. Peter rode shotgun next to Manske while I sat in back, behind the wire mesh cage partition. I felt a little like a prisoner. We rumbled our way along the isolated dirt road that connected to Lyle Almquist's house.

"Voodoo," said Tom Manske after a few minutes. The word hung on his lips like a bad aftertaste. "What was Almquist yammering about? This Vang some kind of witch doctor?"

"Shaman," Peter corrected.

The mention of the word *shaman* caused the hairs on the back of my neck to stand up. Dark chants, magical talismans and secret rituals captured my imagination.

Manske turned the police car on to Black Fir Road. "Witch doctor, shaman. What's the difference?"

"Not a lot. Both are healers. The difference is more points of view, I guess. Moua Vang comes from a line of shaman. Most Hmong these days are Christians, but some still hold on to their old religion, which is based on animism—"

"Ani—what?"

"Animism," I inserted, leaning forward. "They believe spirits inhabit nature—trees, lakes, animals. That kind of thing."

Peter nodded assent. "Right. They believe in protective spirits, wild spirits—"

"And evil spirits?" Manske joined in. "Now that could be important. Does Vang take potshots at things to drive out bad juju?"

"Well, let's just say it's taken him some time to get used to our hunting laws."

"Old habits die hard, eh?"

Minnesota had the second largest population of Hmong in the United States, after California. Which always surprised me, considering the Sunshine State's weather was much closer to the climate of Laos than ours. I had to wonder what the appeal would be to the Hmong, particularly in northern Minnesota. The answer, I suppose, was the same thing that appealed to everyone—dense green forests, clear lakes, and a certain sense of isolation. All things considered, it was probably harder for them to adjust to American culture than to a Minnesota winter.

The wooded landscape rushed by for fifteen minutes before I recognized the spot where we'd found the wolf carcasses, thanks to the stick marker that was still in place. Peter Bunyan leaned toward the windshield. "That's it, Tom. Pull in there."

From the backseat I saw nothing, only the endless row of tamaracks and scrub grass. Then a driveway appeared, as if from nowhere. The police cruiser turned in and climbed the sloping road to the top of the hill.

I squinted through the low tree branches behind us, barely able to see the road below. "This seems familiar. Isn't Bjorklund's house nearby?"

The conservation officer was impressed. "Not bad, Snake. Considering the terrain doesn't change that much. Ivar's house is half a mile down the road."

"So he and Moua Vang were neighbors," I said with significance, though I didn't know what it might be.

"Could be important," Manske agreed. "Sometimes neighbors get along, sometimes they don't. It's not always easy ignoring a troublesome neighbor."

Great. Chief Tom Manske and I were finally simpatico. I could die happy.

Three generations of the Vang family stood in the front yard when we pulled up. An elderly woman wearing a once brightly colored skirt with a faded red sash sat in a chair sewing an intricate story cloth. A wiry old man in a dingy white shirt and baggy black pants sat next to her in a lawn chair badly in need of re-webbing. Several children ran around in a circle, their all-American jeans and t-shirts in sharp contrast to the elderly couple's more traditional Hmong wear. A younger woman, their mother I assumed, bent over a large metal tub. Steam rose from the boiling contents, its smell not unpleasant, but I had a feeling it wasn't tonight's dinner.

The woman recognized Peter and offered him a cautious smile. After he asked about her husband's whereabouts, the old man lurched out of his lawn chair and motioned for us to follow. He shuffled along with quick, easy steps, checking every so often that we were keeping up. After a few hundred yards, we reached the end of the property. There we saw a short yet sturdy man in his late thirties toss a newly split log on top of a neatly stacked woodpile. Beside him, a teenage boy planted his axe into the tree stump he'd used as a brace. He couldn't have been more than sixteen years old, a carbon copy of the older man, except for the Harry Potter glasses perched on his short nose.

"Peter," the Hmong man greeted with a friendly nod and a show of yellow teeth. A suspicious gaze traveled over the rest of us. "Why you bring them here?" His English was clear and heavily accented, his voice confident.

Whatever else he was, Moua Vang was no wallflower. From the way he moved to the way his eyes whipped around and held my gaze, he crackled like a high-capacity battery. As a teenager, I'd studied martial arts for a few months. I was no good at it, but I did learn to assess people by the way they moved, the same way I'd learned to assess a wild animal. This man could be dangerous, like a badger. Swift and intense.

For his part, Peter Bunyan maintained a business-like demeanor. To an immigrant, the uniform would have been intimidating enough. The aviator shades came off, allowing Vang to see his eyes. A small gesture, yet important in the dance of differing cultures. Knowing the Hmong farmer was already distrustful of this incursion on his property, Peter tried to show he wasn't a threat. He introduced Tom Manske and me.

Vang stared directly at the police chief. "You are not Red Iron police."

Manske cleared his throat. "Actually, Mr. Vang, Red Iron Township is too small to have its own police. The township has an arrangement with Wolf Lake. That's why I'm here."

"Arrangement?" Vang turned to the young boy and spoke to him in his native tongue. Then back to Manske. "This is Long. My son. He speak very good English." Vang nodded sharply to the teenager, urging him on.

Long Vang looked like any other American teenage boy. "Chief," he said in an educated voice, "Dad doesn't understand why you're here. Has he done something wrong?"

"Your neighbor, Ivar Bjorklund, was killed two days ago. I'm looking into it."

The elder Vang was taken aback. "Ivar dead? Who kill him?"

"We don't know."

"You find out. He good man. Help out my family."

"That's why we're here." Manske nodded back. "His body was found a few miles down the road in the woods. Do you know anything that might help us? Maybe you saw something."

"What time?"

"Tuesday afternoon."

Vang shook his head. "I not home. Driving goats to man in Hibbing."

"Okay. Maybe one of your family heard or saw something around that time. Like gunshots?"

"Could it have been around two o'clock?" asked the younger Vang.

"It's possible. We don't know the exact time. Why? Did you hear something?"

"No, but my grandfather did. He heard gunshots."

Hope flickered in the police chief's eyes. "Your grandfather?"

"When the weather's nice he likes to sit in the sun in the afternoons. At dinner Tuesday, he was telling us about a pair of hawks he saw soaring over the distant treetops. Then he heard a popping noise. It sounded far away. He said it sounded like a firecracker."

"This was about two, you say?"

"Around then, yes."

"Does he know what direction the noise came from?"

"We can ask him," the young man said matter-of-factly. The old man had gone to rest on a tree stump in a nearby clearing. At our approach his hollow cheeks stretched back a layer of wrinkles earned from years of hard living. After a brief exchange between grandson and grandfather, he stretched a bony arm toward the forest below.

"Grandfather says the sound came from that way."

I tried to get my bearings. He was pointing east, in the general direction where we'd found Bjorklund's body.

Manske gazed out across the treetops. "Is he sure about that, son?"

Long Vang questioned his grandfather. The old man responded with a confident, winsome smile of dull yellow. "He's sure," said the grandson, chuckling, "because he saw the black birds go that way."

"Black birds? You mean crows?"

"Ravens?" Peter got the word out a fraction of an instant before me. We both smiled when the old man nodded back in confirmation.

Long pointed far into the forest below. "Grandfather said three ravens flew that way right after the shots."

I could barely contain my excitement, which annoyed the police chief, whom I'm sure felt left out of what Peter and I had latched on to.

Peter faced the teenager. "Long, some wolves were shot last week. We found their carcasses maybe half a mile down the road from here. D'you know anything about them?"

"No, sir."

"How about you, Moua?"

"Know nothing about dead wolves."

Long translated the conversation for the old man, then turned to Peter and adjusted his glasses. "Grandfather says he doesn't know anything."

"He heard no gunshots a week ago? Or anything that might have sounded like a gun?"

"No, Officer Bunyan."

"Thank you," Peter said with a nod. He seemed satisfied by the answer and, I think I understood why.

I smiled at the elder Vang, who seemed taken by me. "Long, please tell your grandfather he's been very helpful."

"He has?" Chief Manske inhaled sharply.

"He has," Peter agreed. Then to Moua Vang in a more somber tone: "I've heard a report you've been shooting at bald eagles again."

The Hmong farmer shrank at the charge before growing somewhat indignant. "No! Did not shoot at eagle. Shoot to scare away eagle."

"Bald eagles are a protected animal, Moua. I've told you that before."

"Eagle bad spirit in my country. Eagle take chickens for dinner last week. I shoot only to scare away. Not kill."

Peter gave the other a stern look of disapproval. "I gave you a warning once before. No more shooting at eagles, not even to scare them away. You'll get in big trouble if you shoot one accidentally. You could go to jail. Put some netting over the top of your chicken fence. That will protect your chickens better."

Vang bobbed his head respectfully but said nothing more, which I found interesting. The nod was an acknowledgment to an authority figure, not really an agreement he'd comply.

The clearing was at the edge of the hill from which you could see the forest spread out for miles upon miles. Vang would have a clear shot at a flying eagle from here. In front of me two white birch trees leaned toward each other. I instantly recognized it as

146

the white X I'd seen the great blue heron land in when we reclaimed the wolf carcasses.

Taken by a thought, I said, "Mr. Vang, when you scared away the eagle, was it from here?"

"More over there, away from trees. Want to make sure I miss eagle. Want no trouble with Officer Peter."

That proved too irresistible an opening for the police chief. "What else do you try to scare off with your gun, Mr. Vang? Wolves? People?"

Distress flared in Vang's eyes. "No shoot wolves! No shoot Ivar. He was my friend."

"We'll want to see any guns you have."

After a distrustful look aimed between the two lawmen, Vang agreed. He dispatched his son who met us five minutes later as we approached the house. Long presented the firearm to Manske, who barely inspected it before handing the weapon to a surprised Moua Vang. No more surprised than I. Weren't they going to test the thing?

"I'm finished here. How about you, Peter?"

Peter touched me lightly on the arm. "That's a shotgun, Snake. Ivar and the wolves were killed by a rifle."

Okay, so I still had a lot to learn about guns. Even though I felt slightly silly, at least I wasn't a total ignoramus. I knew the textbook difference between a shotgun and a rifle—I just hadn't been around enough of them to see the physical differences between the two firearms. While I licked my wounds, Manske and Peter bid farewell to the Vangs.

As we walked back to the police cruiser, I scrutinized the trees for any glimpse of the road, which remained hidden by tamarack trees and clumps of aspen. A comment made earlier echoed in my mind. If Moua Vang still performed shamanistic rituals on his property, they'd be well hidden from a simple drive-by.

"So what was all the crap about ravens?" demanded Manske five seconds after he turned the cruiser onto Black Fir Road. "The two of you were almost giddy from the old man's story."

I sat back in my seat, trying not to look smug or even mildly satisfied, although I was. I didn't answer the question, waiting for Peter to do it, not wanting to sound stupid in front of Manske again.

Peter said, "Long's grandfather heard a gunshot two days ago in the middle of the afternoon, about the time Ivar was killed."

Manske adjusted his grip on the steering wheel. "Sure. He pointed in the general direction where you found the body. I got that much. What about the birds?"

I leaned forward. "Ravens are the only known bird that will actually fly toward a gunshot."

The police chief jerked his head around to peer back at me. "Really?"

"You bet. Ravens are highly intelligent. They can use tools, can even learn to use tools from each other, which means they're pretty clever at figuring things out. After years of dealing with humans, they've learned to associate hunters with a free meal. Hunters often gut their kills on-site. That's a feast for the ravens. They'll swoop in and scarf up the entrails. For them a gunshot is a dinner bell."

"Okay . . ." Manske puzzled it over. "What does that mean, exactly?"

"It means," Peter offered, "that grandfather Vang helped corroborate our theory of what happened to Bjorklund."

"Sure, but what about the deal with the dead wolves? The old guy didn't hear them get shot."

"Because they were killed somewhere else, too far away for the shots to be heard at the Vang farm. The kill site revealed as much. We found no shell casings because no shots were fired there."

I pressed my nose against the wire mesh partition. "I was wondering if that's what you were thinking, Peter."

Dust flew as the police car rumbled over the gravel road. The air roared with the machine-gun rhythm of loose stones bouncing under the chassis.

Manske raised his voice over the din. "Then, Mrs. Jones, please be kind enough to explain why knowing the wolves were killed somewhere else is so helpful."

Fair question. I hadn't thought things through that far. I said the first thing I could think of. "So we're saying the wolves were shot elsewhere, farther west or east of the Vang farm. Those wolves were from the Red Iron pack. Their normal range was ten miles farther east. Gina Brown from the wolf institute has a database of GPS readings she's collected over the past few months. Two of those GPS positions are promising."

"I still don't follow. What's so special about those GPS locations?"

Seeing I was a little flustered, Peter Bunyan filled him in. "They're where the collared wolves spent a lot of their time."

"And the connection with Bjorklund?"

"The same gun killed them both," I said, inspired. "There's got to be a connection between the wolf slaughter and the death of Bjorklund. The wolf carcasses were moved for a reason. If one of the GPS locations can tell us why the wolves were killed, maybe it'll explain why Bjorklund was murdered too."

Mankse grunted approval. No arguments. Peter smiled. I leaned back in my seat, satisfied by my performance. I'd held my own with these two experts, and that was a big deal. Now we just needed to find proof of that connection.

# CHAPTER 15

No Signe.

I'd hoped to find her at Last Chance Outfitters. After Peter dropped me off, I wanted to check on her and see how she was coping with Bjorklund's death. She'd seemed okay earlier that morning. I'm sure she had plenty of friends and family to help her through her grief, but I still felt the need to do something for her. And if she were doing really well, I might be brave enough to ask what she thought about the message behind the elm twig clutched in Bjorklund's hand. Without emphasizing any connections with her.

But it was not to be. Signe wasn't in and Last Chance Outfitters was in the capable hands of a young college student, Dimitry Sliwinski.

"Signe's running errands," Dimitry told me, half turned behind the front counter. "You can set those by the register," he directed a spiky-haired sales clerk with an armload of freeze-dried food packets.

"How's she doing?" I asked after he turned to me with his full attention.

"Not bad. Not bad. Though it's a little hard to tell. She's being a good Swede and holding back her emotions. She took off a few hours to deal with them."

"It feels really odd. This is the first time I've been here when she hasn't greeted me with her big smile."

A cloud passed over Dimitry's young face. "Signe's always

here. I mean always. She takes one day off a week—if we twist her arm. Most of the time, she just needs to get away by herself for an hour or two. And when you figure she's known Ivar for most of her life, well, I'm glad she took off for a while." A playful smirk pulled at his Slavic cheekbones. "And if she doesn't make it back this afternoon we're ready. We called in the shock troops: Ginger."

The spiky-haired Ginger lifted her nose with mock indignation. She sported four earrings and enough mascara and eye shadow to shame a raccoon.

I liked the idea of Signe taking some private time for herself to get away from customers. When you work with the public you have to staple on a happy face. You don't have to be sincere; you just have to look sincere. The zoo is often underfunded and understaffed. The public can be an uncaring taskmaster. They don't care you're having a bad day. Don't care if someone or something you cared about has died. When one of the young sun bears died at the zoo a while back, I was devastated. I'd hand-raised Chera from a cub, the only keeper he'd readily extend a paw to for blood draws and vaccinations. The day he died, I put in a double shift and then conducted a private tour of the Tropics Trail for the media. Chin up and attentive, answering questions and quite professional. No time for tears. By the time I got home I was more than ready for the glass of Shiraz and hot bath Jeff had waiting for me.

And ready for a good cry.

I wondered what Signe Amunson did for release. Nobody can stay that pleasant all the time. It has to come out somehow. Whatever she was doing, I hoped it was a comfort to her.

A platoon of customers trooped up with their camping supplies as I waited to tell Dimitry I'd come back later to check up on Signe. After the last customer was rung up, his eyes searched the empty store before leaning forward. "Probably a good thing

Signe's not here."

"What d'you mean?"

His long fingers slipped down behind the counter and returned with a flyer I recognized. Printed on green paper were large capital letters screaming out their message:

YOU ARE A POLLUTER. YOU ARE HARMING THE ENVIRONMENT BY SELLING OVERPACKED, NON-RECYCLABLE PRODUCTS. CLEAN UP YOUR ACT! WE'LL BE WATCHING YOU.

The Stewards of Superior! My eyes got big. "When did this get here?"

"Beats me. I found it taped to the back door an hour ago when I signed for a delivery. For all I know it could've been there since yesterday."

"Have you gotten these before?"

"Not that I know of. I'm sure Signe would've mentioned it if we had." The young clerk eyed the flyer as if it were radioactive. "Signe'll bust a seam when she sees this."

"She'll go nuclear," Ginger said, refolding a sweatshirt a would-be customer had left rumpled on a shelf.

I rubbed the back of my head, maybe hoping to stimulate some understanding into it. The Stewards of Superior were getting a lot more active lately. Gina, Bjorklund, now Signe. And those were only the people I knew about. How many others had gotten those warnings?

"Dimitry, what can you tell me about this group?"

"Nothing."

"Know anyone who's a member?"

"Sorry. They kinda lurk in the shadows."

"Yeah, I heard they were secretive. Any idea how many members they have?"

Dimitry shook his head.

Straightening the bait buckets, Ginger said, "I heard they're small, like maybe ten or twenty members."

"You wouldn't know someone I could talk to, to learn more about them, would you?"

"What I've heard is stuff people talk about in bars. I don't know any actual members of SOS."

I tapped my fingers on the glass counter. "I don't understand them. They're a little too secretive. They threaten people, but have they ever actually done anything violent?"

Both Dimitry and Ginger came back with blank looks.

My stomach gurgled. The old watch said it was 11:10. I had nearly an hour before I was expected at the Super 8 for the *Zoofari* pre-production meeting. Enough time for me to grab a quick bite.

Though not quite yet.

"Hey, cutie, aren't you going to say hi?" It was Gus. He and Mooney waved from their table in the coffee "lounge," as Signe affectionately called the four small tables tucked near the coffee bar. Mooney waved me over. The Dukes of Decaf were holding court.

"Hello, boys."

Mooney regarded me with empathy. "Word is you were the one who found Ivar Bjorklund's body. That must've been unsettling." His arthritic fingers stroked the side of his paper cup.

"I wasn't alone. Gina Brown and Peter Bunyan were with me. Did either of you know Mr. Bjorklund well?"

"Not as well as Signe," Gus answered. "They've been friends for most of their lives."

"He was more than a friend." Mooney rolled his eyes suggestively.

Gus swiveled with a sour expression. "That was a long time ago! Keep up with the times, you old fart. That one's so old it grew a beard."

"Maybe things haven't changed as much as you think. I was trying to say that in the old days Signe had a thing for Ivar."

"A thing?" I was intrigued. "Like she was attracted to him?"

Mooney cackled. "We heard she was pretty sweet on him back in school days, and they've been getting pretty chummy again since Lily's death."

"Did anything ever happen between them?"

"You mean like sex?" Mooney happily filled in.

Gus leaned away. "That was blunt!"

"I was cutting to the chase, as they say. That is what you wanted to know, Snake. Am I right?"

It was more information than I needed, but I gave a little nod. "Yes, Mooney."

"Heck, I don't know if the two 'em ever climbed in the sack together. In the old days, though, I hear it wouldn't've taken much to egg them on."

With an air of disapproval, Gus aimed his red bowtie at the other man. He smacked Mooney lightly on the bicep with the back of his hand. "Don't go teasing the young lady, you old fart." Then to me, "There might've been a time long ago, before Ivar met Lily Ferndale, when he and Signe went out a few times. My daughter went to school with Signe. She told me some of this stuff. Can't tell you what kind of fiddle-dee-do they got into back then, except it all stopped once Ivar met Lily. The two of them stayed friends after Ivar got married. That's how I remember it."

Mooney nodded introspectively. "She never married, you know."

"Because of her feelings for Ivar?"

"Can't say . . . I really can't say. Signe doesn't talk much about her private life." Mooney took a long sip of coffee.

I glanced over my shoulder at the front counter, which seemed empty without Signe's effusive presence. Dimitry held up a deerskin jacket from the display rack. To the interested young woman he went into detail about the "exquisite crafts-manship and finely carved wildlife pattern" in the design.

Mindful of the customer, I lowered my voice. "Guys, a question for both of you. Do you think Signe could ever get upset with somebody like Mr. Bjorklund, so upset she might lose her temper and lash out?"

Mooney sucked on his lower lip. "Gee, that's a good one. I can't see her doing that. You?"

"No," Gus said. "She's the last person I'd ever expect to turn into a hot head, if that's what you mean. On the other hand, when she puts her mind to something, she goes and does it lickity split. Like the other day, she just took off."

"Took off? You mean, left the store?"

"You bet." Gus's scratchy voice sounded like it came from an old Victrola. "Right after lunch, she told Dimitry she'd be gone for an hour and she left."

"When was this?"

"Two days ago."

"About what time?"

"Two o'clock."

"You sound so certain, Gus."

"*General Hospital*." He motioned toward the front counter. "She missed it. Signe's got a small TV up front. It's her favorite soap. The only one she'll watch. When that show is on she has one eye on the TV and the other on her customers."

"Tuesday . . ." I repeated, more to myself than them. Tuesday afternoon was when Bjorklund had been murdered. At the front of the store Dimitry was on the verge of making a sale. The young woman, turning this way and that in front of the mirror, liked what she saw in the glass. The leather jacket sparked my memory.

I pulled over a chair from another table and joined the two

old-timers. "How about Lyle Almquist, the man who does those leather jackets? You must know him. He's in here regularly with his leather goods."

"Young lady," Gus sat up with dignity, "we know everybody in Wolf Lake. And if we don't know 'em, they ain't worth knowing! What about Lyle?"

I folded my hands on the table. "He was seen in Zup's parking lot last week having an argument with Mr. Bjorklund."

Amusement from Gus. "I'd be surprised if you told me Ivar wasn't having an argument with somebody! He was a grumpy old cuss." He turned to his cohort for confirmation.

"A week ago, you say?" Mooney bowed his head, squinting his eyes to dredge up the memory. "Ivar was in here a week ago causing a ruckus. He waved some piece of paper in Signe's face, making a lot of noise how he was going to make Lyle pay."

That fit what the leather crafter had said earlier that morning. I could see Bjorklund working himself up into a lather over a refund on a pair of moccasin slippers. No injustice to him was too small.

"How did Signe react?" I asked.

Mooney shrugged. "She took his rants like she always did. Tried to calm him down and told him not to get so worked up over things."

"He didn't like that!" Gus chortled. "The one thing you never told Ivar was not to get excited. That seemed to set him off more'n anything."

"Yep," Mooney agreed. "Right after Signe told him not to get so worked up over it, he stormed out the door."

And went to Zup's Market, where, by chance or design, he ambushed Lyle Almquist in the parking lot. A quick glimpse at my watch told me I still had plenty of time, but if I wanted a leisurely lunch, I should get moving. "Thanks for the conversation, guys."

The two oldsters grinned like a pair of adolescent teenagers on the make. Mooney reached out to touch my sleeve. "Snake, how much longer are you in town for?"

"Not to worry, you'll see me a few more times. We aren't leaving till the weekend. But I'll have to be careful," I cautioned with a wink. "My husband's in town and he gets jealous if I hang out with handsome young men. See ya."

I blew them a kiss, leaving them feeling sky high. I was halfway across the parking lot to my Jeep when I spotted a familiar bulked-up muscle mass at the Gas 'n Go next door. Forrest Hansen leaned against the side panel of his white Grand Prix, watching the gas hose. His head was bowed, his expression somber, as if the life force had leeched out of him and he was merely going through the motions. He and Bjorklund had been thick. My distaste for the man urged me to run away and leave him to his private thoughts. Unfortunately, my upbringing had taught me to acknowledge another person's grief. In the big scheme of things it seemed little to ask, a small balm of civility in an otherwise hostile world. It wasn't even a uniquely human trait; some members of the animal kingdom were known to offer comfort to others of their species in times of distress.

Summoning up my courage, I strode over to pay my condolences. I cleared my throat. "Mr. Hansen?"

Words flopped in the back of my throat like a slippery trout in a mountain brook. I wasn't sure what to say.

At my approach Hansen straightened, the muscles in his neck and chest tightened under his sweatshirt. Rueful dark eyes held me at bay. "What d'you want?"

My feet scuffed to a halt. I took him in tentatively. "I just wanted to say how sorry I am about Mr. Bjorklund."

"The man's dead. Can't you let him be?"

A bark came from the back seat of the car. Bjorklund's sheepdog, Oskar, stuck his head out the open window and whined at me as if reminding me that he, too, was in mourning.

I reached out and gave the dog a pat. "You're taking care of him?"

Hansen seemed embarrassed at being caught in this act of kindness. "Would you rather I let the cops drag him down to the animal shelter? He's a good sheepdog."

His baleful stare made me avert my eyes. I'd said nice things to him and both times he flung my words back at me. I tried to explain. "I'm sorry if I'm upsetting you. I'm not trying to cause trouble. I know you and Mr. Bjorklund were good friends. I just wanted to say how sorry I am for your loss."

"Okay, you said it. Now go."

"Try to be nice to some people," I muttered as I walked away.

"Wait. Hold up. I . . . I didn't mean to be rude."

Better.

I stopped and turned about.

Hansen gently stroked Oskar's head. "Ivar was supposed to drop by the paper mill Tuesday afternoon. Only he never showed up. I tried to reach him that evening but no one answered the phone. It wasn't until the next day when I found out what happened to him."

"It must be a shock to you. You were with him just that morning."

"Twenty-two years I knew him. Since I was a teenager." Forrest Hansen gazed off, as if into the past. "If it hadn't been for Ivar, I might never've climbed out of the hole I was in. He was a good man. He got me my first job at the paper mill . . ."

The gas hose shut off with a loud click, interrupting the moment. It seemed to wake up old hostilities. Hansen slammed the hose back on the pump and skewered me with a fiery glare. "You know what really torques me, lady?"

No, I didn't know what really torqued him, and suspected

this meant our little love fest was over.

His voice turned frigid. "It's how you come up to say you're sorry about Ivar when you didn't know him at all. And just two days ago, you and the rest of your crew accused him of shooting those wolves."

Okay, in the first place, I don't think one extra person constitutes a crew; and in the second place I was cranky about Muscle Boy throwing my good intensions back in my face. Despite my reservations I'd tried to do the right thing. Fat lotta good it did me.

Still, I tried to take the high road. "We didn't accuse Mr. Bjorklund of shooting anything. We—I—asked about his rifle. Officer Bunyan asked him if he knew of anyone who could have killed those wolves. Not accusations. Questions."

Take that!

Hansen snorted. "Don't make me laugh! Ivar's views on wolves were no secret. You must have suspected him of killing those animals."

My eyes became green lasers. "You're way off base, Hansen. Listen, Mr. Bjorklund was a person of interest because of things he'd said. That's all. Why would I automatically assume he killed those wolves without listening to his side?"

"Because you're a tree-hugging animal rights Nazi!"

I felt my cheeks flush. A jolt of adrenaline surged through me. I really wanted to smack the guy over the front end of his chick-magnet car and turn him into a hood ornament. Yet before venom had a chance to spew from my mouth, I counted to three and willed the toxin back down my throat. Somewhat calmer, I zinged back in a voice not wholly devoid of sarcasm, "When have you ever seen me hug a tree? And speaking of groundless accusations, take a gander in the mirror, buddy. If I were the animal rights Nazi you say I am, I wouldn't have hesitated to accuse you or Mr. Bjorklund of that wolf slaughter.

But—I—didn't." I jabbed my finger at him, emphasizing each of the last words.

The thick cords in Hansen's neck tightened. I half-wondered if he were thinking of using those tree limbs he had for arms to snap me in two. Clumsily, he screwed back on the gas cap. When he spoke again, it was in carefully measured tones. "All I know is an old friend is dead. He suffered a lot in his later years, more than most folks. The last year with Lily was really bad. After she was gone he struggled to keep his sheep ranch working, then you and Bunyan show up to harass him. And later that day he's killed."

My jaw dropped. "You can't possibly think we're in any way responsible!"

"Not that I can prove. Let me put it this way, lady: you're bad news. Now get out of my way, I have to check on the sheep. Ivar may be gone, but he had a lot of dependents—nearly a hundred of them."

Without another word, Hansen slid into the Grand Prix and peeled off into traffic. Alone by the gas pump, I mumbled at his receding bumper, "We weren't harassing him."

"That didn't go over very well," said a sympathetic voice.

Cole Novak, across the parking lot at Last Chance Outfitters, held a metal rasp against a newly installed hand rail. "I could hear the windbag from over here."

I walked back, mindful that Novak was not only a member of the I Hate Forrest Hansen Fan Club, he was the president. At our last meeting, he'd called Hansen a "lying son of a bitch." Frankly, I was in a mood to agree with him.

A group of customers emerged from Signe's, arms loaded with fishing nets and camp stoves. I waited for them to pass before addressing Novak's statement. "Is he always that touchy?"

The perpetual cigarette at the corner of his mouth dipped. From the opposite corner came a long purge of smoke. "Hansen's always had anger management issues since I've known him."

"That juvenile arrest for assault?"

"Bingo." Novak smiled with purpose.

"Well, at least he's taking care of the animals. I commend him for that."

"Ani—oh, the sheep. Well . . . yeah, I guess you could look at it that way."

"What other way is there?"

He removed his wire-rimmed glasses and pinched the bridge of his nose. Slipping them on again, he eyed me as if I were Little Naive Riding Hood. "Watching over Ivar's sheep isn't entirely a selfless act. He owns half of them." The embers of the cigarette turned bright orange as he drew in a lungful of smoke. "I'm not saying the guy isn't interested in the welfare of those critters, but he could also only be interested in protecting his investment. In fact,"—Novak gestured with the rasp—"now that Bjorklund's out of the picture, Hansen probably owns those sheep."

"Hansen was a business partner?"

"Oh yeah. A major investor. Signe too, albeit a small one. She was trying to help old Ivar get over a rough financial patch and she bought a piece of his operation. I heard her tell your friend that."

"My friend?"

"The pretty girl from the wolf institute. Dark red hair, sweet face."

"Gina?"

"Yup. Signe was talking to Gina a few weeks ago about it."

My skepticism had a gag reflex. "Cole, where do you get this stuff?"

"People talk, voices carry. I'm standing around. I hear things." He gave an indifferent shrug. "People say things, but you can't always believe what they say. They aren't always what they seem."

"Hansen?"

Novak leaned in to smooth out a burr. "Hansen'll tell you he's doing things for Ivar's estate, like keeping the Icelandic sheep together. My bet is he'll unload the flock as soon as he can to get back his investment. Hansen's no sheep rancher. The guy's already taken off a bunch of personal time from the mill to help Ivar out. He'll probably be happy to be rid of them."

Novak was hardly an impartial source. He was a disgruntled ex-mill employee who had been fired by Hansen.

"Gee, Cole, I have to say it's hard to believe all the stuff you tell me. After all, you do have an axe to grind when it comes to Forrest Hansen."

In reply, he offered a philosophical shrug as he continued to work on the rail. "Your call. I was only sharing information. Hansen's got things he'd rather have stay in the shadows. No different than the rest of us. We all have secrets and we want them to stay that way. Like him, for instance."

Novak jerked his chin toward Sheridan Avenue. On the sidewalk across the street, Justin Trudeau ambled along toting several shopping bags.

"Justin?" I asked. "You know him?"

"Since high school. Went to Duluth Central with him."

"If Justin has a secret, Cole, I really don't think it's any of my business." I held my hand up, hoping to ward off any information I didn't need to know.

His lips pulled back into a wicked smile of bemusement. He actually removed the cigarette from his mouth for this. "You think he's Native American?"

"I don't care what he is. It's none of my business."

Novak ignored me. "Justin's French and Armenian. The guy's no more Indian than I am."

"You're not serious!" I was dumbfounded and felt a surge of guilt at giving any credence to Novak's accusation.

"Ain't I?" Novak chortled, taking perverse pleasure in undercutting my beliefs. It was as if he'd just told me Marilyn Monroe was really a male transvestite.

"Why would he pretend to be Ojibwe?" My curiosity had overcome my discomfort at being burdened with this secret.

"For the books."

And then I got it. A Native American writing about nature had more cachet than yet another Caucasian. The at-one-with-the-land imagery worked in his favor. Yet for all that, I couldn't see Justin Trudeau lying about his heritage in order to sell books. It seemed so . . . so . . .

Calculated.

Then a horrible thought reared up. Would protecting that kind of secret be worth killing a man over? Except then he should have killed Novak, not Bjorklund.

It didn't make sense!

I was about to put Novak's feet to the fire on the matter when a car horn from behind brought me up short. Chief Manske's white police cruiser whirled into the parking lot and slid to an abrupt halt near me. Peter Bunyan sat in the seat next to him.

"So you are here! Get in!" he ordered.

"What's up?"

"We got a call about the killer. A tip. C'mon, we have to roll."

# CHAPTER 16

Like a hunter with an eight-point buck in his sights, Chief Manske was primed for action. I barely got the camcorder bag and
myself in the back seat before he peeled off onto Sheridan.

"An anonymous call came into the station. The guy—we think
it was a guy—said he had info on who killed Bjorklund. Said he
was afraid of being found out by the killer, that he couldn't talk
on the phone long or be seen talking to us. We're supposed to
meet him at the junction of Highway 1 and Radcliff Road."

"We?" I asked.

Manske almost smiled. "Yeah, our tipster asked for you and
Peter specifically."

"Really?" Enough skepticism filled my voice to pack a muck
bucket. "Seems a little fishy, doesn't it?"

Peter grunted. "More than a little." He turned in the front
seat toward me. "I don't know what this guy's angle is. Maybe
he's scared. Doesn't matter, we can't ignore this."

"You don't really need me, though."

Manske frowned back at me. "Like I said, the tipster wants
all three of us. He said he has information about those dead
wolves. He wanted to show us something at the meeting site."
Manske steered around a road-kill skunk on the highway,
dispersing the crows feeding on it.

"I guess. Although Peter's the conservation officer in charge,
I still don't see why I'm so essential. You have no idea who the
tipster was?"

Manske shook his head. "He wouldn't give his name. Whoever it was spoke in a broken whisper. Our dispatcher couldn't tell if it was a man or woman, only that he sounded nervous. The caller said he'd wait in the woods by the junction of those two roads. When he sees our car he'll come out. We have to be there by eleven-fifty or he's gonna walk."

It was almost 11:30. A pang of guilt ratcheted through me. In thirty minutes I was supposed to be at the motel meeting with Jeff and the others. I hoped we'd get back in time, but it dawned on me that this meeting could take longer than I'd guessed. I'd been so caught up in the moment, in the chance to help catch a murderer and resolve what had happened to those four dead wolves, that I'd completely underestimated the time. There'd be hell to pay if I let this morning's foray into crime investigation interfere with my *Zoofari* duties. Of course, I could've refused to go, something Billie Bradshaw would be more than ready to point out.

I sighed, hoping I'd made the right choice.

We weren't long out of Wolf Lake, cruising along Highway 1 at a good clip, when I felt compelled to return to a topic from earlier in the morning. "Peter, tell me more about Moua Vang."

"Why the sudden interest?"

The pine trees whipped by the window as I strained against my seat belt to press my face closer to the wire mesh partition. "I was thinking about earlier, when you and the chief were talking about animalistic practices."

"I said voodoo," Manske corrected with humor.

"Yes, exactly. Is he still doing that? We didn't really see anything to suggest it on his property."

"And you won't, Snake. But it's there."

"Why do you say that?"

The cruiser tooled along the highway, taking a series of S curves without slowing down. Peter Bunyan swayed in his shoulder harness at each turn. "The old practices aren't something Moua wants to talk about. And he doesn't do a lot of it. It's part of the old traditions. As I said, most Hmong are Christians these days. However, for Hmong like Moua, who came from the old country, the old traditions still have a pull. He doesn't want to offend the spirit of his ancestors, which means he still occasionally sacrifices animals to appease them. In his culture, the soul of a sacrificed animal is connected to the human soul."

The image of four dead wolves played in my mind. "Go on," I said with growing disquiet.

"I've had to remind Moua that the state of Minnesota doesn't condone animal sacrifices. Now, he has made some concessions. Farmers butcher chickens, hogs, and livestock all the time for food. We don't call it animal sacrifice. So on the rare occasion when a cow or goat is offered to the ancestors, it's done as part of a celebration barbecue."

I held on as Manske took us through more curves. "As long as the animals are treated well and humanely killed, I don't have a problem with it."

"And Moua does that. I was invited to a ceremony and the feast last year."

"What about the other stuff?" Manske asked. "One of my officers worked with a Hmong guy in Duluth. Name's Shue Lorr. Lorr told him about other practices—polygamy, bribery."

Peter laughed. "Tom, you'll find true blue Americans who practice those same things. Look, the Hmong are adapting, trying hard to integrate into our society. And like every other immigrant group who came before them, they're succeeding. But it takes time."

"Sure. My point is some of these other practices involve breaking the law. Maybe Vang's a good guy. I don't know. Does he understand our laws? And does he obey them? You talk about old traditions and that stuff. How far will this guy bend the law?"

"He's okay," Peter came back. "I think we can trust Moua. Two years ago I had to straighten him out about hunting out of season and without a license. Since then he's followed the law."

"As far as you know," grumbled Manske.

"Yes, as far as I know."

"Could he be doing things on the sly?" I asked. "Like shooting at eagles for feathers?"

"Good question. There is a healthy black market for eagle feathers. They're hard to come by. Native Americans want them for ceremonies and rituals and by law, they're the only people allowed to have these feathers in their possession. I know one CO who caught a poacher some years back shooting eagles to get their feathers." Peter shrugged. "You want my honest opinion, I don't see Moua doing that. Particularly after I dressed him down last year for taking pot shots at eagles. I told him about the fines and jail time."

"You don't sound entirely convinced."

Peter smiled at me. "Sometimes it's hard to tell if you're getting through. With Ivar Bjorklund I knew where I stood. He'd tell me off, complain, but we'd reach an understanding. With Moua, who comes from a different culture, you can't be sure how he's filtering what you're saying."

"Jackpot!" Tom Manske gave a decisive nod. "There's your million-dollar question. If Vang is still shooting at eagles to scare them off—he says—how do we know he isn't shooting them to sell their feathers? And if he's doing that, he could also have shot those wolves. They were found close to his property."

There it was.

The eight-hundred-pound gorilla in the room. We all saw it, yet no one quite knew how to wrestle with it.

"I know," Peter said after a pause, his voice conflicted. "It's a possibility, though I find it hard to believe. Part of my job is establishing trust with people—sizing them up quickly and working with them. I go with my gut. And my gut tells me I should trust Moua Vang."

"My gut talks to me too," the police chief piped in. "And it's suspicious. The wolf carcasses are found near Vang's property. Bjorklund's his neighbor. And he ends up getting killed, too!"

"Coincidence," Peter said.

Manske looked at the DNR officer with mild derision. "In my world there are no coincidences. You peel back the wrappers on a coincidence and you'll find—"

"Moose!" My fingers clutched the wire mesh partition, as my eyes locked onto the car buster in the road ahead.

With NASCAR-like adroitness, Manske tapped the brakes and yanked the wheel, lurching the car around the bull moose in a heart-stopping arc. I twisted to catch a glimpse of one of my favorite animals trotting to the other side of the road and into the pines.

"That was close!" I said, catching a whiff of burnt rubber.

"Way too close," Peter agreed. "A split second later and we would've had an extra passenger. Good driving, Chief!"

Manske, white knuckles gripping the steering wheel, grunted back something unintelligible. His face in the rearview mirror told me he'd caught a glimpse of the afterlife. We were lucky. I doubt we would've survived an adult male moose hurtling through our windshield. Needless to say, all eyes were glued to the road in the event of another Bullwinkle incursion.

"Peter," I said after things had calmed down, "do you know if Moua Vang is a smoker?"

"I don't think so. Any particular reason you asked?"

"His teeth. They were very yellow."

The DNR CO regarded me curiously. "You think there's some meaning there?"

"Don't know. Only that Ivar's teeth were yellow, too. It's something they had in common."

"Heads up people, we're almost there." Manske turned on to Radcliff Road, a wide expanse of compacted dirt leveled out of the forest. "I'll pull over by—shit!" He slammed back violently in his seat.

Something smacked into the windshield at high velocity. It left a spider web of splintered cracks. Then another impact. And another.

"Jesus! Get down! Those are gunshots!"

I gulped down a scream as my head snapped back in response to the car. Manske jerked the steering wheel to the left and jammed down the accelerator.

More shots. Each impact hammered like an ice pick in my spine, killing me one ping at a time. The hot breath of a bullet whizzed by my shoulder and I recoiled the other way. I ducked for cover—as much as my seat restraints allowed.

The tires squealed as the car swung out. Manske swore. A tire blew out. The police car shuddered violently. We lurched off the road and my world turned upside down as the car bounced and tumbled hard. Once. Twice. Slamming to a sudden, bone-jarring halt. My body exploded into the shoulder harness, knocking the wind out of me. I felt as if I'd been head-butted by a mountain goat. I fought the urge to throw up.

As the world slowly reeled back into focus, I realized the car was in a gully nearly on its side. And I was still alive! At least I thought so. Only the seatbelt had kept me from crashing into the passenger door beneath me. My neck protested as I turned my head to check for blood. None. No holes either. Guess I was still in one piece.

"Peter? Chief?" I croaked.

No reply. The woods were silent. No birds. No crickets. Only the quiet hissing of steam boiling off the hot engine.

169

I hoisted myself up with a grimace, discovering a throbbing pain in my left shoulder. Then stopped. What if the shooter was still out there? God, we were sitting ducks in this car! I undid my seat restraint and fell against a hard square object. The camera bag had tumbled into the car door. I froze, listening for danger. My heart thudded against my ribs like it was desperate to burst through my chest and run off to safety without me.

I waited ten seconds and peered through the broken windows for signs of movement outside.

"Peter? . . . Chief Manske?" I tried again. No response. I sucked in a lungful of air to calm myself. My hand probed the partition screen to find it securely in place. Tom Manske's head rested against it. I wiggled a finger through the mesh and felt his neck. I was thrilled to find a faint pulse. Peter was slumped away from me. I couldn't tell if he was still breathing.

Now I could clearly see we were in a ditch, the driver's side of the car up in the air some thirty degrees. The door on my right was jammed against the ground, so I struggled to right myself and crawled up to the opposite door handle. My heart sank when it barely opened. Stuck. The door was caught on something, a result of our tumble. The rear bar restraints offered no hope for the windows. I was literally inside a cage. The door was my only chance. I moved the camcorder bag behind me and braced my back against it, grabbing a firm hold of the wire mesh partition. I brought my legs in position and double-kicked the door.

I stopped with a fearful realization.

My banging was making a hell of a lot of noise. If the shooter was still out there, this would alert him, bring him back. On the other hand, if he was already coming down to finish us off, it didn't matter. Remaining inside the car was a death trap, I decided. I started kicking again. The door groaned open a little further. Good thing I wasn't the dainty daughter Mom had wanted. Her Lavender would have burst into tears right now, whereas Dad's girl Snake was a feisty kicking machine. Thank God I had on my hiking boots! I kicked like a maniac for half a minute before the car door creaked open.

I wriggled and twisted my way out the opening, broken glass cutting my hands as I hoisted myself up and out. I fell like a sack of bricks, hitting my right shoulder on the hard ground. White spots popped before my eyes from the pain. "Go ahead, put me out of my misery," I muttered through clenched teeth.

The shooter didn't respond.

I sat up on the ground and leaned against the car as my head cleared. I looked around. Nothing down the road. Nobody in the woods. At least that was a good sign. My ears strained for the sound of footsteps. All I heard was my own heart pounding in my ears. Fear coaxed me to my feet. I had to get Peter and Manske out of the car. The smell of antifreeze warned of broken lines. If a wayward spark caused a fire—

I scrambled to the front of the upended cruiser and let out a groan. No way could I get them out by myself. I was going to need help. I patted my jeans' pockets and whipped out my cell phone. I flipped it open, the lights came on and . . .

And . . .

No signal!

Damned phone! Other people got service in Wolf Lake. Soon as I got home, I promised myself, I was going to switch my cell phone provider. I fought the urge to heave the worthless hunk of junk into the forest. Instead, I tucked it back in my pocket and climbed over the hood of the car.

Against all reason, I thought of the *Zoofari* production meeting I was going to miss. I'd never make it now. Billie was going to kill me. And Jeff would worry about me, then he'd kill me. Maybe they'd cut me some slack once they heard why I was late, but I knew better. Taking off with Peter and Manske had been mistake number one. Getting shot at and nearly getting myself killed would earn me no brownie points with either one of them. I uttered a little moan of self pity and continued to crawl along the slanting hood.

The cruiser's windshield was shattered. With some effort and much swearing I managed to crawl partway through the opening. Peter and Manske were both alive and unconscious. To my relief neither showed signs of gunshot wounds. Now what? I reached for the police radio. It was dark. No power. Fortunately, luck hadn't totally abandoned me, for I spied the police chief's cell phone tucked in the seat cushion beside him. Wiggling in farther, I willed my arm to grow longer. I barely managed to snag the device.

It came right up and found a signal!

I dialed 911. Three rings later and a feminine voice gloriously answered.

Breathless, I blurted out what happened before the phone had a chance to die on me. I gave her our location, said we'd been shot at and needed medical help. My shoulder felt like it was going to fall off but I didn't mention that.

I shook off the throbbing pain and listened at a faint moan coming from the car.

"Peter? Do you hear me?"

His eyes cracked open. "Snake?" I could hardly hear him.

"I'm here"

"Am I dead?"

"No, just banged up. Are you in pain?"

He didn't answer, shutting down. I checked to see if he was still breathing. Yes! He hadn't left me yet.

"Snake!"

I slid off the hood to see who had called my name, belatedly thinking it might have been our attacker. Justin Trudeau stood by the open door of a hatchback twenty feet away. I hadn't even heard him pull up. Justin trotted over, glancing with alarm between me and the crumpled police car in the ditch. "You okay?"

"I've had better days." God! I was glad to see him.

"What the hell happened?" He nodded to the battered cruiser.

"Someone was shooting at us. He might still be out here somewhere." I gave him the quickie explanation as we took refuge behind the car frame.

"Seems to be gone now," Justin said, peering cautiously into the woods.

I struggled back to my feet. "Help me get these guys out." We went to the front of the vehicle. "It was a setup," I added. "This spot was chosen because it's isolated. The shooter could see us coming from those trees ahead. And they weren't warning shots. He wanted us dead."

Justin climbed on the hood, while I scanned the surrounding forest for any sign of our shooter. "Maybe this isn't about you, Snake. The chief works on so many cases—"

"No. Manske said the caller specifically asked for Peter and me. The shooter wanted all three of us in the car. Now we know why."

"Jesus!" Justin was halfway through the open windshield. "Getting these two out will be tough." He slipped back to the ground and smoothed his long black hair away from his face. "So you think you got shot at by the same guy who killed Ivar?"

"Who else could it be?"

# CHAPTER 17

"You're lucky to be alive."

"I know," I said.

"Those other guys got pretty banged up."

"I know, Billie," I said, not feeling talkative. I felt ambushed by the sudden appearance of Billie, Arthur, and Gina at our booth. Having missed lunch, I was famished. I sure wasn't going to let a squiffy shoulder and a few facial cuts ruin my dinner at The Chocolate Moose. I'd also hoped to have Jeff to myself for a while longer.

Without asking if we wanted company, Billie plopped down on the bench across from me next to Jeff. I know she was concerned. The timing just sucked.

"Your guardian angel must have been watching out for you," Billie grumbled. "Being in the back seat's what spared you."

"Yeah. Peter and Chief Manske got the brunt of the impact."

"Snake's one tough sheila," Jeff said with pride, unaware of the full story. I hadn't been sure exactly how to tell him, so had decided on a quiet dinner. I'd fill in the details around dessert.

Billie huffed. "She could have been killed, Jeff. The police chief has a concussion, a broken foot and a herniated disk. And her friend from the DNR has two cracked ribs and a broken collarbone."

"Damned lucky!" Gina shoved into the booth next to me, blocking all avenues of escape. Arthur slipped in beside her. "You were amazing, girl!"

She flashed me a wide smile. It was the smile of a co-conspirator, of an ally. Not so with Billie, whose stern countenance made me feel like Cinderella before one of her stepsisters. It didn't matter. Both of them were going to drag me out of the frying pan and toss me into the fire if I didn't stop them.

This wasn't how I had envisioned my dinner with Jeff. The anguish in his face when he rushed into the hospital still seared my memory—his worry and dread that I might be seriously hurt compounded my guilt.

Jeff had wanted to take me directly to the hotel to get some much-needed rest, but I'd brushed off his concerns, insisting I was fine. What I really needed, I joked, was a hot meal in a quiet place. Late in the afternoon, before the dinner crowd, the log cabin décor of The Chocolate Moose offered a comfy, public spot to tell him the rest of the story. I hadn't exactly lied to him at the hospital. I'd simply omitted the part about the gunshots.

I should have known better. Should have remembered how quickly bad news travels in a town the size of Wolf Lake and that Gina Brown would be plugged into the pipeline. Hell, she'd be pumping the fuel! I just hadn't expected the three of them to invade our table and spill the beans before I had a chance to tell Jeff my side of the story.

Jeff began to catch on that we were talking about more than a simple traffic accident. He looked askance at Billie.

I took a forkful of my Walleye pike. "Gina, any news on Rufus?" I tried changing the subject. "Weren't you checking out some leads today?"

"Rufus? Aren't you the cool one after what you've been through?"

I stared hard at Gina, rolled my eyes toward Jeff and shook my head. Shut up! I bombarded her with thought rays.

She didn't take the hint. She leaned forward, looking past me to Jeff. "Can you believe her? A few hours ago someone tried to kill her, and she's cool as a cucumber. I guess hunting crocs with you makes getting shot at seem easy."

Oh God! It was out on the table now.

Jeff sat opposite me. He'd been leaning on his elbows toward me. Now he pulled back, his questioning gaze a dagger to my heart.

I couldn't bear to look at him. I tried to focus on scooping up a forkful of wild rice. My left hand was in a sling and I was right-handed, but my shoulder throbbed and complained at the small movement. Funny how much of your body is involved in performing the smallest of tasks.

Billie had seen Jeff's reaction. "Jeff must not be privy to the local gossip, Snake. Maybe you should fill him in."

"Yes, please do." His voice took the temperature of the room down twenty degrees.

My hands shook. I didn't want to talk about it. Not here. Not like this. Someone had tried to kill me this afternoon. Talking about it just made it more real, more frightening. Last summer I'd been shoved into the crocodile pool at the zoo. There I'd had a fighting chance with our feisty saltwater croc. Knew what I was up against. This was different. What chance did I have against a sniper in the forest?

Jeff rested his forearm on the rustic table, fingers curled tightly. He tilted his head toward me expectantly. Billie leaned against the tall-backed bench, arms crossed. Even Arthur eyed me with some puzzlement. They waited for me to explain why I hadn't told Jeff the whole story. Keeping my eyes on my rapidly cooling food, I wrapped up the details quickly, skimming over the shooting as if it was of no consequence.

Arthur sat back, agog. When he spoke it was with well-chosen words. "Snake, that rollover was dangerous! You could've been crushed. And worse, you had some psychopath shooting at you at the time. I would've been scared shi—um, terrified."

I wondered if this was what a mother felt like when she first realized her child was growing up. The former Shaggy had traded in the Scooby-mobile for *Masterpiece Theater.*

I squirmed. "It's hunting season. Things like this happen all the time."

"Happen all the time?" Billie scoffed. "Mistaking a police car for a deer. Sure, makes sense."

"It was nothing."

My hand reached for Jeff's, seeking reassurance. He pulled away, his eyes trained on the table top.

"Snake," Billie added softly, "if you'd been seriously hurt . . ." She sighed, unable to finish. "You had us worried. Do you know how scared we were when we found out you'd been in an accident?"

"I know. I'm sorry."

She shook her head. "That's not good enough. You owe us more." Billie was working up to a point she wanted to make, setting up her facts methodically before me. "You put your nose where it doesn't belong."

"Chief Manske asked me to ride with him."

"You could have said no."

Gina rushed to my defense. "Lighten up a little. Snake's been trying to help. If this killer—"

I elbowed her in the ribs and shot her a murderous look. Jeff stabbed a fork into his prime rib. His eyes were glued to the food on his plate, unwilling to cast so much as a glance in my direction.

"No, I won't stop. I'm sorry, Snake. I don't think you did anything wrong. This bastard killed four wolves in cold blood. Then he killed Ivar. Now he almost got you—"

"Gina, please!" I pleaded. With a brooding husband across from me, I needed her to ease up on the gore. She wasn't helping.

"No." She stared at me resolutely, placing both hands flat on the table. "This is too important. Your friends should appreciate that. It's payback time."

My jaw set. "Payback who? Don't go reading too much into what happened."

Gina appealed to Billie. "Do you believe this? The woman gets shot off the road by some nut case and she doesn't want me to read too much into it."

"Bull's eye!" Billie drove the blade in a little deeper.

The clatter of dishes rang around us as the place started to fill up from the late afternoon crowd. Our waitress came by to refill our water glasses and bring Gina a slice of blackberry pie. After the waitress set down a Chablis for Billie, Gina continued, "With Peter out of commission, who's going after the wolf killer? And there's the murderer. What about the cops?"

Billie cleared her throat. "Yes, Snake. What about the police? What exactly were you doing with them? Besides research for *Zoofari*, that is."

The tone was uncomfortably familiar—or should I say, familial? I half wondered if Ms. Bradshaw was a long lost sister to my mother, the woman who liked to keep me up to date on what my old high school boyfriends were up to. Like did I know Scott Kaplinksy was now a vice president for Target Corporation? And pointing out how I was just a zookeeper married to just another zookeeper.

The parental disapproval in Billie's manner came a little too close to one of my tender spots.

"Wait a second." Gina sat up, deciphering the conversation. "You mean Snake hasn't told you?"

Arthur's water glass hovered near his mouth. "Told us what?"

Jeff lowered his head, as if preparing for a blow.

"Told you about the headway we've made." Through bites of blackberry pie, Gina told them of finding the wolf carcasses, how studying the GPS position of the Red Iron pack caused us to stumble upon Ivar Bjorklund's body. Then there was the excitement of who cut the fence at the wolf institute and Rufus's vanishing act. All of it she tied together into the climax of getting shot at in the chief of police's squad car.

I saw their faces and realized my mistake earlier. I shouldn't have trivialized being shot at but hadn't wanted to make it into a big deal. Thanks to Gina's rousing telling of the event, it was now one very big deal.

I sighed and prayed for an asteroid to hit The Chocolate Moose. One had put the dinosaurs out of their misery. If it was good enough for them, it was good enough for Snake Jones.

I stole a look at Jeff, who was now silently picking at his plate. His silence was killing me. I would have preferred some yelling. Anything would be welcome, anything but freezing me out. I'd never seen him like this and didn't know what to make of it.

Billie sipped her wine and fixated on my sling with an expression drier than her Chablis. "I have to admit, Snake, you did some good work. Can we assume now that you've almost been killed and your shoulder's banged up that you're going to put your extracurricular activities aside to focus on why we all came to Wolf Lake?"

Kaboom! A warning shot across my bow. Billie was playing her producer card, reminding me, in her own delicate way, of my *Zoofari* responsibilities.

Gina became agitated. "Wait." She waved her fork at me. "You can't quit! Not now. We've got to get that slimy bastard!"

Billie leaned over. "Isn't that what the police are for?"

"Chief Manske's in the hospital."

"There's got to be somebody to take his place. I'm sure the Wolf Lake police can handle things."

Eyes down, Jeff exhaled sharply into the table. His lips parted momentarily then closed again.

I nearly said something to him when Gina reached over and grabbed my hand, the one in the sling. "But they don't believe in the dying message clue! Manske blew off Snake, so what makes you think anyone else wouldn't do the same?"

Three pairs of eyes swung to me like search lights in a prison yard.

Arthur set down his water glass, a spark of the old Shaggy curiosity glinting in his eye. "Far out! A clue? What clue?"

My mouth opened, but it was Gina's voice that answered him. "This is so cool!" she blurted. "When we found Ivar's body he was clutching a little elm branch in his dead hand."

"Don't think I follow you." Arthur rubbed his whiskerless chin.

"We think he was naming his killer."

We?

All of a sudden Gina and I had become a team. Not a good thing. Bjorklund's killer could be anywhere. Two tables away sat a group of four grizzled men, unshaven, unwashed, and wearing clothes that were obviously slept in, each sporting the same half-delirious look of campers who had just gotten back from the BWCA wilderness and were seated for their first real food in a week. One of them might be the killer, waiting for the right moment to shut me up.

Billie made a face. "What makes you think he was naming his killer? A stick in his hand? That could mean anything!"

"Like what?" I challenged, annoyed at having my observations put down yet again. Billie had the same dismissive attitude as Officer Hernandez when he interviewed me at the hospital after the accident. "You tell me, Billie. What does it mean?"

"I—I don't know—something."

"Not good enough. You don't like my theory, then come up with something more plausible. Well?"

"Um, maybe he already had the twig thing in his hand when he was shot."

"No. The man had dragged himself over ten feet to get to that little stick. The marks in the grass were plain. As I told the police—and they agreed with me—Bjorklund passed by other sticks and leaves. It seems like he went out of his way to get that elm branch. Why?"

Billie was at a loss. She shook her head, slightly intimidated by me, I think. I was pissed.

"You're Ivar Bjorklund"—the fingers of my right hand spread out in the air—"and you've been shot and left to die, with only seconds left to live. You can't get help so you decide to leave a message. What message?"

No sounds emanated from our table. Around us the rattle of plates, flatware and table chatter echoed off the rustic pine paneling. Billie's brown-penciled eyebrows crawled up beneath her silver bangs. "I don't know . . ."

"Was he leaving a goodbye message to a loved one? His wife was dead. He had no immediate relatives."

Silence.

"And he wasn't spilling the beans on Deep Throat's identity. That came out years ago."

That earned me a hard look from Jeff, as if he were seeing me for the first time. The harsh appraisal nearly did me in. I faltered but forced myself to continue. I leaned against the table, wincing as the pressure on my forearm sent a shockwave to my shoulder. "What message would you leave in the last seconds of your life? What would matter most to you at that moment? Maybe naming the person who killed you?"

Billie was a hard sell. "Maybe it was a reflex thing. A muscle spasm. His hand reached out and clutched the ground."

"I'd go with that," I conceded, sagging against the back of the booth. "Except what Gina didn't tell you was that he had pulled it out by the roots. No, he went for that particular stem on purpose."

If not appeased, Billie was at least silenced.

"Okay . . ." Arthur frowned at his hands, which drummed on the tabletop. "But what does it mean?"

For all the fuss I'd just made, I came up empty. "I don't know."

Gina tingled with inspiration. "Hey, it's a piece of wood, right? Wood. Trees. The forest. Forrest Hansen." Her pretty round face glowed with triumph. She explained the significance to the others.

I'd thought of him before. Certainly he was hot-headed enough to kill the old Swede and then shoot at a police car. "Nice try, Gina. The thing is, why pass by all those other sticks? Wouldn't they have given the same message? Maybe it's got nothing to do with the wood. Maybe it's the leaves. Was he naming the Stewards of Superior? One of their flyers was found under his body. Though I don't know how that fits in . . ."

Jeff slammed his crumpled napkin to the table. He surged to his feet. "You're not letting this go, are you?" Without another word, he set down three twenty-dollar bills and squeezed past Billie for the door.

"Jeff!" I called after him, struggling to my feet. Only Billie's restraining arm stayed me.

"Snake, let him go. He needs time alone." The fret lines around her mouth deepened, allowing her maternal side out at last. Her white hair fluttered from the breeze caused by a group of exiting customers. "This isn't a game. You're in no condition to track down a killer—of wolves or humans."

"Let me go. I need to talk to Jeff."

She grabbed my good hand. "And I need to know where your priorities are. We all do."

★ ★ ★ ★ ★

I closed the door to our room at the Super 8. The window curtains were closed and the TV on, it's spectral light the only illumination in the darkened room. Jeff sat on the edge of the closer queen-sized bed, brooding like he'd lost his best friend.

Where to begin? At that moment, I would've preferred facing a charging rhino to what I dreaded was about to happen. I snapped on the light. Jeff turned off the TV, eyes averted.

"Wanna talk?" I approached the bed.

The tension in the room spiked as his vivid blue eyes latched on to me. I read the misery in them. Jeff's voice was low, controlled, but the anger came through loud and clear. "You lied to me."

The accusation went into me like a knife. "I didn't—"

"Then what exactly do you call it?" He was on his feet. "Everyone in the town knows you were shot at except me. Do you have any idea how that makes me feel?"

"Jeff, I'm sorry. I was going to tell you—"

"When? When were you going to tell me?"

I took in a deep breath, forcing down my sense of panic, of feeling cornered. "I was afraid of how you were going to take it. I thought if I softened you up a bit with a good meal and some wine, it wouldn't seem like it was that big a deal."

"It is a big deal." His hand jerked toward the sling hanging off my left shoulder and my bum arm. "Wake up, Snake. You're hurt. What you're doing is reckless. After what happened today, it's bloody dangerous."

"It's important."

"More important than your life? Someone almost killed you! The car was cracked up. Your friends are in hospital! It's only by the grace of God you're not there, too."

"Jeff," I implored, "you've got to understand. Gina made me realize we're too close to totally give up. With both Manske and

Peter out of the picture, we can't let whoever did this to them, to Bjorklund and the wolves, get away with it."

"No, you have to understand." Jeff began to pace like a caged tiger. "It's not your job! Let someone else investigate. You've done all you can."

"But they're not listening to me! They gave me the brush off."

"For good reason!"

"No! For no good reason." I searched for a way to make him understand how important this was to me. "They aren't going to concern themselves with the dead wolves. What about Rufus? It all ties into Bjorklund's death. We must be getting close to the answer—"

"Because some crazy bloke with a gun almost killed you?" Jeff braced himself in front of me. "What about *Zoofari?* We came all the way up here to film a wolf show. And now you want to do a walkabout and play bloody detective. Snake." His tone turned to quiet anguish. "We mortgaged everything we own to keep the show going. That was our dream. We're on the verge of going national if we play our cards right . . ."

"Animal Planet!" I had forgotten all about Jeff's call on my hopelessly inept cell phone. I hadn't had a chance to get him alone and talk about it since he'd arrived.

He shook his head, baffled. "It's taken you this long to ask about that. It's like you don't care anymore."

I stepped closer, my eyes filling. "I care, Jeff!"

"And so do I! You could've been killed today!"

My hand reached out for his. He tried to pull away, but I held it like an anchor rope. "I'm not abandoning *Zoofari*. I'd never do that. I've already worked out shooting locations with Gina and Debbie Wong. You know I don't always get involved during the actual film shoot. That's you." I squeezed his hand. "I get involved again in post-production. Most of our stuff is being filmed at the wolf institute. You don't need me there for all of it."

"What if we want to shoot at other locations, follow the story of the missing wolf? We need you." He grabbed me gently by the shoulders. When I winced he let go instantly with a pained, apologetic expression. "When Gina called to tell me you'd been involved in a car accident and were hurt, I thought I'd lost you. Then I find out later about the shooting. If Gina's right, the bloke's still out there. If he finds out you're still alive, he may try again. If that happened, luv, I couldn't bear it."

The big lug still cared! I blinked back the wet haze. "I'm sorry I put you through that. I really am. I hope you can understand why I did what I did. A man's been killed. Four wild animals were killed and their carcasses dumped in the woods so nobody would find them. For me it's about doing what's right, Jeff. That's why I hung out with Peter Bunyan. He asked for my help. That's why I went out to that rendezvous with Chief Manske, because he asked me to, and we might've caught a killer. You see that, don't you?" I searched his face for understanding but saw only an implacable barrier. "Nobody cares for wildlife more than you. Whoever killed Bjorklund and those wolves might kill again. One thing I've always admired about you is your sense of fairness. I think I can help stop this. You understand?" My eyes entreated him.

He backed away a step. "It's too dangerous! You can't put yourself in that kind of danger again."

"You do it all the time," I shot back. "That first year we were in Australia together. Every time you dove out of your boat to relocate a saltwater crocodile, my heart would stop. I was terrified."

"That's different! I've worked with crocs me whole life."

"They're still out to kill you, Jeff. They don't understand you're helping them. You're invading their space and they show no mercy. Yet you deal with it."

Exasperated, he said, "It's not the same."

"Yes it is! You put yourself on the line for wildlife all the time. But I've accepted the risk because that's what you do. Can't you see I'm willing to do the same thing, only in a different way?"

A heavy silence followed.

I thought I noticed a thaw in Jeff's demeanor, a relaxation in his neck and shoulders. In two quick steps he reached out and crushed me to him. My shoulder protested, but I didn't move, didn't want to leave the comfort of his arms. He kissed me long and hard.

Finally, he stepped away and sized me up with a wary eye. "You're a sly vixen. That's what I've always loved about you. You're right. The way you're sticking your neck out to help others is like what I'm doing. I still don't like it."

Taken by a thought, I smiled back flirtatiously. "You could help me. We were searching for the GPS coordinates when we found Bjorklund's body. We never did take up the search afterward." My finger tapped him on the chest. "You're the expert tracker in the family."

# CHAPTER 18

"You're looking at the most hated, most misunderstood animal in the history of the planet—the wolf."

Arthur Lutz stepped back with his camera for a wider shot of Jeff, who crouched near the pond inside the main enclosure at the wolf institute. In the background, Cheyenne, the most people-friendly pack member, observed him from ten feet away, while Lakota paced anxiously in the distance, unhappy with the intruder in his territory. Out of camera range but close by, the wolf care staff watched the animals with a laser-like focus, ready to intervene at the slightest ear flick.

"An apex predator, wolves were designed to run for miles. They can bring down an animal more than ten times their size." Jeff looked over his shoulder at Cheyenne. "Once the most pervasive mammal in the world next to human beings, the wolf has been hunted to near extinction, with the exception of places like northern Minnesota."

Arthur, lowering himself to one knee, zoomed in on Cheyenne while Jeff continued his monologue.

"It breaks my heart what we humans have done to these magnificent creatures. The wolf was the first animal to be domesticated, our first nonhuman friend." He turned toward Cheyenne. Arthur moved in closer, filming a tight two shot. "New genetic evidence reveals our relationship with them may go back ninety thousand years farther than previously believed. Please join us for the next hour as we learn about the conservation efforts to save one of the world's most mysterious and iconic animals, the gray wolf."

While the camera now trained on the wolves, Jeff focused on me, assuring himself I was still within the field of his protection. He had conceded my points last night, but ours was an uneasy truce. He was scared to death for me and I didn't blame him. I was scared, too.

"Great!" Billie Bradshaw nodded, lowering the gun mic. "That's our lead-in. Let's do the next setup."

Debbie Wong and I stood near the enclosure fence as we watched Claudette and Danny shepherd Cheyenne, Aila and Lakota away from the pond. I was grateful they were hand-raised wolves. They weren't out to kill us, unlike the ill-tempered saltwater crocodiles I'd helped Jeff relocate in the backwater estuaries Down Under. The wolf care staff did a bang-up job making sure we were safe. We were never in danger. Still, out of habit, I kept tabs on where each wolf was at all times. You never take those things for granted.

Truth was, I was on edge. Any loud noise made my heart jump. And though my brain confidently assured me there was practically no chance of the murderer shooting me here, the sailor knots in my belly were not persuaded. I tried one of Gina's calming mantras.

Charmed, Debbie turned to me. "Jeff's passion is contagious. Any more at home like him?"

I could honestly say Jeff Jones was one of a kind. Jago, his elder brother, ran the family's reptile park in Beerwah. I didn't care much for Jago, who was one of those stereotypical hard-nosed, smart-mouthed, talk-with-his-fists Australians. He talked down to Jeff, which annoyed the hell out of me, though Jeff took it in stride. The youngest of the Jones boys, James, I adored. Sweet baby James. Quietest of the brothers, he had a cheerful disposition and a wry wit that allowed him to skewer Jago without the latter being aware of it half the time. None of this I shared with Debbie, just tossing her a simple "no" in answer to her question. I'd leave the discussion of my in-laws to another day.

"This is a nice distraction," Debbie confided. "I spent two hours last evening following a lead on Rufus, which turned out to be a wandering Siberian Husky."

"That's disappointing."

"I'm fine with it. We asked people to call in any wolf sightings. They are. I can't complain, even when they're off."

"You seem to be holding up well, Debbie. I'd be a nervous wreck."

"I am. You just don't see it. I've got too many other things to deal with to implode. I'll do that later." She gave a little laugh. "Actually, I'm thrilled you guys are here. Your visit will give some positive attention to the wolf institute. It'll get us on the news again this evening, which means another chance to ask people to help us watch out for Rufus."

"Glad to help."

"I didn't tell you before." Debbie leaned in, slightly chagrined. "But I've never seen your show. I can definitely see why Jeff's so popular. Look." She extended her slender arm toward the viewing windows of the auditorium, behind which two dozen people watched us, some clearly recognizing the guy from TV. A young mother pointed at me, then leaned down to say something to the little girl with her. I searched the crowd, wondering if one of those happy faces belonged to the killer. Was I being studied from the other side of the glass like the wolves?

Thankfully, most of the attention focused on Jeff. People grinned at the man in the khaki shirt and shorts. I marveled at him. For a native of the tropics, he handled late September in the North Woods very well. The mornings were getting frostier and the days cooler as the transition to fall progressed. Rugged though he was, soon Mr. Southern Hemisphere would finally have to make the transition to long pants.

We snapped to attention as Billie called Debbie over. The next shot included an interview with her. I studied my clipboard, forcing myself to concentrate on the job at hand.

Last night Jeff confessed he hadn't actually talked to Animal Planet. He'd played phone tag with one of the assistant development coordinators. But they had called him! Our demo tape had gotten past the first hurdle. Somebody wanted to talk to us. Very cool. Now I had to make sure I didn't blow the deal. I needed to keep my mind on my work, which wasn't so easy right now with all the graphic images from the last few days ping-ponging in my head. And my shoulder bothered me. The sling took some getting used to and a few Advils helped the soreness. Still, I was relieved we'd filmed most of our schedule for the morning. The exterior soft shots would be done when the late afternoon sun made for richer colors and better shadows.

Arthur poised the Canon DVCam on his shoulder and trained it on Jeff and Debbie, who stood by the tall chain-link fence that separated the main enclosure from the wolf lab.

Jeff jumped into the sequence with his usual exuberance, as if this was the most special moment of his life. "I'm with Debbie Wong, wolf curator here at Minnesota Wolf Institute. A bit later, we'll get to see how these animals are fed. It's a different experience, I understand, than what we do at the zoo."

Debbie nodded, a broad, enthusiastic smile hiding her nerves. "We feed the animals once a week in order to simulate the conditions they'd face in the wild. Wild wolves don't eat every day."

"Wolves at some zoos get a product called canine chow, made by the same people who produce your dog's food. What do you feed the animals at the institute?"

"Road kill."

Jeff feigned shock and Debbie actually laughed, relaxing for the first time since the camera had been trained on her. "Minnesota has too many deer. Sadly, a lot of them are killed by automobiles on our highways. We're able to use some of these deer to feed our wolves." Arthur circled his subjects. Debbie's attention left Jeff and followed our cameraman's movements as she went on. "We're able to collect and freeze some of the carcasses. On Wednesday we hang one outside to thaw. The wolves smell it and get excited for their dinner."

"Cut!"

With more diplomacy than I knew she had, Billie suggested Debbie should keep her attention on Jeff and forget what Arthur was doing. Easier said than done when you're not used to speaking in front of a camera.

Everyone took a deep relaxing breath and they picked the scene up where Debbie was speaking about the deer.

Jeff lightly touched her hand and asked, "What d'you do in the winter? It gets below zero up here, much colder than your freezer. How do you thaw the deer then?"

"During the winter the carcass is thawed in my office."

Jeff grinned. "Now that's got to be a conversation piece!"

Debbie, now quite at ease in front of the camera, went on to explain how the institute operated on limited days during the harsh winter months and she was rarely in her office then.

The life of an animal caretaker was never dull.

Another shot in the can. Another setup.

"Billie," I said as she, Jeff and Arthur converged to discuss the next take. "I'll be in the wolf lab. I want to make sure it's ready for the next sequence."

Which was true. I also thought I'd caught a glimpse of Gina headed that way. I hadn't seen her since last evening and I needed to talk to her.

Inside the lab, I found Gina at the back counter, several full plastic sandwich bags lined up along the Formica top. She offered a muted smile when she saw me.

"Wolf scat?" I leaned forward.

"I was crawling around a couple rendezvous sites this morning. Thought I'd bring in some samples for testing."

"Did you manage to get in a little search time for Rufus while you were at it?"

Gina glanced up furtively. "Of course. I checked all the traps at sun up. Empty." She sighed.

"You'll find him," I said with more confidence than I had a right to claim. It had been two days with few reported sightings, none of which had proven to be Rufus. The stress on the staff was eating them up.

From a cabinet, Gina slid out a sealed display box with a clear plastic cover, which she placed on the counter. "This should add visual interest. Comes in handy for school presentations. Nice yuck appeal." The display contained a collection of bone shards, claws, teeth, feathers, and other goodies found inside wolf scat samples. "You want me to talk about biomass calculations and that sort of thing?"

"Sure. Keep it short and simple." I was distracted by the ball of panty hose she'd plopped down in front of her. "Dressing up for the camera, are you?"

"No," Gina laughed. "This is the sort of pricey cutting-edge technology we use in the wolf lab. It's how I usually process scat. It goes in the panty hose and I run it through my washing machine, which removes all the fecal matter, leaving only the good bits."

"I love it!"

"Wish I could take credit for it. Got the idea from a DNR wolf manager in St. Paul. I'll empty the contents on camera. For the stuff I collected this morning, we'll do it the old-hand sort way." She pulled a pair of green latex gloves from a box. When she turned back it was with a more subdued manner, almost pensive. "Jeff wasn't happy last night at the restaurant. I know I didn't help matters."

"No, you didn't," I agreed, half joking. "Your timing sucks. I was trying to have a quiet dinner with Jeff. Tell him about the car accident in more detail, ease him into the idea of me getting shot at—"

"But we barged in on you."

"Well, yes."

"Sorry. We were all so worried about you." The gloves squeaked as she pulled them on. "I mean, you could've been killed."

"Now don't you start!"

Gina swung about and met my gaze, her liquid brown eyes apologetic. "I screwed up. I shouldn't have got on your case about quitting the investigation. You were right. It's not your job to find out who killed those wolves and murdered Ivar."

"Thank you."

Sometimes all you want from a person is a simple acknowledgment they went too far.

In a glum voice, she added, "Jeff was pretty upset when he left the table. My fault, I'm sure. I hope you guys didn't have a fight because of something I said. Are you two okay?"

"We're good, Gina," I assured her.

"Good." The worry lines relaxed around her eyes.

"And you'll be glad I've had a change of heart. I'm not giving up the investigation."

"Way cool!"

"Don't get too revved up. There might not be much I can do"—I lifted my sling arm—"but I'll give it the old college try. Jeff's offered to help."

Gina smiled. "So . . . I've been thinking. You must've pissed off someone enough for them to take a shot at you. Any ideas who it might be?"

I reached over and took a pair of gloves for myself. "I've thought of very little else. Of the people I've talked to, one person's been the most hostile: Forrest Hansen."

Gina approved the choice. "You mean Forrest Grump? The creepy bodybuilder guy."

"Yeah, he was really nasty yesterday when I offered my condolences."

"You saw him yesterday?"

"At the Gas 'n Go next to Signe's." I eyed the bags with their furry pieces of dried wolf excrement. "I was impressed. Did you know he's taking care of Oskar?"

The admiration in my tone prompted Gina to set me straight. "I'd hold off nominating Hansen for Humanitarian of the Year. Maybe he's doing a nice thing. Maybe not. Oskar's a valuable animal. I can't tell you how many sheep trials he's won. And he's sired some champions himself. Oskar's worth money."

"Guess that makes it easier for me to dislike the guy and keep him as a suspect."

Gina set a small tray on the counter and emptied the contents of the first bag onto it. "He and Ivar have been friends since Hansen was a teenager. I can't see him hurting the old man; Signe says Ivar was like a father to him."

"All I can say is Oedipus killed his father. And Hansen has a history of violence, beating up Justin Trudeau, even if it is in the distant past. What if the financial partnership he had with Bjork-lund soured? It happens."

"True." She picked at the scat with a dental tool. "Looks like raven feathers and bones. Must've been a snack. Aila's caught a raven or two in the enclosure."

My foot brushed against a twig someone had tracked into the lab. I bent down to pick it up, twirling it between my thumb and forefinger. "Gina, how well do you know Cole Novak?"

"Signe's handyman?"

"Yeah. Can I trust him?"

"This sounds juicy! Trust him with what?"

"With the stuff he's telling me. Can I believe what he says?"

She inspected me carefully. "What's he been telling you?"

"He used to work at the paper mill. Hansen fired him. Novak called Hansen a lying son of a bitch."

Gina whistled softly. "I wasn't impressed with Mister Biceps before. I'm really not feeling any warm and fuzzies for the man."

"Oh, and speaking of firing, remember Hansen was a sharpshooter in the army."

"Good with guns, huh?" Gina nodded. "Well, Hansen's a guy I'd keep my eye on, that's for sure."

"Except the man who's telling me he's a liar is the guy Hansen fired. He's obviously carrying a grudge. Thanks to Hansen, it's hard for him to find work."

"Or so he says."

"You think he's lying about that, too?"

Gina turned her attention back to the scat on the tray. "There's a different breed of people up here in the Northland, Snake. People who don't want to work for 'The Man' as Danny would say." Her eyes met mine, determining whether I caught her meaning. I must have fallen short because she went on, "Novak isn't dumb. It's possible he works as much as he wants to work. There are a lot of craftsmen and artists up here like that. They do what they need to do to get by, and then the rest of their time is their own. They don't need money for big fancy houses and cars. They prefer the simple life. Prefer being their own man or woman."

I nodded enthusiastically. "So, if Novak is one of those guys, and it sounds like he might be, then he's throwing stuff out just to see if he can get a rise out of me. The crazier it is, the more he likes it."

"Guess he's having a bit of fun at your expense."

It was more than fun. I hesitated, not knowing how to tell her about the other gem Novak had cast at my feet, so I blurted it out. "Yesterday he told me Justin Trudeau isn't really a Native American."

"Say what?" Gina paused in the act of dissecting a piece of scat. She glared at me, incredulous.

"Novak said Justin's really French Armenian."

Gina blinked. "And you believe him?"

My good hand underscored my words. "This is what I'm asking you. Can I believe him? Novak said he went to high school with Justin."

"I don't believe it." She set down the scalpel, disturbed by the implication. "Not about the high school thing. I mean the other. About Justin's heritage. I can't believe he'd make that up." Gina faced me, a sharp glint in her eyes. "I think you're right, Snake. Cole's messing with you. Could be he's trying to deflect suspicion away from himself. It's no secret he had issues with Ivar."

"And Forrest Hansen."

"And Hansen," Gina said with conviction. "He's making everyone else sound suspicious except himself."

"Right. If Novak had all these suspicions, he could've gone to the police. But he didn't."

"Maybe he knew the Wolf Lake police wouldn't take him seriously. Maybe he didn't want to stick his neck out. Or maybe he was hoping you'd take his suspicions to the cops for him."

"Too many maybes there, girl!"

Gina laughed and returned to her work. With a jack knife blade she cut the scat into sections, picking out a few small bones. "I'm glad you're still in the game. It's like I said, with

Manske and Peter banged up, the investigations are in limbo. Thinking you'd packed up your sleuthing bags, I decided the trail shouldn't go cold." She looked askance at me. "So I did some digging into the shootings."

I wasn't sure if I liked the sound of that. Only yesterday someone had tried to kill Peter, Manske and me. Gina was no more immune to bullets than the rest of us.

A stream of sunlight glinted off the nearby window. I lifted my hand to shade my eyes. "Did you find out anything?"

A rush of crimson touched her cheeks. "Let me tell you, Cole Novak isn't a forgive-and-forget kind of guy. As I heard the story from Signe, it was Ivar who got Cole fired. Ivar was his supervisor at the mill. Hansen was merely the executioner. I bet Cole didn't tell you that?"

"No, he didn't, the little turd."

"Maybe he didn't know. What if Cole found out Ivar was really the one responsible?"

My thoughts drifted away from the furry nugget in front of me. If Gina was right, Novak had plenty of reason to resent Bjorklund, but was it enough to push him to murder?

There was another problem. "If Novak is the shooter, why kill the wolves? He's got a low opinion of nearly everything and everybody. Wolves are the only living thing I've ever heard him say anything favorable about."

"I know!" Gina tossed up her hands. "It doesn't make sense, if the two things are connected. But"—she resumed with full steam—"there's a two-hour gap Tuesday afternoon when he wasn't at Signe's. He was getting supplies." This last with dark emphasis, as if Novak had sneaked off to his Lair of Evil to conjure up his flying monkeys. "Tuesday was when Ivar was murdered."

"Doesn't mean he did it. For all that, you can say the same thing about Signe. She was away from the store on Tuesday afternoon, too."

"Signe?" Gina was taken aback. "You think Signe had a hand in this? Are you sure? Next you'll be saying I had something to do with it."

I opened my mouth and closed it again. Well, you did lie to me about going back to the wolf institute. Though you didn't. You went flying. I bit my tongue. After yesterday's bullet derby in the woods, I didn't have the heart to stir things up with Gina. I'd already riled up too many people in Wolf Lake; I didn't need to make my old friend feel I suspected her. I didn't.

Not really.

I smiled thinly at her. "Relax. It's all conjecture. Just holding up the ballots to the light and looking for hanging chads. My point is it's really easy to get swept up by a few details and be carried off by the wave." I knew whereof I spoke. I'd been on that conjecture wave so often myself, I was in danger of being crowned Surfer Queen.

"I take your point," Gina said, squeezing a few drops of water into a test tube with ground-up scat. She corked it and shook it up.

It brought a smile to me. "Too bad we can't do that with people!"

"We can." She smiled impishly. "Haven't you ever watched that reality diet show from England? The nutritionist makes all her victims poop for her so she can analyze it. Why do you ask?"

"Would be nice if we could analyze Bjorklund."

"Shouldn't there be serum workups and that sort of thing done on him?"

"I don't know if those things are done automatically. Bjorklund was an old man who died of a gunshot wound. The BCA might not do those kinds of tests on him if the investigating officer doesn't want them."

She accepted that. "What're you hoping to find?"

"Oh, I don't know. I keep wondering what happened to him. It's hard to imagine the young man Signe talked about. She said he was built like an ox—hell, the way she tells it, he could practically carry an ox! Bjorklund changed so much in his later years, really went downhill."

"Don't forget what he'd gone through, Snake. First the accident at the paper mill, his son dying in Iraq, and after that running himself ragged taking care of Lily."

"Pretty tough stuff," I admitted. "Then trying to run the sheep ranch on his own after she died."

"Not so alone. I heard Ivar hired some part-time help a month ago."

"Good. He needed it. He looked in such poor health. Say, d'you know if he was a smoker?"

Gina shook her head. "Ivar was a clean Baptist. No cigarettes, no booze."

"Then I'm stumped. His teeth were yellow, like a smoker's."

"Maybe it's something in the water," she joked with a dismissive wave of her hand.

Before I could reply with something witty, Danny Hoffman burst through the lab door, his face flushed. "Whoa, there you are!" His voice reverberated off the walls. "I've been looking all over for you."

"What?" Gina grew worried, the color draining from her cheeks. "Have they found Rufus?"

"No. No news there." His eyes shifted between us. "You haven't heard then?"

"Heard what?"

"I just got some heavy news from a pal. His sister works dispatch at the police station." Danny's slender body was swaying and shifting like a sitting cobra, as he gripped the side of the door. "There's been another shooting. I thought you'd want to know since you're kind of involved." He waved at my sling.

"Who, Danny?" I said impatiently. "Who got shot?"

"Ivar's neighbor. Forrest Hansen. And it's way more serious than getting shot. The dude is dead!"

# CHAPTER 19

"What!"

Gina and I both stared at him, dumbfounded. The knots in my belly constricted tighter.

"Are you sure?" I finally asked in a small voice.

"I'm positive. Hansen's body was found at Bjorklund's place yesterday around dinner time. He'd been shot. Murdered."

Gina's hands flew to her mouth. A second later they came down again. "Oh my God, that was when we were at The Chocolate Moose!"

"Are the police still at the crime scene?" I asked.

Danny shrugged. "I don't think so. Some BCA dudes from Brainerd left this morning. Gene's sister said not much else is going on there what with Manske out of the picture."

He made a move to leave and I stopped him. "Who else have you told this to?"

"Only you guys."

"Do me a favor and don't tell anyone else. Please?"

"Sure, Snake." Light dawned finally. "Your friends won't find out. Not from me, anyway. Rock on!"

Twenty minutes later the *Zoofari* crew broke for lunch. By then I'd joined them, my game face on and my nerves tingling. Quite casually I told Billie I had an errand to run and would be back before the next setup. Jeff saw through my subterfuge but said nothing. With a quick kiss, he whispered in my ear, "Be careful, luv."

Thankfully, he didn't know about Hansen's murder or he wouldn't have been so obliging. Less so had he known what I was planning on doing.

I wasn't sure what to expect as I pulled my Jeep into Bjorklund's driveway. An open door with a big banner saying, "Welcome Snake Jones! Please Come In!" I don't think so. The yellow Do Not Cross police tape across the front door gave me second thoughts.

Every turn on Black Fir's twisting road, every bump had brought a fresh clutch of apprehension. What if the killer had seen me leave the wolf institute and had followed me? Constant checks of the side-view mirror didn't allay the fear. The fact I'd made it safely to Bjorklund's house didn't set me at ease.

What the hell was I doing? Could I really justify entering a closed crime scene? Even in my mixed-up head I knew it was wrong. Who was I to snoop around in hopes of scratching up a bit of evidence the experts had missed? How presumptuous was that? More to the point, how much trouble could I get into by crossing the yellow tape? Plenty! Yet, like a lemming charging over a cliff, instinct drove me on. If Chief Manske and Peter Bunyan were able-bodied and on the job, I told myself, I wouldn't have to do this. Right?

Well, it sounded good.

Still, I wasn't sure I was brave enough to face the wrath of the Wolf Lake police if they caught me messing around their crime scene.

The key phrase there was *caught me*. Leaving my Jeep parked out front wasn't such a hot idea. To a passing patrolman it would glare like the bat signal in the night sky of Gotham: Intruder Inside! No, I needed to be as stealthy as a jungle cat. And believe me, one thing you learn tracking wild animals is to be stealthy, so I put my Jeep in reverse gear, turned around, and drove back along Black Fir Road. After a quarter of a mile, I pulled off-road behind a stand of jack pines and left my vehicle. I picked my way back through the trees, careful when I got near Moua Vang's property, keeping in the shadows and out of sight.

In no time, I emerged into Ivar Bjorklund's backyard. I waited and listened for any unusual sound. All I heard were song birds. I moved quickly across the patchy rye grass and approached the rambler with its peeling paint. At the front of the house rested a box frame filled with stones. Once a flower garden, the only greenery it supported now was a few rogue weeds. That and the faded decorative landscape edging suggested at one time the house had been a showplace of bright colors and flowers, now left to fend for themselves.

I avoided the front door, peering through every window and trying each sash. All locked. So were the back door and the bulkhead cellar doors, and all the basement casement windows—

Except one!

At first jiggle, the basement window appeared as bolted down as the rest of them, until I nudged it once more and heard it creak, then partially give way. Not locked, only stuck. The old sash had swollen over the years. The bad news was the window was on the driveway side of the house, so I'd stick out like a humpback whale on the beach to any passing car. Or any madman with a gun. The good news was there were no passing cars. Nor likely to be any. As I'd noticed earlier, Black Fir Road was isolated and heavily wooded. By the time any vehicle pulled into the driveway, I'd hear it in time to run to the back of the house. In theory, at least.

I jiggled and fussed with the sash, not easy with an arm in a sling and glancing anxiously over my shoulder every two seconds. Finally, a splinter of rotted wood broke off and the window came loose. Slipping my arm out of my sling, I pushed the window up, positioned myself carefully and shimmied in feet first. I dropped to the basement floor with a thud and cried out as a sharp blade of pain ripped through my arm. My shoulder hurt like hell. But I was in!

My palm had a smudge of grease from the window. I wiped it off on my thigh. That's the beauty of blue jeans. Low maintenance, and now they were accessorized.

I stood silent in the damp basement, waiting for my heart to stop pounding and my arm to quit throbbing in tempo. I could still leave now, I told myself. No harm done. Just go.

But I was stubborn. I'd already come this far. Whatever reservations I had for being here were trumped by my determination. I moved on.

Conscious of the ticking of the clock, I treaded quickly across the bare cement floor. I shot up the stairs to the kitchen, where I paused. Neat and clean, it was tidier than I'd expected for an elderly man living alone. As if waiting for him to return, dry dishes leaned against a wire rack on the counter next to the ceramic sink. The sink itself was empty except for a greenish stain running below the faucet. Inside the cupboards were the usual flour, crackers, sugar, canned goods and macaroni and cheese. Lots and lots of mac and cheese. Poor Ivar Bjorklund must've been living on the stuff. More surprising was the inside of the fridge: a quart of milk gone sour, two containers of fruit juice, a block of cheese and eggs. Some leftovers I couldn't identify in clouded plastic containers. And two dozen bottles of water standing upright in a tight squadron on the bottom shelf. Who knew the old man would be a fan of the bottled-water craze? Particularly when he had his own well.

My boots squeaked on the hardwood floor as I entered the main hallway. I came to an abrupt halt at the living room. Blood, or what was left of it, lay ahead of me, a dried pool to mark the spot where Hansen had been killed. I winced at the sight, feeling my intestines turn. I didn't dare go any farther and risk contaminating the crime scene. Black powder marks were everywhere, the wood furniture, the walls, where the BCA had dusted for latent prints.

I didn't want to get any closer. My objective was to see the layout of the room and get an impression of what had happened. Even so, I wish I'd grabbed a pair of latex gloves from the wolf lab. You can bet the police would be darned curious to know how my prints ended up at their crime scene. I just had to be careful not to leave any.

From what I could tell, the pool of blood marked the spot where Forrest Hansen was killed. He was shot from about where I was standing. He'd crashed into a coffee table that still sat upended. A throw rug was scrunched against the opposite wall. No blood stains marred the brown and rust braiding, so it must have slid away when Hansen fell. I wasn't sure what else to make of the situation. The kitchen door was behind me, so the murderer could have come in that way, or by the basement stairs, also behind me. Unless he'd come in with Hansen.

I retraced my steps and ducked into a little alcove in the dining room, drawn by a handcrafted, built-in walnut cabinet with an oval mirror. Bright with cheery knickknacks, it gave me a sense of peace and familiarity, a nice change from my gory imaginings in the other room. A small postcard with a Swedish flag was tucked in the edge of the mirror's frame. I ran the back of my hand along the pastel table runner and wondered if Lily had done the Swedish huck embroidery herself. Sitting on the runner was a ceramic troll eating from a basket of tiny krumkakes, the crisp and crumbly cone-shaped cookies I used to help my grandmother make.

A decorative plate from Göteborg and a brightly rosemaled washboard declaring *Välkommen* decorated the pale yellow walls. Three wooden horses of different sizes festooned the display, the largest of which was the traditional red dalahäst.

The Dala horse. I'd seen the same at Grandma's and now kept her collection on display in my kitchen. Every time I had picked one up, she would remind me that they were made in Dalarna, the province of Sweden my great-great-grandparents had come from.

This, I knew, must have been Lily Bjorklund's doing. She'd been the one who gave the Icelandic sheep Swedish names. She was the one trying to preserve her heritage. All lovingly kept by her husband. Not a speck of dust dared rest on these objects, which meant the old man regularly tended to them.

Two photographs sat up in silver oval frames. One showed the Bjorklunds as a young couple, vibrant and happy. The second was more recent, Lily obviously ill, while Bjorklund still looked strong and robust, though having lost a little weight.

The hairs on the back of my neck twitched. My unconscious mind was kicking me in the shins. At times like this I wished the animal part of my brain worked better. There are moments when having a highly developed frontal lobe is overrated; it tends to elbow the old reptile brain aside. It means sometimes we overinterpret an event or completely miss something an animal might notice instantly.

I had nothing.

With a sigh, I left Lily's alcove and ventured back to the basement, giving it a thorough search. Nothing in the laundry room except laundry. Baskets of it. Here was one trait Bjorklund and I shared; we both waited till the last possible moment to do our wash, then we did loads of it. Next to the laundry was a workshop. A metal lathe and drill press were well cared for. Grinders and a host of other unfathomable tools hung in neat rows on the wall. Judging by the tools, it appeared he could still manage to use his old machinist skills from time to time despite his mangled hand.

A rack of hand tools caught my eye and I felt a rush of excitement. I hurried over to inspect the handles. None matched the gouge Gina'd found at the old Swede's murder scene. Different handles. Different set. Too bad. It made perfect sense for the former machinist to carry a tool like this. If the v-gouge wasn't Bjorklund's, then it must've belonged to someone else.

Probably the murderer.

I turned my attention to the neighboring office, little more than an ad-hoc work area jammed in a corner near the water heater. This held more promise. The small desk pushed in the corner held none of the neatness evidenced upstairs. Papers and envelopes covered the top of the desk and spilled onto the floor. Wide-open file drawers met my gaze, all of them empty. Latent prints and powder dotted the metal cabinets and desk. Either the police had taken the files with them or the killer had.

Frustrated, I glared at the empty cabinets. Nothing for me there. And, I realized, Hansen was Bjorklund's partner in the sheep business. If he'd been searching for records down here and was surprised by the murderer, there should've been blood here. On the other hand, if the murderer had been the one rummaging through the files and Hansen surprised him as he was leaving, that would explain why Hansen was shot upstairs.

Why had the murderer come to Bjorklund's house unless it was to get something? All the file cabinets were wide open. Had the police opened them? Or the killer? If the police had found the file cabinets ransacked, it'd explain their interest in them.

So the murderer had been searching for something in Bjorklund's records. Maybe a letter. A bill of sale. The only thing I felt certain of was that Ivar Bjorklund and Forrest Hansen had been killed over something they knew. And the killer thought I knew something as well, for he'd wanted me in the squad car along with the others when he shot at us.

What did I know that was so threatening to the killer? Beats me!

Discouraged, I swung round. My gaze scanned the basement walls and floor. In front of me was a pantry. More bottled water. Cases of it. Even some gallon jugs lined up against the cinder block wall. Several feet away, on a raised carpeted platform rested an old dog bed with chewed corners and a wrinkled old blanket.

Hansen must've forgotten the dog bed when he got Oskar. I smiled at the thought of Bagger, my Golden Retriever and his favorite "banky." I turned to go, walked two steps and halted. I glanced over my shoulder at the dog bed. A thought niggled in my brain. I'd seen the plaid blanket before. But how could I have? I'd never been in Bjorklund's house until now. Curiosity drove me to check it out.

A big whiff of dog hit me as I bent down. Lifting the blanket, I discovered it was, in fact, a shirt, the same shirt I'd seen Bjorklund wearing the first time I'd met him at Signe's. That explained it. Satisfied, I dropped the shirt and left.

I took only four steps, then stopped. Something very unflannel-like had crinkled when the fabric fell to the bed. Picking up the shirt again, I found a folded envelope in the front pocket. It was addressed to Bjorklund from the St. Louis County Department of Public Health.

My mind raced back to the morning Peter and I had come here to interview the old man. There'd been something in his pocket. Something he kept touching as if to assure himself it was still there.

Something from the Department of Health?

Curious.

My gaze shifted to the bottles and jugs of water. Water. *Maybe there's something in the water.* Gina was only joking, but could she have been right? Was there something in the water? I thought of the greenish stain in the kitchen sink, the same stain I'd seen on my first visit with Peter Bunyan. The foundation wall in the front of the house had the same greenish tint by the outside water faucet.

I gasped at a brain wave. The old flower bed! Was it covered with stones because nothing would grow there now? If Bjorklund had been so meticulous at keeping up other mementos of Lily, why not her garden?

The Department of Health was responsible for many things. Birth and death certificates, emergency preparedness, recycling, the medical examiner, and environmental safety, which included testing water quality.

An image flashed before my eyes. The second photo of the Bjorklunds upstairs. Lily had died of cancer. Stomach cancer. Had their water supply been responsible? If Bjorklund's well water was contaminated, it might account for his rapid weight loss. Maybe it hadn't come from the stress of taking care of and losing Lily. Maybe he'd been sick, too!

All that bottled water upstairs and down here. He must've known! Had the test results for his water been in this envelope?

I ran my fingers through my hair, stretching my scalp, trying to keep all my thoughts from bumping into each other. It shouldn't be difficult to find out if Bjorklund had sent in a water sample for testing. A telephone call might do it. From me or, better, the Wolf Lake police. Soon as I got back to the wolf institute I'd see if—

I stopped breathing.

The sound of tires crunching on gravel screamed impending danger. A car had pulled into the driveway.

## CHAPTER 20

I was frozen in place, my ears straining for the sound of footsteps heading toward the house. Was it the police? One of the news crews that had descended on Wolf Lake after Bjorklund's murder and the escape of the wolves? Panic fluttered in my belly, forcing me to move.

Hustling my buns to the same window I'd entered by, I pressed my hand against the cool cinderblocks and strained my ears. Two car doors slammed and footsteps crunched against the stones. I reached above my head for the window and winced at the stab of pain in my shoulder. Getting out was going to be harder than getting in; I'd need something to stand on. Obviously, I hadn't thought this breaking-and-entering thing all the way through. A cornered rat had a better shot at escape.

Happy now? They'll arrest you for sure! If I was lucky.

At that particular moment an ugly thought reared its nasty head. What if it wasn't the police out there? What if it was the killer?

Oh.

I stood motionless, my ears pricking at every sound, straining to hear above the wild thumping of my heart. Voices rumbled outside. Two men talking. Rushing to the workshop, I grabbed a folding chair and set it carefully under the window. I didn't need the sound of metal scraping against concrete alerting my visitors to my presence, no matter who they were. I used my sling to wipe my prints clean. Then I stood on the chair, peering through the dirty window into the side yard.

A Wolf Lake police officer I didn't recognize stood talking to a stocky, dark-haired Hispanic man who was listening attentively while Oskar trotted alongside. The man with Bjorklund's border collie must be the hired help Gina had mentioned. Oskar strained at his leash, wanting to go to the house—toward me! The Hispanic man, whom the officer called Eduardo, snapped a command, and the dog fell back into step with the two men as they angled toward the barns. Soon all three disappeared from sight.

If they'd brought Oskar along, they were here for the sheep, not to gain access to the house. This was my chance! Wasting no time, I lifted up the window and used both arms to hoist myself up, my mouth clamping down hard at the pain.

A tearful moan huffed out as I twisted my body through the narrow opening; my shoulder screamed in protest. Halfway through the window, my foot slipped and I crashed against the metal frame. My eyes jammed shut. It felt like being kicked in the gut by a steel-toed boot. When my watery eyes opened again, it was to the sight of the officer and Eduardo standing in the distance among the meandering sheep. Luckily, the men had their backs to me.

But I was in plain sight! All they had to do was turn around and I was dead meat. I struggled until the toe of my boot found purchase against the inside wall. Slowly, using what little upper body strength I had left, I oozed myself through the window. A little more. A little more. Then a brainwave hit me: I could've gone out the kitchen door!

Geez! What a stupe!

I felt as ridiculous as Winnie the Pooh getting stuck in Rabbit's hole. Which didn't help me one iota in my current situation. My eyes burned into the backs of the two men, watching their body language, anticipating any movement toward me.

Their attention was trained on Oskar, who was busy rounding up the sheep. If he hadn't been, I was certain he would have alerted the men to my trespassing as soon as my butt had hit the hard ground.

Of course, I had no idea what I'd do if the men unexpectedly turned my way. I couldn't go back inside. Maybe I thought if they turned, I'd freeze and blend in. You know, like the big black spider motionless against the white bathroom tile when you flick on the lights.

Yeah, that kind of blending in.

Fear of being discovered spurred me to slither forward until I managed to roll out onto the grass. I worked myself up to a low crouch and crept slowly along the side of the house toward the back. Oskar barked once and I froze, terrified. To my relief, the border collie's attention was directed toward a group of ewes. I inched along, watching the two men follow the dog's herding motions. Still in full view, I shuffled along the side of the house until I could safely round the backside.

Thank God! I was finally able to exhale. I sucked in breath after breath, steeling my nerves, then dashed across the side lawn for the woods.

In the shelter of the trees, I sagged against the comfort of an old birch. My hands trembled; my knees were like gelatin. Last summer in the Black Hills, I'd nearly been trampled by a bison while filming *Zoofari*. People hear the story, shake their heads, and tell me what a dangerous job I have. Well that experience wasn't half as harrowing as the last five minutes!

Dry wood snapped behind me and I froze. A dark figure stepped out from a line of trees in front of me.

A silent scream lodged in my throat.

Moua Vang!

He stood beside the knotted trunk of an elm, suspicious, his attention for a moment directed beyond me in the direction of

Bjorklund's backyard. Riveting his gaze back on me, distrust clouded his face.

"Mr. Vang." I forced a friendly smile. I kept the volume low in hopes my voice wouldn't carry far.

"What you do here? You sneak around." His voice was hard, unfriendly.

This was the man Lyle Almquist had accused of quirky voodoo rituals. He was Ivar Bjorklund's neighbor and lived near the spot the dead wolves were found. What was he doing here? Spying on me? Or the police? Or hoping to find more wolves to shoot at?

I straightened up to my full height, doing my best to project authority. Inwardly, I braced for a mad dash to my Jeep. "I could ask you the same thing. Why are you here?"

"I see many police cars. They come yesterday. Now you come with more police. I want to see what happening."

Was he annoyed or merely curious? I couldn't tell, other than he seemed unhappy I was there. He tilted his head to the side, sizing me up. Vang had no weapon, which made the mad dash still appealing, though with my arm in a sling I didn't like my odds of outrunning him.

He was waiting for me to answer. I tried sounding official. "Forrest Hansen was killed in Mr. Bjorklund's living room yesterday." I was aware I might be telling him something he already knew.

Vang didn't flinch at the news. In fact, he took it in stride. He raised an eyebrow. "That what you doing now? Helping police?"

The sarcasm wasn't lost on me. Moua Vang might not speak the King's English like a native, but that didn't mean he wasn't sharp as a razor.

"Yes," I answered, somewhat truthfully. "I'm helping the police find out who killed Mr. Bjorklund. Did you see anyone drive to the house yesterday? Did you see Mr. Hansen drive up?" It just occurred to me that Hansen's car wasn't in the driveway. The crime lab folks had probably towed it to the BCA for analysis.

He weighed my words, but his face gave away nothing. If I'd been him I wouldn't have believed me either. I hoped, that having seen me with Chief Manske and Peter Bunyan, he'd assume I had some authority to be here, particularly if he believed I'd come with the officer on the scene.

Vang crossed his arms. He wasn't buying it. His lips curled back derisively and showed his teeth. Yellow teeth.

I saw an opening, hoping to distract him. "Did Mr. Bjorklund talk to you about your well water?"

His eyes narrowed with interest. "How you know that? Ivar say my water bad like his. He show me paper that said so."

"Paper? From the health department?" I fumbled for the envelope I'd crammed into my back pocket.

One glimpse at it and Vang nodded.

I smiled back. "Mr. Bjorklund sent them a water sample to analyze, didn't he? That's why he had all those bottles of water in his house. He couldn't drink the well water."

"That right. He had rain water in the barn for the animals."

"How long had he known about the bad water?"

"Ivar guessed it was bad for many month. When the letter come, he knew he was right."

"When did he get the letter?"

"Two, maybe three weeks ago. He say he was going to make big trouble."

"Trouble? For who?"

Vang shook his head. "He not say."

Images rushed through my head. Ivar and Lily Bjorklund wasting away for years from contaminated water. Moua Vang, his neighbor across the road, with the same yellow teeth. For the first time, I thought I might know why the old Swede had been murdered.

# CHAPTER 21

For the rest of the afternoon I barely thought of anything else. I got back from my "errands" in time to help with the setups inside the wolf lab. I was feeling anxious, expecting the police to come in at any moment and arrest me for trespassing on a crime scene. If Moua Vang had mentioned seeing me to the Wolf Lake police, my ass would be in another sling.

Despite this, I did feel a sense of accomplishment. My gut told me I'd kicked the lid off something important at the Bjorklund house. Now I just had to make sense of it.

While Billie and Arthur discussed the flow of the next sequence with Jeff, I stole back a dozen steps, pulling Gina aside.

"Know anyone at the St. Louis County Department of Health? Bjorklund sent in a water sample. Think you could get a copy of the report?"

"For Ivar?" An impish curl pulled at the corner of her mouth. "Gee, I was only kidding when I said there must be something in the water."

"I know, but you might've been right."

"Really?"

"His fridge and basement are full of bottled water. I think his well was contaminated."

Her eyebrows leveled. "How d'you figure that?"

"Moua Vang." Omitting the exciting details, I told her about my encounter with the Hmong farmer.

"Interesting." Gina nodded, her sweet round face coaxing me further. "So what does Ivar's water have to do with anything?"

I was mindful that at any second the film crew would start the next segment and they'd be calling on me for help. I had a job to do and didn't want to let them down. Jeff had been right. As an owner and producer of *Zoofari*, I needed to remember my responsibilities. It wasn't just that we had mortgaged the house; it was that other people were counting on us to make a go of this, too. Which was not to say I couldn't squeeze in a few extracurricular activities on the side.

"The toxins in the Bjorklund's well made them sick. They gave Lily cancer and turned the old man into a shadow of his former self. He'd lost a lot of weight in the last five years. I saw a photo of them in their prime—"

"Still not getting it . . ."

"It was like a tornado had hit his office, every file cabinet open, loose papers every which way. The rest of the house—at least the inside—is nicely kept. Even Bjorklund's workshop is clean and tidy. His tools were put away, the floor was clean. But the office was a mess."

Gina appraised me with a quirk of her eyebrows. "You got this info from the police?"

She still didn't know I'd entered the house. I hesitated telling her, the lie rolling easily off my tongue. "Something like that," I said, purposely being vague. It was better she didn't know the particulars of my lunch detour. Knowing what I'd done could make her an accomplice, which I didn't want to risk.

Gina tried fitting the pieces together. "Either Hansen or the murderer got at those files."

"I think it was the murderer and Hansen surprised him."

"Why's that?"

"Because of the mess in the office. Hansen was Bjorklund's business partner. You'd think he'd know where the files were kept. While a stranger would have to tear through all of them."

"Okay, that makes sense. But what was the murderer looking for?"

"I don't know," I confided, "but it might've been this." I pulled out the folded envelope from my back pocket. I showed her the return address. "St. Louis County Department of Health. See why we need to get our hands on that report?"

"Gotcha. I've got a friend in Duluth I can call later."

I stole a glance across the wolf lab. Billie, Arthur and Jeff were just about ready for us.

"Gina, could you call after this segment? It's Friday. They'll be closed tomorrow. And we're leaving town on Sunday."

She nodded, then remembered: "What about the dead wolves? How's this figure in with them? And cutting the fence?"

"No idea." I shrugged. "I don't know enough to make a connection, if there is one."

"Maybe the water analysis will show a connection."

"My thought exactly. The report will either prove I'm right or that I'm full of—"

"Imagination," she chuckled.

"A nice way to put it. Thanks. Can you do it? Get the report, I mean?"

With a saucy turn of her head, Gina Brown grinned. "You forget. Think back to Northland. Remember the weekend when Sigurd Olsen's canoe went missing and nobody figured out who took it? That went off with military precision. I can be pretty single-minded when I want to."

That she could. Like an avalanche running down a mountainside.

"I wouldn't be dead for quids!" Jeff beamed with gusto, a mischievous glint in his baby blues.

Gus and Mooney blinked back in confusion, each checking

to see if the other knew what to make of the reply to Mooney's "How things going?" comment a moment earlier.

I'd just introduced the Dukes of Decaf to my husband, who shook their hands and shined them with 1,000 watts of personality. Seeing a translation was necessary, I reassured the two old timers. "He just told you he's doing great."

Filming was done for the day and I had brought Jeff to Last Chance Outfitters to meet Signe, Gus and Mooney before we met up with Billie and Arthur at the Super 8. I also wanted him to see the leather jackets Signe had for sale.

"Coulda said so in the first place and saved us a lot of trouble," Gus muttered loftily.

When he's in a playful mood, Jeff likes to lay on the accent a bit thick. "You're the blokes Snake's been telling me about. I want to thank you for making her feel welcome. 'Twas good onya, mates."

You could tell neither had a clue what "good onya" was, but whatever it was it seemed a positive thing, so they smiled at him like two school boys getting praise from their teacher.

Jeff waved back, moving to the front counter where Signe had taken down a few buckskin jackets from the display rack. He draped one over his arm, stroking the lusciously smooth leather with his hand. "Have a go at this! Softer than a koala's bum. Finest leatherwork I've ever seen. A local bloke makes these?"

"Lyle Almquist."

"And he can put on any design?"

"I think so. He's done all sorts of patterns and animals on his jackets, even a few people."

"I can vouch for that." A wiry man in a baseball cap stepped over from the map counter. He turned around to show off the back of his jacket. A small airplane flying above a forest lake was embossed in vivid detail. "Lyle made this a couple years ago from a photo I gave him."

"Oy! Me dad would love one of these. I could get a photo of old Barnaby, dad's favorite croc. Ship the jacket back to Australia for his birthday."

"You'll pay dearly for it, but it's worth every penny. It'll last a lifetime, they say." The other man extended his hand, pale blue eyes crinkling with his ready smile. "Scotty Winston."

"Jeff Jones." He shook Scotty's hand and then began to introduce me.

"Snake Jones." Scotty finished for him. "Gina's told me a lot about you."

"You're Scotty the pilot! Nice to finally meet you. Gina's told me a lot about you, too."

"Yeah, I take her up in Nelly here"—He pointed his thumb at the plane on the back of his jacket—"every so often to track some of her wolves from the sky. In fact, we're going up tomorrow. See if we can find the one that went missing."

"Bit of a long shot, isn't it, mate?" Jeff said.

A shock of dark curls fell across Scotty's forehead as he pushed his Twins hat back from his forehead. "That's all we've got left, I'm afraid. Long shots."

"I'm sorry I didn't get to go up with the two of you on Tuesday," I said.

"Tuesday?" Scotty frowned. "I haven't been up with Gina in over three weeks. In fact, would your film crew like to come up with us? She'd mentioned you'd be interested."

"Reckon!" Jeff was all over it, ready to seal the deal.

"Scotty?" I was confused. "Gina wasn't with you on Tuesday? Could she have gone up with someone else?"

He gave me a dimpled grin. "Not likely. My Cessna Skyhawk's the only plane outfitted for aerial radio telemetry."

I didn't smile back. I'd lost track of the details, but knew Gina had lied to me about where she was the day Peter and I went to visit Bjorklund. She'd told me she had things to do at the wolf institute, but when I arrived there, no one had seen her all morning. When she finally showed up, she'd told me she'd gone aerial tracking with Scotty, who was now saying she'd done no such thing.

I let out a pent-up breath, about to ask Scotty for more details when—

"Hey, check out the parking lot!" Dimitry called out from the coffee bar, gesturing with the whipped cream dispenser. "Looks like a fight!"

We all crowded to the front windows. Even Gus and Mooney got up from their table, a rarity.

It was quite a spectacle. Lyle Almquist's beater white pickup truck had barricaded Danny Hoffman's Chevy Cavalier by the pumps at the Gas 'n Go. Danny stood outside his car, hands braced against the hood, shifting his weight, ready to jump at a moment's notice. His eyes locked on Almquist, who thundered up to the wide-open driver's door, red-faced beneath the white whiskers.

"What the hell d'you call this!" Almquist grabbed a cardboard box from inside the car and threw it at Danny. It struck him in the chest, hitting the ground and scattering loose papers on the asphalt.

"Dude! Don't blow a gasket on me, man. I can explain—"

"Explain what? That you're part of 'em? I don't need any more lies, you little shit face. I just wanna bust your head!"

Almquist did a side-step to the front of the Cavalier. For a large man, he moved with agility—though not far, limping heavily on one side and slowing down after the first four steps. Danny, twenty years younger and ninety pounds lighter, easily moved out of Almquist's reach. The latter glared back, then pounded the car hood out of frustration, really wanting a piece of Dan-O.

"Hey man, don't abuse the vehicle!"

Bad idea. You could see it in Almquist's eyes. The middle-aged rocker may have been too hard to catch, but his car wasn't going anywhere. Almquist went to the bed of his pickup and retrieved a rusty crowbar. With unabashed pleasure, he pummeled the hood of Danny's car to a dented, twisted mass.

"Jesus, Lyle! Stop!"

Danny made to intervene then pulled back, reconsidering his chances. The odds were against him. Unarmed, skinny rocker dude versus furious, large, white-bearded man with a metal club. Mad Santa, I thought, although the resemblance to St. Nick was quickly dissipating. All Danny could do was watch the other brutalize his car again and again.

Jeff and I shouldered through the crowd of spectators, which had gathered in the parking lot.

"That's enough, mate." Jeff reared up in front of Almquist like a king cobra, grabbing hold of the crowbar.

Almquist struggled to get the weapon free. When that failed he went nose to nose with Jeff. "Who're you? This ain't none of your concern."

"He's with me." I stepped forward. "If I were you, Mr. Almquist, I'd stop struggling. My husband wrestles twenty-foot crocodiles for a living."

The big man might not have believed me, but he took a moment to scope out Jeff. Maybe it was the fact Jeff was obviously very fit. Maybe it was the scars on Jeff's forearms, tokens of past reptilian encounters. Or maybe it was that he wasn't backing down. Whatever the reason, the fight slowly left Almquist, but not the anger.

He pointed toward Danny. "Don't let that punk get away! He's the guy to blame."

Several onlookers had moved in closer. A few picked up the green flyers at their feet, only to glare at Danny afterward.

I didn't understand. "Blame for what?"

"For this!" A woman in the crowd thrust the flyer toward me. The opening words seared into my retinas.

YOU ARE A POLLUTER, COMMITTING A CRIME AGAINST NATURE.

I stopped reading. My gaze flicked to Danny, asking for an explanation. "What are you doing with these?"

Others in the crowd echoed my question, most not as polite. "Yeah!"

"Did you dump one of these at my daughter's house?"

"We ought to string you up, you little shit!"

It was Lyle Almquist, of all people, who waved for the others to quiet down. "He's been leaving these things all over town. I got one last week."

I still couldn't believe it. "How'd you know it was Danny?"

"Stupid little twerp was driving with his windows open. He passed me down the road a few minutes ago. One of them flyers blew out and landed on my windshield. Plain as day, I saw what it was. He's one of them damned eco nuts."

Danny looked like he'd love a hole to crawl into, if the crowd didn't turn ugly and do it for him.

My gaze drilled into his. "Is this true? Are you a member of this Stewards of Superior group?"

He shifted his weight and jammed his hands into his jean pockets. "Sorta."

Gina Brown pushed her way to the front of the crowd. It wasn't until I saw her petite frame launch forward that I knew she'd been part of the throng. She stood toe to toe with Danny, ready to spit fire. "Snake asked you a question. Yes or no? Are you a member of this group?"

He squirmed. "I was trying to tell you, it's not really a group."

"What're you talking about?" Gina grabbed one of the leaflets and crumpled it under Danny's nose. "Somebody put one of these on my door. They've been leaving them all over town. You bet there's a group! And if you know who they are, you'd better tell us."

A chorus of assent rumbled from the spectators.

Danny couldn't meet Gina's eyes. His gaze locked on his scuffed-up work boots. "There is no Stewards of Superior. Just me."

"What d'you mean 'just you'?"

Now Danny's eyes met hers. "There never was a group. It was only me."

"You! It was you who left that piece of crap flyer on my door?"

Lyle Almquist grunted with vindication. "There! I told you."

Gina crossed her arms. "You fucking asshole! We work together. I thought you were my friend."

Danny grew defensive. "Gina, look at the stuff you buy. D'you know how much of that packaging gets dumped into a landfill? Every year—"

"God, I can't believe this! You're lecturing *me?* Now? All along it's been you putting up those flyers and threatening everybody!"

"I never threatened anybody!"

"The hell you didn't!" Almquist stepped closer; Jeff laid an iron hand on his chest.

Disgusted, Gina shook her head. "I can't believe you're that big an idiot!"

Angry mutterings from the mob agreed with her. Mild alarm flashed across Danny's face and he backed away a step.

"Danny," I pressed. "Why the pretense?"

"Like—duh! If people knew it was only me, they wouldn't pay attention to the flyers. But if they thought a secret group was watching them, maybe they'd really think about the issue."

"Danny, Danny. Not a good idea."

"Well, if people knew it was me leaving the flyers, they'd freak out. They'd come after me with pitchforks and torches."

"Not a bad idea," Gina grumbled. "I can't believe what you did! You accused people of being polluters, good people, scaring them into thinking some eco terrorists were after them."

Lyle Almquist, who was still on a slow burn, pressed against Jeff, and this time my husband let him pass. By this time, he probably thought Danny deserved whatever he got. Almquist lumbered toward the aging rocker. He came to an abrupt halt at the brief burp of a siren.

A white Wolf Lake police cruiser pulled into the lot. Officer Lomax climbed out and headed toward us. Someone must have called the police. My money was on Signe, who was watching us from inside the doorway.

"What seems to be the problem here, folks?" he asked, taking in the tense crowd.

Almquist, with help from a few spectators, was more than willing to fill in the facts. Afterward, Officer Lomax held up one of the green flyers to Danny. "You write these?"

"Hey, man, I left messages. I never hurt anybody."

That was more than Gina would take. "You don't get it. By doing what you did, you put a black mark against all environmentalists. Who'll take us seriously if you go around doing cowboy tactics like that? Oh, gee"—she clamped her hand on top her head—"you're in a shitload of trouble. You know what Debbie's gonna do to you when she hears about this? You're dead meat, man! You'll be lucky if you aren't fired. The bad publicity could really hurt the wolf institute. What the hell's the matter with you?"

"I think you'd better come with me," the officer said, taking Danny by the elbow.

Confusion filled Danny's face as he was spun around and handcuffed. "Under arrest? For what?"

"There must be something we can charge you with," Lomax answered optimistically, then escorted Danny to the squad car. After securing him in the back seat, Lomax turned to the crowd. "Show's over, folks. Please move along. If any of you want to file a complaint against Mr. Hoffman, call the station."

The crowd dispersed like a hill of ants in a rainstorm.

Jeff gently guided me away. We had to meet Billie and Arthur at the motel and catch some dinner.

"I can't believe Danny's responsible for all those messages. What was he thinking?"

"Obviously, he wasn't."

"No," I mumbled, my mind elsewhere. My emotions were too raw to sort through right now. I told Jeff about the SOS flyer we'd found under Bjorklund's body, wondering what, if anything, it had to do with his murder.

As we walked to my Jeep, Jeff turned to me. "I can't read your mind, luv, but it sounds like you think Danny might be the killer."

"No—well, yes. Maybe. Oh, I don't know! The problem is Danny loves wolves. He'd never've killed those four animals."

"Would he go after the blokes who did?"

"That," I said, hedging, "I couldn't tell you."

Or didn't want to admit. People with as much passion as Danny Hoffman could be unpredictable. How—or even if— Danny fit into the murders I couldn't begin to figure. If I was right about the Bjorklunds' well water, one common thread between the old Swede and the rocker was pollution.

But I couldn't dismiss Danny's skewed logic for his actions. What did I really know about what he was capable of or how violent he could be? Though he seemed so mellow, he played angry, violent music. Could Danny Hoffman have killed two men out of a corrupted sense of justice?

# CHAPTER 22

"Collar 8042 is emitting a mortality signal," Scotty Winston told us as we crossed the tarmac to his red and white Cessna Skyhawk. Conventional radio collars emit a mortality signal if the wolf doesn't move after a certain amount of time. "Could be a malfunction or one of his pack mates chewed it off him. It's happened before."

I hurried to keep up. "What are the chances of that?"

"Not good. Most of the time the signal means they're dead."

"Gina won't be happy to hear that," I practically shouted to be heard above the roar of a Piper Cub overhead, which had just left the runway.

My sadness at the news of another dead wolf was mitigated by the dread of sitting in a cramped flying tin can with a volatile Gina Brown for several hours. Or a volatile me. I was angry she'd lied to me. The more I thought about it, the angrier I got.

Gina had pulled a vanishing act after the police took Danny into custody. I'd hoped to corner her at the wolf institute this morning. For one thing, I wanted to know if she'd called her contact at the Health Department about that report. But it wasn't to be. Scotty's call to our hotel at the crack of dawn had roused us from our beds and sent us flying out the door. A chance to film wolves from the air had been too enticing to pass up.

As a small production company—make that puny—we had to be multitalented. With only four seats on the plane, simple math

227

showed there wasn't room for all of us, so Jeff pulled rank on our cameraman, and he and I would be filming the sequence.

Up close it was evident the Cessna had seen plenty of air miles, its paint job faded and scratched in places, a bird-sized dent near the engine cowling. The Yagi antennas mounted on both wing struts looked worn.

Scotty waved to a parked car. Debbie Wong emerged and strode toward us, one hand jammed into her jacket pocket, the other clutching the binoculars hanging from her neck. Head down, black hair streaming behind her, she hurried toward us.

"She needs an escape," Scotty confided, explaining that Debbie would be flying with us instead of Gina. "I don't know how she's managed the last couple of days, what with Rufus on the lam, dealing with the press, the public, and reporting to the institute administrators."

The fret lines softened as Debbie offered us a wide smile, one wider still for Scotty. Her eyes were puffy from lack of sleep.

"Hey, Debbie!" I greeted. "Nice surprise. I was expecting Gina."

"It was her idea I take her place. Gina thinks I need to get away for a morning. Maybe I do. Anyway, she wanted to stay behind to help Danny find a good lawyer."

"What? Gina was one of his victims. Why would she want to help him?"

Debbie pulled a strand of her long black hair away from her mouth. "You got me."

Scotty interjected. "It'll be a minute, guys. I need to do a quick check of the plane." He pulled down his baseball cap and went to inspect the wings.

"Danny's been charged then?" I asked.

"Not yet. He's being held on suspicion of making terroristic threats."

"Terroristic threats?"

Her black eyes were hard as diamonds. "What else would you call what he did? He snuck on people's property in the middle of the night, came right up to their doors and left threatening messages. That's bad enough. You have to wonder what else he's capable of doing."

The venom in her voice took me aback. Anger, frustration, betrayal: they were all there.

The early morning chill nibbled at me. I zipped up my jacket a little more. "Not murder, though. You don't think he could've killed those two men?"

"I don't know, Snake. I don't know what to believe about Danny. I thought I knew him."

"Sounds like the police didn't charge him for the murders."

"No. Seems he's got an alibi for both killings. He was at the institute during the first one and practicing with his band during the second." Her troubled voice sounded like she'd wished it had been otherwise.

For me, it was a relief. I hated the idea that Danny could be the killer. And, deep down, I believed Debbie did as well. She was simply weary of dealing with all the crap thrown at her the last few days. Danny's nocturnal adventures being yet one more turd ball in the road.

Scotty rejoined us and opened the Cessna door. Debbie and I climbed into the back, Jeff and the camera sat in front.

"Here you go, Deb." Scotty handed her an antenna switching box, which would allow her to zero in on the signal. He also handed each of us headphones after he took his seat.

Debbie slumped back. Her eyes jammed closed, as if shutting out the ugliness of an uncaring world. "The phone didn't stop ringing all night. Reporters, the board of directors, donors, staff, friends. Danny's put the MWI smack in the middle of it with this stunt."

"You look like you've been up all night."

"I was. One of the reporters camped out on my lawn referred to Danny as a dangerous environmental fanatic. They don't know if Danny is actually dangerous or not, but for him to be branded like that doesn't help us. It causes ripples."

I could empathize. "The zoo went through a media feeding frenzy when our director was murdered last year. Open wounds always bring out the flies and scavengers."

Debbie managed a thin smile.

"It could've been worse," I added. "We were there when Lyle Almquist caught Danny with the evidence. It didn't take long to draw a crowd and believe me, some of those people wanted blood."

Jeff, who'd been listening patiently, turned toward us with amazement. "Danny was lucky Almquist didn't get his hands on him. If his hip hadn't slowed him, he'd've torn that skinny little bloke to shreds."

Debbie stared at her scuffed hiking boots. "I almost wish he had," she mumbled, her words nearly drowned out by the Cessna's engine, which roared to life. We put on the headphones and Debbie gazed at me with a heavy solemnity. "Danny's finished at the wolf institute. I'm sure not many other businesses in Wolf Lake will hire him either."

We braced ourselves as Scotty taxied the small plane to the airport's only runway, a bumpy ride.

The news about Danny's dismissal saddened me, which made a lousy situation only worse because I understood the bind it had put Debbie in. "You did the right thing. Danny had to go. Keeping him on would have been a liability."

"Thanks, but it still feels lousy." Muted anguish filled her expressive dark eyes. "The chief administrator wanted him gone ASAP. The sad thing is his job performance was wonderful. I could always count on him. The problem was his private life got in the way."

"You think the public will hold the institute responsible for Danny's actions?"

"It's not fair, but that's how people react. If we didn't fire Danny, people would automatically assume that we condoned what he did." She let out a plaintive sigh. "It's going to be hard on the wolves."

"How so?"

"He was a nanny for the exhibit pack when they were pups. They bonded with him. If you don't interact with them within those first critical months, it's too late. Which is why all our wolf care staff commit to nine years. At a zoo like yours, staff can usually change more often without any negative impact on the animals. No offense."

"None taken."

"Wolves won't tolerate that sort of personnel turnaround. To work with them the way we do requires a long-term commitment."

"So they've lost one of their best friends," I said.

Scotty got clearance from the tower and throttled the engine. The Cessna vibrated as it sped down the runway, the deafening sound of the engine slightly muffled through the headphones. Without the mic system, we would've gone hoarse trying to be heard. Within seconds we were airborne, climbing and banking over White Iron Lake. Jeff aimed the Canon XL1 over the shining water, getting some establishing shots. Debbie turned on the antenna switchbox in her lap.

Scotty's voice was clear over the headphones. "My guess is we're ten minutes from the source of the radio signal, so enjoy the scenery."

"Wouldn't it be easier to just track from land?" I scribbled on a clipboard, taking notes which I'd later use for the voiceover of this segment.

Debbie shook her head. "On land we only have a range of two miles at most. We can cover a larger area from up here. Besides, you're in the land of ten thousand lakes. Many of them are in this part of the state. Kinda wet down there. Not a lot of roads."

The green forest stretched beneath us to the far horizon, dotted by countless lakes for mile upon endless mile. Between the waterways, spreading patches of gold and rich red caught the morning sun like holiday ornaments. In a few weeks, only the conifers would still be wearing green.

"Lotta trees down there," I commented, face pressed against the window. The purpose of this flight, as officially logged in the report, was to locate the source of the mortality signal and learn the status of the wolf associated with it. But we all knew there was another reason. "It'll sure be hard to see Rufus loping around from way up here."

"More than likely we won't." Scotty turned in his seat and offered a smile of encouragement to Debbie. "But stranger things have happened. We could find him strolling along the highway or scrounging through someone's garbage. After we finish with our official mission, we'll do a number of fly-bys near the MWI and Wolf Lake. Rufus may be close to home."

"You're the best," Debbie said.

"Glad to do it. With any luck, this won't take too long. It'd be easier in the winter because of the tracks. If we can pinpoint the location of the signal, get an idea of the terrain, then the ground staff can go with their truck to examine the carcass."

Arthur had mounted a gyro stabilizer to the camera to offset vibrations from the plane. Jeff did a long panning shot of the terrain. Filming without the door would make for better television, but it would've required prior permission and there'd been no time. No doubt, Arthur could work his magic in the editing room later.

My stomach pitched as the Cessna banked again, putting White Iron Lake well to the rear. Riding in a small plane was a much more sensory experience than riding in a big commercial jet. You didn't need your eyes to know what the pilot was doing; you felt every dip, roll, and bump. It became a carnival ride as the nose dropped and the trees rushed up until we seemed in danger of eating pine cones.

"I've got something," Debbie said, adjusting the telemetry box. "Turn left."

Scotty nodded and banked ninety degrees to the left.

After a second, Debbie came back. "Okay—now the right. Damn. Lost it."

"It's the trees," Scotty explained. "VHF waves are line-of-sight. Dense vegetation and hills deflect the signal. Too bad it wasn't a GPS collar. No problem, I'll swing around and do three-sixties until you pick up the signal again."

Wonderful. My stomach was already doing belly-flops and for once, I was thankful there hadn't been time for breakfast. I concentrated on the scenery below, the acres of forest and clear blue lakes that symbolized what was best about living in Minnesota. I tried to block out the image of finding another dead wolf. Hopefully, death would be from natural causes: disease or fighting within its pack. I prayed to a god I didn't quite believe in that it would not be from gunshots.

Thinking of gunshots reminded me of Gina. It still seemed odd she'd pass on an opportunity to search for Rufus from the air. Particularly when one of her main job functions was tracking wild wolves, assembling and analyzing databases. How could she miss this ride? When you considered she hadn't actually gone up with Scotty earlier in the week as she'd claimed, it made her decision today more puzzling.

And to miss it for Danny Hoffman? To help him find a lawyer? After what he'd done to her?

It made no sense.

Actually, a lot about Gina's recent behavior didn't make sense. On Tuesday she'd skipped riding with Peter Bunyan and me when we went to ask people about the wolf slaughter, something that mattered to her deeply. The morning after the shooting, when I was all banged up, I'd expected some sort of mother henning from her, the way she'd been in college. Maybe her seeming lack of concern was because Jeff was with me by then. Or maybe she was preoccupied by other things. She'd gotten in to the wolf lab late on Friday morning with some story about collecting scat in the woods. Old scat. Not one of the samples she'd supposedly collected that morning looked fresh. They could've been weeks old.

My mind was taking a nasty turn I didn't like. Gina had been my best friend at Northland, loyal to a fault. I studied my reflection in the window and wasn't sure I cared for the woman staring back at me. Who was I to pass judgment on her? If I were a real friend I'd try to understand.

Wouldn't I?

"Hold on! I've got something." Debbie sat up. "Scotty, turn right." She worked the antenna box. After a minute of the plane maneuvering back and forth, she said, "That's it! We're on top of the signal."

My face pressed against the glass. "I don't see anything. Too many trees."

"There's a clearing down there," Scotty reported.

"I see it!" Jeff said, zooming in with the camera lens. "Something's on the ground. It could be a moose."

Scotty circled the plane. "Over there! See where the trees thin out around the clearing . . . I think that's a wolf. He's not moving."

I squirmed in my seat. "Where? By those logs?"

Debbie brought up her binoculars. "Those aren't logs. Those

are wolves! They're lying on the ground. I count three of them. No, five!"

Scotty banked again, bringing the Cessna around for another pass.

My heart sank. "Okay. I see them. Damn, they all look dead." Silence.

"Wait! I see movement."

"Debbie?"

"An ear flick. Scotty, go lower. . . . Yeah, now someone's raised his head to look at us. And another. Ah, that moose, it's a half-eaten carcass." Debbie laughed. "They're sleeping! They gorged themselves on that moose and are sleeping it off. I bet none of them have moved in a day. That explains the mortality signal!"

Jeff let out a "Who-hoo!" and swiveled the camera onto Debbie's beaming face.

I tried to join in on the jubilation, but couldn't. Despite my attempt to see the glass half full, my thoughts lingered on Gina's deception, and I wondered if there wasn't another predator among us.

# CHAPTER 23

Our main mission accomplished, we circled the greater Wolf Lake area for nearly an hour in search of Rufus. A slim hope at best, it felt good to try, even though we never caught a glimpse of him.

It was late morning by the time we returned to the airport. Jeff and I weren't expected to hook up with Billie and Arthur until after lunch. They'd spent the morning filming at two known wolf rendezvous sites. Peter Bunyan, though up and about after the accident, wasn't up to taking them as planned. He enlisted the help of another DNR conservation officer to take our film crew twenty miles northwest of Wolf Lake.

With a couple hours to ourselves, Jeff and I decided to check out the Great American Bear Center. We'd pulled into the parking lot when I noticed Gina's powder blue Tacoma rocketing out of town along Highway 1.

"Wonder where she's off to in such a hurry," Jeff said for the both of us.

A crazy impulse came over me. "Let's find out. Ever do any car tracking?"

Jeff didn't hesitate. "I'm on her tail." He grinned, cranking the wheel. I'd voiced my misgivings about Gina during our ride back from the airport and now he was as curious as I. Cutting in front of a putzy sedan, he went in pursuit of the Tacoma pickup. "How're we going to explain ourselves when we catch up with her?"

"Depends on what we catch her at."

"Seriously, sweetheart, what do we say?"

"We could say we thought she was acting on a Rufus tip and we wanted to help. Who knows? That might even be the truth!"

It was great to have this discussion with someone I trusted, someone who'd give me a rational, thought-out response. Not like Gina, who jumped at every conclusion with the agility of an Olympic hurdler.

Or—

I sat up in my seat, a nasty thought crossing my mind.

Was she playing me? Trying to throw me off the scent by making everyone else appear guilty?

We kept at least two cars between us, though it was difficult at times. At Soudan we nearly lost her, thinking she'd pulled into the old mine complex, but it turned out to be another blue pickup.

"That's her!" I pointed at a blue dot far in the distance. "Geez, she's got a lead foot. Better gun it or we'll really lose her."

Jeff put the pedal to the metal. "This might be a wild kangaroo chase."

"You could be right. Well, it's only been twenty minutes. Let's give her another ten. If she doesn't pull over by then, we'll turn around."

Traffic slowed at the city limits of Tower. I thought we'd lost Gina again until I peered down Spruce Street and glimpsed her car in the parking lot of a Mexican restaurant, La Cocina and Cantina. I turned in my seat as Jeff kept driving. Gina jumped out of her car and sprinted toward the restaurant. Was she meeting someone? Not Rufus, I knew that much.

"Jeff, circle the block. Gina's back there."

We parked by the side of the restaurant behind a trash dumpster, just out of view of her parked truck. I stepped out of my

Jeep and walked a few steps to the corner of the building, waiting. The warm and spicy smells of tortillas and refried beans was a cruel reminder I hadn't eaten yet today. It almost offset the dirty feeling I had for spying on Gina. I did not like what I was doing.

Before I could beat myself up too much, Gina's petite frame charged out of the restaurant, hugging two large brown bags, hurrying toward her pickup. For an instant I thought she might've seen me as she leaned in the passenger side to set down the bags, but her long auburn hair fell in front of her face. I darted behind the building and raced back to the Jeep. "She's on the move!"

"I'm feeling a bit foolish here," Jeff confided, as he switched on the engine and slowly pulled out.

"Me, too."

Jeff waited until Gina had turned back on to Spruce before following her. He kept as far back as was safely possible. "What's she doing out here?" he wondered.

"Good question. Her family are in Bemidji, Duluth and Minneapolis."

"She could have friends in Tower."

"But why so secretive then? Why not tell us?"

"Did you ask her?"

Jeff had me there. "Nope. Guess I outsmarted myself. Or I figured I wouldn't believe her. She lied to me on Tuesday, after which Bjorklund was found murdered."

"You think the two events are connected?"

"I don't think so, Jeff, but—man!—you should've seen the way she yelled into the forest after we found those wolf carcasses. She was screaming for vengeance. Even Peter was startled by her ferocity."

Gina was two cars ahead of us when she turned into the Tower Medical Center.

"She's off to see a sick friend is all," Jeff said with relief. I was grateful his voice was devoid of any "I told you so" intonations.

We parked at the end of the lot next to a massive Ford Expedition, hoping Gina wouldn't see us as she circled for a spot closer to the front entrance.

"I'm going in." I opened the door, determined to confront her. It was now or never.

"I'll come along to tie you down."

I stuck out my tongue at him.

Jeff and I hung back, making sure Gina was well ahead. As soon as we entered the lobby, my nose was hit by Eau de Hospital. That unmistakable scent of antiseptic and fear.

"Hello," said a pudgy volunteer from behind the information desk, grinning at us. Impossibly thick red hair dangled in her eyes. Multicolored bracelets jangled from her wrists when she moved her hands.

I gestured with my sling hand, playing on her sympathy. "Um, we were supposed to meet a friend here. We got lost. I'm sure she got tired of waiting for us."

"The patient's name?"

"Gee, I can't remember. My friend is Gina Brown."

"Sure, Ian's sister. Second floor, room 203."

Her voice belonged in a cartoon, one featuring squeaky mice and chipmunks. I pitied anyone who had to listen to it all day.

"Thanks." I waved, pulling Jeff with me. "Holy shit," I whispered as we headed toward the elevator. "Gina's brother's here!"

Jeff angled toward me. "You didn't tell me she had a brother."

"An older brother. The sun rose and set on him back when I first met her." I pushed the button for the elevator. "Funny thing, Gina hasn't mentioned him once since I got here. Our talks centered around Northland College, wildlife, wolves, and what we've been up to since we last saw each other. Ian never came up. In fact, she had an old photo of him at her place. When I asked her about Ian, she changed the subject."

By the time we got to room 203, I still wasn't sure what I was going to say after we barged in. Except we didn't barge in; the angry voices from inside held us in check in the hallway.

"You're not leaving!" Gina's shrill tone was all too familiar lately. "It's too soon."

"Quit treating me like a cripple."

Jeff grabbed my arm and tapped the nameplate on the doorway: Ian Brown.

We stepped noiselessly into the doorframe and Gina froze. The shock of seeing us seemed mitigated by confusion at what to do. For an instant, I thought she was going to put her body between Ian and me, like a lioness protecting her cub.

I expected her to go ballistic when she saw us, incensed we'd followed her. Instead, she was surprisingly subdued, almost relieved.

"Snake, you remember Ian." Her face flushed red. She gestured toward the man in the wheelchair.

If I hadn't seen the nameplate, I wouldn't have recognized Ian Brown. Older and thinner, his once thick head of curls had thinned to a wispy combover. It was the eyes—the deep amber of a lion—and the dimpled smile that were unmistakable. It saddened me to see how pain had creased permanent lines around his mouth and behind his eyes.

"Snake!" He held out a hand that was more like a claw, the fingers locked together in a parody of Mr. Spock's blessing.

I grabbed his hand, and knelt down to give him a hug, hoping he hadn't seen the shock on my face.

"And this must be that husband Gina's been telling me about."

"G'day, mate!" Jeff stepped forward and gripped the other's

hand in both of his.

"I just watched an episode of *Zoofari*. You were at the National Zoo's research center."

"It was an amazing place."

A heavy silence fell around us until Ian waved at the untouched paper bags on the bed. "Anyone want to join me? I've been craving the chili rellenos ever since I got here. Gina always buys enough to feed a football team."

The irresistible aroma of Mexican food filled the room as Jeff opened the bags. Poor guy was as hungry as I was.

"I shot him." Gina said with a matter-of-fact casualness that belied the color in her cheeks. Her eyes held mine steady, daring me to disagree with her.

I was speechless, too startled by her comment for words.

"Knock off the Greek tragedy crap, will you, sis?" Ian scolded. "It's getting frickin' old." His body jerked to the left and I noticed that both of his feet were strapped down to the wheelchair.

Gina clenched her jaw muscles and dug into the bag.

"What happened?" I asked, taking the wrapped burrito offered to me.

Ian gave his sister a sidelong glance. "She didn't tell you? Still the skeleton in the closet, am I?" he mused around a mouthful of chili rellenos. His crippled hands struggled to hold the foil-wrapped pepper, red juice dribbling down the side of his mouth. "This is a maintenance check." He indicated the room.

Gina scowled. "He makes light of it. He fell out of his wheelchair."

"It happens. Nothing to get worked up about."

"Tell them how it happened, Ian."

He came back with a devilish smirk. "I was trying a new yoga position. Part of my therapy."

"And you got hurt!"

"A bruise. Doesn't mean I can't take care of myself."

"Oh!" Gina threw up her hands in exasperation and stared out the window.

"Yoga?" Jeff was intrigued.

"Don't let the wheels fool you. I started practicing yoga five years ago, and even Gina has to admit it's made a difference. It won't help me walk again, but its helped me reconnect with a part of me I thought was dead." He waved awkwardly at his legs.

"So he's been following your advice?" Gina had given me the impression yoga and meditation was the cure-all for life's ills.

"It wasn't my idea."

"Sometimes I think Gina would prefer I was housebound. That way she could assuage her guilt by being a martyr who takes care of me."

Gina dropped her jaw and turned away.

Ian's face softened, rolling his chair a little closer. "Sorry, Gina. I shouldn't have said that." He angled the chair to face Jeff and me. "This"—he poked at his legs—"happened a long time ago. An accident. Shit!" He glowered at the glob of chili that had dropped from the relleno onto his pants. "A stupid accident."

Jeff handed him a paper napkin.

"We'd gone hunting," Ian continued. "Peter, Gina and I."

My ears twinged. "Peter Bunyan? He was with you?"

"Little sister had a big crush on him in those days." Ian's golden eyes leveled on Gina with affection.

"We were drinking," she said.

"I was drunk," Ian corrected, his voice calm, as if he were telling someone else's story.

"You were drinking and hunting?" Jeff sounded as incredulous as I felt.

"Young and dumb, that was us. We were celebrating. I was done with graduate school and taking a job out east. Peter was on his own career path. The three of us wanted to have one last hurrah. You know how it goes. We were afraid of drifting apart, so we wanted this one last outing together. And we'd always liked hunting. We used to go all the time. Gina was always the one you could count on to get a big buck."

Pride flashed in Gina's eyes, then quickly disappeared.

"Peter and I had challenged her to take a drink from Peter's hip flask." Ian raised the last of his relleno in a toast to his sister. "Well, the kid wasn't going to be shamed by her big brother. She took a few shots just to prove she was one of the boys."

"No," I protested. "Gina? You used to avoid booze at parties. In fact, you'd mock the girls who got wasted."

Gina hung her head. "I wasn't wasted. Didn't even feel drunk. Doesn't matter, though, if I hadn't done it Ian wouldn't—"

"For crying out loud! Will you drop it?" Ian lashed back. "I'm so tired of hearing you beat yourself up over this. It was a stupid, stupid accident. If anyone's to blame it's me for egging you on to take a snortful and then expecting you to handle a firearm after."

Gina sat down on the edge of the bed, her eyes moist.

Calming himself with a few deep breaths, Ian turned his attention back at us. "The three of us were in a tree stand for five hours and full of nervous energy. Like I said, young and dumb. After we'd passed the flask a few times we started horsing around. Gina moved to set down her rifle when it went off. The shot knocked me out of the stand. I hit the ground hard. Broke my back."

"My fingers slipped," Gina murmured. "I saw the rifle dropping but couldn't reach out to catch it." She looked at us with reddened eyes, her cheeks damp. "Ian will never walk again. Mom and Dad—"

"The hell with Mom and Dad. I don't blame you."

"You used to . . ."

Ian slumped in his chair, as if they'd had this argument before and he'd grown weary of it. "That was a long time ago, kid. I was lashing out. Mad at the world. You were an easy target, so full of guilt. You still are. What I've been trying to tell you for years is I'm not that guy anymore. I've moved past all that. Can't you?"

"How can I?" she choked, clamping her hands over her face.

I stepped over to put my good arm around her shoulder.

"Gina," Ian said in a heartfelt voice. "You've got to forgive yourself. I did, a long time ago. I'd like my kid sister back, the one who used to tease me and was happy to listen to her big brother."

"I still do that," she blubbered.

"Not really. You walk on pins and needles around me, afraid to poke fun at me 'cause it might hurt the crippled guy's feelings. You're killing yourself with all this guilt and all the stuff you do for me. You want to really help me?"

Gina wiped her eyes and looked at him intently.

"Forgive yourself and be my happy, dorky kid sister again. I miss her."

Gina laughed and was embarrassed when snot came out her nose. She wiped it with a napkin, then went to Ian's wheelchair and hugged him.

I glanced at Jeff, who leaned against the wall, smiling his usual encouragement to me. My rock.

"This is where you were on Tuesday afternoon," I said, realizing why Gina had lied to me. "And Wednesday." She had been here visiting her brother, not murdering Ivar Bjorklund or Forrest Hansen. I felt foolish for having suspected her.

"Yeah. Ian lives in Tower. A couple times a month I run over to his place. Because of the wheelchair fall, he stayed at the hospital for most of the past week. The first few days he had some neurological problems in his left arm. The doctors wanted to keep close tabs on him. It seems to be getting better."

Ian raised a can of Coke by way of illustration and then took a slurp.

"Sorry I lied to you," Gina said with contrition. "I didn't want to tell you where I was really going, because then I'd have to explain why Ian was hurt. It was dumb. Peter wanted me to tell you."

It all made sense now. Gina's reaction to finding Bjorklund's body. He'd been shot, a brutal flashback to the day she'd shot her brother. The tension between Gina and Peter. He knew about Ian's injury, was the only other witness to her guilt, and she resented him for it—or was shamed by it. Peter Bunyan was the keeper of a dark secret for which she had never found her peace. Remembering how evasive Peter had been when I asked about Ian, I could only assume that he, too, felt responsible for what had happened that day.

"Here." Gina shoved a paper in my hand, one she'd produced from her pocket. "I got this fax."

"You've turned my sister into some kind of secret agent," Ian quipped.

"What is it?" Jeff asked.

I scanned the report. "Chromium six!"

"Chromium six?" Jeff peered over my shoulder.

"Erin Brockovich," I answered.

"That movie with Julia Roberts?" Ian was attacking the last of the burritos.

"It was based on a real event. She played a law clerk who helped bring about a multimillion-dollar lawsuit against the Pacific Gas and Electric Company of California."

Jeff scratched his chin. "Wasn't the town's drinking water contaminated?"

"Exactly. By hexavalent chromium. Chromium six." I held the paper up like a trophy. "And this is Ivar Bjorklund's water test report."

# CHAPTER 24

"That's the last big one." Billie Bradshaw indicated the camera case on the ground. "I'll get the little stuff."

"I'm on it." I stepped forward. The reinforced, padded and water-tight bag was bulky and I didn't want Billie to lift it. Although two inches taller than I, she was also nearly thirty years older. I was the young pup with the sturdy back, albeit with a bum shoulder.

Jeff had broken speed limits trying to get us back to Wolf Lake in time. We met up with the crew to film Debbie doing her daily health check of the wolves: inspecting teeth, eyes, ears, paws, fur and the fullness of bellies. A highlight was watching her hand out supplements and meds, all deliciously wrapped in individual meatballs for each animal. The wolves snarfed up the treats in one gulp. Ordinarily, Debbie would've done this inspection first thing in the morning; but due to our early morning foray into the sky, she'd postponed it for us.

By 2:30 we were packing things up in the wolf institute's parking lot.

"Good job, Snake." Billie held open the spacious trunk to her sedan. "We're done here."

With a grunt, I hoisted the bag into the trunk, knowing it held Arthur's precious cameras, lenses, battery packs and view-finders.

The trunk closed with an authoritative thud. Behind me Jeff and Arthur were speaking animatedly with Debbie Wong. The three stood by the field stone and timber–framed entrance of the institute, saying their goodbyes. Arthur, whose chinos were less sharply pressed than when he first arrived in Wolf Lake, now sported a newly acquired MWI sweatshirt.

"Sorry you guys have to leave," I lied, secretly happy they were on their way. Billie would not approve of my next plunge into the investigative pool.

"It'd be fun to have dinner with you and Jeff. But if Shag—oh, you know—and I get back late this afternoon, we can get those extra pickup shots we talked about. Plus we've got a crack-of-dawn appointment with that freighter."

"That's dedication."

"Nit-pickiness, as my mother used to say," Billie said acerbically. "Besides, you and Jeff could use a little more private time together."

"We had a nice drive this morning. I promise I'll have the script ready for you by the end of next week." I wanted to make it clear to our director that I was still capable of holding up my end of the business in spite of my adventures.

"He's worried about you, Snake." She nodded toward Jeff. "You were almost killed in that car shooting."

I rested my eyes on the endless track of pines that rose up behind the parking lot. "I know. We talked about it. Worked things out."

"There's more to it, Snake. I've never seen you so distracted. It's like you weren't really with us on this trip."

Her words stung. "Billie, I handled all my obligations—"

"You did," she agreed, though not happily.

I jammed my hands in my back pockets and looked her in the eye. "I'm sorry I let you down. If I've seemed distracted, I'd like you to understand why." I moistened my lips. "I saw the carcasses of four wolves dumped in the woods like so many bags of garbage. Thrown away. As if their lives were meaningless. I was shocked by the cruelty behind their deaths. A conservation officer asked if I wanted to help find out who was behind the shootings. Hey, I jumped at the chance! It also tied in with the theme of the episode we were filming."

She let me say my peace without interruption. Then spoke. "And that's the real reason you and Jeff are staying behind. Unfinished business. Though nothing to do with *Zoofari.*"

Her tart Gallic features suggested she knew it all. She'd make the supreme hotel concierge, in my opinion, for she knew where all the secrets were buried and how much dirt was on top of them. "You're a lot like me when I was your age." She offered a placating smile. "You do your birth sign proud. Cancer the crab grabs hold of what it wants and won't let go, no matter what anybody says."

I couldn't have gotten a better compliment from her. A woman I admired, Billie was the most perceptive person I'd ever met. Nothing got past her. If I could attain half her insight by the time I was her age, I'd be well ahead of the game.

She tilted her head toward me, a twinkle in her eye. "Be careful. Don't get in over your head. And make sure you don't lose sight of the big picture. Listen to your Aunt Billie."

She called herself Aunt Billie whenever she felt protective of me. She had lost her only daughter eighteen years ago in a boating accident, a subject she never discussed. Ever. I'm sure the incident had been the major contributor to the care-worn lines around her eyes.

"Thanks." I smiled back. "Part of me works on common sense, part on emotion. Sometimes the two don't mix. Either way, I have to do what I think's right."

"I know you do," she said. "My problem is I'm a director. I make my living telling people what to do and they have to do it. I just wish it worked that way in real life."

★  ★  ★  ★  ★

The sun was skimming low against the western treetops when Jeff parked the Jeep in front of Signe's. He ran next door to get us a couple of dinners to go from Zup's, a chance for us to sample Wolf Lake's ethnic history. I'd been told the Welsh pasties had been a staple of the miners back in the day when iron ore was king in the Arrowhead region. Jeff had his stomach set on the Polish sausage.

For once Cole Novak wasn't wielding wood and saw in front of Last Chance Outfitters. Good. I wasn't in a mood to talk with him. Only after I drew closer did it occur to me that he might've finished his construction fix-up. The sawhorses were gone, the curls of shaved wood and sawdust swept up, the long electrical extension cords coiled up and removed. Someone's muddy shoes had already tracked up the new steps. They didn't creak when I stepped up them.

As I reached for the door handle, my eyes drifted up to the new sign Novak had painted for Signe. The pine bough in a circle with a blue lake in the background. A pine bough with three furry branches. No, it wasn't like Ivar Bjorklund's elm twig, only superficially. And yet there'd been that connection with Signe's name.

A sign. Her name meant that. Was there something Bjorklund had wanted us to know about Signe?

I hurried into the store before my imagination got the better of me. For a late Saturday afternoon the place was busy. Gus and Mooney were gone by now, so I had no one to chat with while the queue at the register worked its way down.

"Snake!" Signe greeted, surprised to see me when the burly giant in line ahead of me had moved on. "Doing some hiking?" she surmised by the trail map I was buying, not the candy bar.

"Tracking wolves," I replied with a suggestive undertone. I didn't take my eyes off her.

She averted her gaze. "Bit late in the day for that, isn't it?" Her fingers punched the keys on the ancient cash register, one with an actual bell for when the drawer opened.

"Hopefully, it won't take long. I've got a couple leads."

"On Rufus?" She lit up, full of hope. I felt guilty for baiting her.

"No, Signe."

She shook her head, disappointed.

No one was behind me in line. The nearest customer rummaged by the Coleman camp cookers a good twenty feet away, engrossed in the choices. I pressed my belly against the counter, leaning in closer for privacy. "You knew about Mr. Bjorklund's water test."

No answer.

The stuffed deer head on the wall behind her regarded me with expressionless eyes. The color faded in Signe's cheeks.

"Signe," I pressed, "you're not answering me. Mr. Bjorklund's well water was contaminated. Something toxic got in his well. What used to be a flower garden is now covered in stones. Nothing'll grow in it."

I grabbed her hand before she could turn away. Defiance glared back at me. "I don't know what the hell you're talking about."

My fingers gripped tighter. "The water made Lily sick. Gave her cancer. Made them both sick. He lost a lot of weight. You, of all people, must've noticed that. People don't lose that much weight so fast over stress alone."

She jerked her hand free. "I've got a store to run. And if I'm not mistaken, you've got a husband waiting for you." Signe nodded toward the main window, where Jeff could be seen standing next to the Jeep.

I didn't budge.

"Why won't you talk to me? You know more than you're saying. Is it because you invested in Mr. Bjorklund's sheep farm?"

"What's the big secret in that? After his hand got mangled at the paper mill he had to do something with his life. His disability payments only went so far. I wanted to help the man out."

"And now he's dead. And his other investor, Forrest Hansen, is also dead."

"Exactly what are you implying?" She folded her arms across her chest and eyed me circumspectly.

"That the land would be worth a lot more money if it wasn't contaminated."

"You think I'm after Ivar's land?"

"No, Signe, I'm not. All I'm saying is whoever owns that property now has a vested interest in keeping the status of the well secret. Mr. Bjorklund knew who contaminated his well, didn't he?"

She stood her ground, remaining silent.

"Signe, whoever that person was might have killed him."

The hardness in her face eased up a bit.

I pushed a little. "The water in that well is what killed Lily."

Signe stirred. She searched deep into my eyes as if seeking assurance I was trustworthy. After a moment, her big shoulders relaxed. "No way to prove it without an exhumation. Ivar wasn't about to do that. But it seems the likely cause. For his decline as well."

I nodded. "Their well must've been contaminated for years."

Her eyes narrowed. "How do you know so much about this?"

"I've seen the water analysis he got from the county health department," was all I said. No point in telling her I'd been sneaking around his home. "Did he figure out how his well went bad?"

"He kinda knew. Or had strong suspicions, but he wouldn't say." She began moving the boxes of candy around beneath the counter as she spoke. "Ivar could be a closed-mouth son of a bitch. Very private. Very old-school Swede. Don't make a fuss if you don't have to. Stoic people look up to us." She smirked. "A tornado could've been ripping apart his house and thrown him in the air, and Ivar would've told you it was getting a little windy."

I smiled thinly. She was treading on familiar ground. My maternal grandparents were like that.

Signe shrugged. "It's how you survived up here in the old days, with four feet of snow and thirty below zero temps."

I laughed. Some of my East Coast and West Coast friends wouldn't understand. To many, the Midwest is flyover country. Nothing of interest. Nothing of value. They don't know that the hardest-working, most resilient, down-to-earth people in America are from the vast midsection of the country. No, Ivar Bjorklund wouldn't have told Signe his suspicions until he was sure.

"And you have no idea who he suspected?"

She shook her head, staring at some point over my head. "Sorry."

Off in the book and music section, a customer punched the button on the CD sampler. Moments later, the bone-chilling howl of a wolf filled the quiet corners of the store.

I spun around. I stared so hard at the man who'd started the music that he backed away from the samplers. I didn't know what it was, some primeval jolt to my system, the call of the wild, but I realized I was wasting my time here. And running out of daylight. I snatched up the map and candy bar and bolted out the door.

# CHAPTER 25

"That way."

Jeff motioned toward our left, eyes glued to the handheld GPS device as we tramped through the underbrush. He reminded me of Mr. Spock with his tricorder. Except instead of an impassive pointy-eared alien with shiny black hair leading our "landing party," my alien (resident-wise) was a boisterous, blue-eyed, sandy-haired bloke decked out in khakis.

We ducked under the spreading branch of a tamarack as Mr. Jones led us further into Superior National Forest. I was a bit nervous at the sun's rapid sink into the west, but this was something we had to do today. Our last chance.

"The signal keeps breaking up," he said, eyes focused on the treetops. "The trees are too thick, and they're blocking the satellite. We need to find more open areas."

Picking our way through the pines and tamaracks, we progressed another forty yards. Sixty. Eighty.

After leaving Signe's, we'd taken our dinners to enjoy at a park overlooking Shagawa Lake. We gulped down our meals, then took off for Black Fir Road in search of GPS coordinates. Earlier in the week Gina had isolated two radio collar signals for the Red Iron pack. Our search for them had ended abruptly upon the discovery of Bjorklund's body and Rufus's escape. Before Jeff and I left Wolf Lake, we wanted to find those two GPS points. The first had revealed nothing except a few paw prints, dried scat and several gnawed deer bones. We now searched for the second location.

"We're on the spot," Jeff announced. "47.582 north latitude, 91.915 west longitude."

Well, I was unimpressed. We'd found the exact coordinates, thanks to the global positioning system doohickey Gina had loaned us. Both Peter and Gina had felt a wolf den was likely to be near this second location. Our task was to find it. Perhaps then we'd finally know why the animals had been shot and killed.

Jeff turned off the GPS and slipped it into his pocket. Reacting to my puzzlement, he explained, "These things are only accurate within ten yards. Now we need to look for signs."

"That's why I brought you with me, Tarzan," I called back, my attention directed to the patchy ground.

The two of us stepped carefully around the site, scanning the grass, dirt, and shrubs for tell-tale signs of animal visitations. The late afternoon sun cast long shadows across the grass. I grew more concerned that twilight would descend on us too soon.

We spent several minutes bent low over the ground before Jeff grunted at something in the distance, squinting. He briskly strode to a clump of crimson sumac. "Have a look at this!" He rubbed his fingers along the wounded bark. They lingered in the deep scars. "A white-tailed deer was here." He grinned, as if this occurrence was something rare and wonderful. "A deer's made these marks with its antlers."

I couldn't help but smile. Jeff's stance on life was that nearly everything in the natural world was special and amazing. "It's been a while since the blighter was here. This rubbing isn't new."

My eyes scanned the area. "If there's a wolf den around here, then he wasn't the smartest buck in the herd."

"If he was in full rut he mightn't have been paying much attention."

"Guess I shouldn't be so quick to judge. Look at us. We're rummaging around an area known to have wild wolves. How smart are we?"

"I thought you said this place was abandoned?"

"No, I think I said Gina suspected it was abandoned after the shooting, provided any of the pack members survived. One thing we should—a paw print! And it's wolf, not dog, Jeff." The two front toes were nearly parallel, a telltale sign. The print was much larger than the average dog's. "It isn't all that old, either."

Jeff knelt down to inspect the track and agreed. We searched for others, but without success.

"Too much grass," I complained. "If a wolf passed through this stuff I sure can't tell."

Jeff tossed me a raffish smile. "Don't give up yet, sweetheart." He studied the patch of grass from different angles before dropping to his knees. He squinted at it and then lowered himself onto his belly, keeping himself at this gopher-eye view. Extending his arm out, he delicately moved his hand over the top of the grass blades. Back and forth. Back and forth. He paused every now and again, eyes shut tight, as if the green shoots spoke to him. I knew better than to interrupt, despite my insatiable curiosity. He inched forward, his open palm sweeping ahead.

"Something's been here," he finally said. "And it went that way." He nodded toward a group of aspens at the other end of the grassy field.

My hands rested on my hips. "What the heck are you doing?"

"Feel tracking."

"Feel tracking? You're kidding."

"Wrongo. Learned it from one of me best mates when I was a youngster. His granddad was full aborigine. Georgie and I played together for three summers in Kakadu in the Top End before his family moved to Brisbane. His granddad taught us how to track and follow game, how to stand perfectly motionless so the animals would come to us and how to feel a track when you can't see it."

I shook my head. "Just when I start thinking I know everything about you."

Jeff gave a dismissive shrug. "I'm passable. Georgie's granddad was a master. Took me two whole summers to learn how to do it. Didn't really get the hang of it for a long while after that. For months that's all me and Georgie did, we'd be on our stomachs for hours and hours tracking game through the para grass, usually rabbits."

Stretched out on the ground, Jeff closed his eyes, feeling the green blades. "What you can't see with your eyes, you might read with your hand. You feel the bent blades and impressions left by what's walked over it. Very delicate. Doesn't always work, but you said there should be a den nearby. That means regular traffic patterns. Lots of animals—maybe wolves do this, too—favor specific paths." His eyes opened and crinkled with satisfaction. "Some of these blades of grass have been permanently bent or pushed down from being walked on regularly."

"Mr. Jones, you amaze me."

"You should've seen Georgie's granddad. Now that bloke was amazing. He would've had this figured out in seconds."

"I'm still impressed."

"Trouble is," Jeff said, sliding forward, careful to avoid the area he was surveying, "if you're not careful, you can destroy the track." He closed his eyes again and fell into a meditative silence. Eventually, the corner of his mouth curved up with satisfaction. His eyes snapped open and he sat back on his haunches, pointing. "The path goes that way."

"We're lucky it was wolves and not dogs," I said, hurrying

along the projected path. Dog tracks meander, going every which way because they're easily distracted by each new scent or curious object. Wolves are much more businesslike. They tend to move in a straight line. I maneuvered to the edge of the grass to an area behind a stand of aspens whose yellow leaves quivered in the light wind. "Eureka! Wolf tracks. Lots of 'em. And scat!"

Jeff hurried to join me.

It was a small clearing, about eighteen yards in diameter, with large patches of bare earth contained within a perimeter of various hardwoods, shrubs and fragrant pines. The pine needles that littered the ground infused the air with their enticing scent.

I bent down, touching a few paw prints. Two different sizes. However, their alignment told me they were from the same animal. The forepaws of a wolf are larger than the rear. "Some of these tracks are new. Hold on." My ears pricked. "Hear that? Running water! Must be a creek nearby."

I turned about, scanning the site as my pulse quickened. A wolf den needed a ready supply of water. "Jeff, this has to be it." Then a small mound caught my eye. Covered in grass and moss, it propped up an ancient and decaying log. My hiking boots beat a hasty path toward it. I grinned back at him. "There's a burrow here! It's the den."

Without a second thought, I dropped to my knees and peered inside. The opening was about two feet wide, enough for me to shimmy part way into. I uttered a tiny yelp of pain when I bumped my slinged arm against the opening on the way out.

"Definitely a wolf den." I brushed the sandy soil off my sling, adjusting the cloth. "I found some bits of wolf fur. The question is . . ."

The question was what had happened to Jeff? I was talking to myself. A warbler twittered in a nearby pine, while behind the den mound a critter scurried into the scrubland, but no sign of my husband. A cold worm of panic slithered across my skin.

"Jeff?"

"Over here, Snake!"

To my relief, Jeff emerged from behind a clump of bushes ten yards behind me. I rushed over and was brought up short when he displayed the contents of his open palm. "Shell casings. From a rifle."

The cold worm writhed in my belly as I stared at those six casings, remembering the four wolf carcasses. "Two misses. Four hits. No doubt now. This was where those wolves were killed."

We stood in silence as the discovery sank in. I tried to visualize the moment as the first shot rang, some of the animals running, others frozen with uncertainty, not knowing where the threat came from and therefore not knowing in which direction safety lay. Tried to visualize the shooter or shooters—

"Jeff, do all the casings match? Are they from one or two rifles?"

"All the same, far as I can tell." He jiggled the brass cartridges in his palm. He'd lived some of his formative years in the more rugged parts of Australia, areas that had retained a flavor of the American Old West. He, his dad and brothers had fired a few guns in their day. While no expert in ballistics, Jeff had enough of a working knowledge of guns to answer my question.

"One shooter then," I said, turning. "We're about—what?— four hundred feet from the road. How'd the killer move the carcasses? Do you think he rode in here on an ATV? I don't see any tire tracks."

"He dragged them." Jeff's blue eyes twinkled in the fading sunlight. Mr. Outback seemed quite amused. "While you had your sweet little arse in that den I was taking a little walkabout. Over that way are drag marks. Your killer must've used a blanket or tarpaulin to move the carcasses."

"Good. That explains how they were transported. I must say I'm a little surprised to find a wolf den this close to a road."

"Oh?" Jeff was a herpetologist, a lizard and reptile man. Northern climate animals were not his specialty.

"Wolves do their best to avoid people. They want nothing to do with us."

"Well, it is isolated out here."

"True. Black Fir Road is a fairly deserted stretch of nothing. The few times I've been on it I've rarely seen another car."

Jeff scanned the area. "Surrounding us are dozens of miles of raw wilderness in nearly every direction. This den would only be used a few months out of the year."

"Yeah. I guess the chances of them seeing a human being on foot would be pretty slim."

Jeff scratched the side of his face. "This place really is isolated. Yet someone went to a lot of trouble to get rid of these animals. Why? To hide something? There's nothing here, luv."

"The radio collars. Those were the only things that told people the wolves were here. Whoever killed them removed and destroyed their radio collars, afraid someday Gina or someone from the DNR or U.S. Geological Survey would come looking for those animals."

"To find what? Nothing here but trees. And more trees!"

"It's a good question."

We combed the den site in hopes of making a discovery. But we found nothing out of the ordinary. At one point I turned to find Jeff gazing into the sky, mesmerized. "Snake, it's a bald eagle. What a beauty!"

Sure enough. Right above us. A wonderful specimen of the American bald eagle soared on the winds, its huge wings outstretched. Even though I'd seen no less than five eagles in the Wolf Lake area in the past week, I never tired of them.

I smiled to the sky. "Jeff, remind me when we get home. I

promised Cricket I'd take her to the National Eagle Center in Wabasha."

"Snake?" Jeff looked at me oddly.

My brow furrowed. "Somebody else recently said something about eagles. Who was that?" My good hand clamped to my forehead. "It's important. I can't tell you why, but it has something to do with the wolf killings." Stymied, I let out a frustrated sigh. "We've got to figure out what's so special about this place. And we don't have much time." The shadows were gathering, the sun already swallowed by the trees.

"Hold on a tick." Jeff narrowed his eyes. "The tops of those trees over there don't look right."

I followed his line of sight. Through a gap in the trees we could see a hundred feet beyond. In one place the continuous swatch of green crowns was interrupted by a tight clump of bare branches.

"You're right," I said. "That's not the fall color change. It's something else. Disease?"

"Whatever it is, those trees are sick. Maybe dying. Let's check them out!"

Jeff wasn't much interested in being a sleuth. However, his love of justice—and me—made him a half-hearted accomplice at the best of times. Seeing him show real enthusiasm for this task helped mollify my guilt for dragging him along.

It took a while to pick our way through the trees but we found the spot, another small clearing where the trees had begun to thin out. A small gully lay before us, into which grew five tightly huddled birches, all with varying degrees of lost or damaged foliage, like a clutch of white-haired bag ladies in tattered overcoats.

My eyes appraised the sickly trees. "You're right, Jeff, there's something wrong with these guys. They aren't healthy at all."

"Smell this." He was on all fours, nose to the ground. "This dampness isn't just water."

My nose crinkled from the pungent aroma. "Chemical?" My head snapped toward him so fast my pony tail whipped across my face. "Get away from it, Jeff. It's toxic. I'm willing to bet this is the stuff the health department found in Bjorklund's well water."

"Chromium six?"

"Shit!" The sun might have been setting in Superior National Forest, but daylight was breaking through the fog in my head. "Lyle Almquist was the guy I was thinking of before, the guy who talked to me about a bald eagle. He was going on about Moua Vang, the Hmong man who lives across the road from Ivar Bjorklund. Almquist made some comments about Vang's so-called voodoo ways, his Laotian customs. He said he saw Vang shooting at a bald eagle."

"Okay . . ." Jeff said, not fully understanding.

"When Peter mentioned this to Vang later, he claimed he was only trying to scare away the eagles from his chickens."

"Do eagles eat chickens?"

"Not usually, but that doesn't matter. What's important is Vang was shooting from the back lot of his farm. I stood there. It's a small hill that overlooks the forest. From there you can see for miles and miles. But, because of all the vegetation along Black Fir, you can't see into Vang's property from the road. The trees are too thick. So how did Almquist see Moua Vang shooting at an eagle?"

Jeff lifted his shoulders.

I gestured with my sling arm. "The only place he could've seen Vang was from the forest. Where we found the wolf carcasses. That area. I saw that hill from a break in the trees. A great blue heron flew toward some trees on Vang's property. At the time I didn't know the hill was on his land, not till later. You see what it means?"

He nodded. "Almquist had to be standing in the same spot as you, or pretty near."

"Right. Which begs the question, why was Lyle Almquist at the site where the carcasses were dumped unless he was the one who dumped them?"

"Makes sense."

"So, let me think this through. We must be . . . five miles from where the carcasses were found. It's early in the morning. Almquist is getting rid of them in a wild, wooded area where he figures no one will ever find them. He hears a shot. He turns to see who's shooting." I turned toward Jeff, imagining Almquist's actions. "Maybe he thinks he's being shot at. Through a gap in the trees he sees movement. A hill in the distance where he sees Moua Vang taking shots at an eagle."

"And later he tells you what he saw."

"Yeah, trying to make Vang look guilty, I bet."

Jeff picked up the thread. "From what you've told me, this site is much more remote than where you found the carcasses. It was the radio collars he was afraid of. The collars meant the pack was being monitored. Eventually, someone would come out to study the wolves and might find the chemical dump. And he didn't want that, which is why he killed the animals and destroyed the collars."

"Uh-huh. He hoped the researchers would think the wolves had moved on. And now we know why. Jeff, it's right in front of us!" I locked my gaze onto the toxic gully a few yards away. "Lyle Almquist worked with leather. He often tanned his own hides. Geez, his pickup truck has these fifty-five-gallon barrels strapped to the bed. Who knows what kind of chemical sludge he has in them? Nonorganic tanning methods use chemicals and leave toxic residue. He'd have to dispose of that stuff someplace." Annoyance edged my voice as I considered the dying trees. "Like right here. Guess he wanted to avoid paying disposal fees. Do it on the cheap. Use the forest for a dumping grou—"

I stopped dead, frozen in space and time.

"Snake? You okay?"

"Omigod!" I stared at Jeff, thunderstruck. "Oh, my God."

"What?!"

"Bjorklund's message. Remember the clue I told you about? What he had clenched in his fist?"

"The branch thing."

"An elm twig with three leaves."

"Right. You thought he was naming his killer."

"My mother would have a fit for me not getting this earlier. I should've known! I'm half Swedish. Bjorklund was Swedish."

Confusion lingered. Not Jeff's fault. I was rambling. Too excited to be coherent. "I know a bit of Swedish. Mr. and Mrs. Johnson from next door when I was growing up. They were from Sweden and they taught me some. And for my genealogy project in school, I learned the meaning behind some of the family names. In Swedish Almquist means elm twig. Bjorklund means something like birch grove. Why the hell didn't I remember that?"

Jeff could only lift his shoulders in sympathy.

I was on a tear, talking faster. "Knowing he was going to die, Bjorklund sees the one thing that will name his killer and he crawls across the grass to get it. That's why he passed those other leaves and branches."

"Crikey! It fits. I think you've done it."

I nodded back, slightly numb from the realization. Though I didn't allow myself long to celebrate. The sinking sun meant twilight was approaching fast. "Let's get going before it gets dark. We can tell the Wolf Lake police what we know. Let them deal with it."

We worked our way through the forest, spurred on by the

thrill of discovery. By the time we got back to our SUV, the gunmetal blue in the western sky was smeared with orange. Jeff tossed the GPS device onto the back seat.

"We should've taken a reading at the dump site," I said.

Jeff shrugged. "No problem, sweetheart, we'll just bring the police back here in the morning."

My heart stopped at the sound of a rifle bolt slamming back. And the harsh voice that came after.

"That's far enough, you two! Don't move!"

# CHAPTER 26

Lyle Almquist!

The big man lumbered out from behind the drooping blue-green branches of a large black spruce. He scowled behind the snow-colored beard, as the murdering end of his rifle pointed at us. At me, to be more specific. Jeff was on the driver's side of the Jeep and could potentially duck out of harm's way. I was caught in the cross hairs.

"Mr. Almquist," I greeted pleasantly. If I pretended I didn't know he'd killed two men, maybe he'd think I didn't—know, that is. I hoped I gave off the persona of being calmer than I felt.

"What're you two doing here?" Almquist demanded. Cold and direct. Not a shred of the affability I'd seen when I first met him.

Jeff, quick on his feet, gave a big Aussie grin. "I hope we weren't trespassing, mate. We were havin' ourselves a look for a wolf den to film."

"Then where's your damned camera?" His fingers nervously adjusted on the gunstock.

He had us there, but Jeff didn't miss a beat. "It's in the back of the vehicle. I'll get it if you like."

"Stop right there." Almquist threatened with his rifle.

Jeff complied, taking a step back.

"Mr. Almquist," I said, "we don't want any trouble. As my husband said, we're scouting the area for a wolf den."

266

"What makes you think there's a wolf den around here?"

Jeff held out his hands and spoke in a soothing voice, similar to the one he used when calming a cornered animal. "Radio collars, mate. We used a GPS locator to home in on an old signal coordinate."

Almquist spat on the ground. "Fucking collars! I knew this would happen!"

To be honest, I wasn't sure it was the best strategy to let the man with the gun know we'd been scouring the woods. There was no need to tip our hand and let him know we'd discovered his secret. Still, it was the most plausible story we could tell, simply because it was true. At least half true. The part about finding the toxic waste dump we'd keep to ourselves. If we could convince Almquist we'd only found an abandoned wolf site he might let us go.

Only he wasn't going for it, his predatory smile widening. "I've been watchin' you for the last ten minutes. You may be a good tracker, young man, but you don't know beans about moving around a forest unnoticed. You found my dump."

"What dump?" I shot a puzzled look at Jeff. "What are you talking about?"

Almquist's eyebrows bristled like white caterpillars. "I ain't stupid, so don't play me like I am. You were standing there smelling the ground. I saw you."

My hopes sank. There'd be no talking our way out of it now. We'd been caught with our fingers in the cookie jar. And I saw no clemency in those steely eyes.

"Lyle," I addressed him by his first name, seeing if I could catch him off guard. "I think there's been a mistake. Jeff and I came here for the wolves. We aren't interested in anything else. Since we didn't find what we were looking for, we'll go. We're on our way back to the Cities."

Jeff, who'd slowly walked around to my side of the Jeep, took hold of my good arm. "That's right, mate. Let's not do anything rash. Whatever's going on in those woods is none of our business. Snake and I'll leave and forget about it. We'll just get in the car and leave town. You'll never see us again."

Almquist snorted, his contempt showing how that was never going to happen. "Move." He waved us back into the forest where nobody could see us. Where nobody would find our lifeless bodies.

Dusk was poised to fall, with only a few last ribbons of salmon-colored sky remaining. The dimming light made walking trickier. We marched several paces head of the rifle barrel.

"Jeff," I whispered. "What are we going to do?"

"Don't know, luv. We're up a gum tree, that's for sure." He reached for my hand, then stumbled forward as hard gunmetal jammed into his back.

"Keep your hands to yourself. And keep your damned mouths shut. Don't let this hip fool you. I can't run, but I'm a dead shot with this rifle. First one who tries anything will drop on the spot and the other one'll get it before the first one hits the ground."

No doubt he would, judging by how quickly he'd dispatched those four wolves.

My ears caught everything behind me, taking in every crunch of Almquist's shoes against the dried grass as we pressed deeper into the trees. Away from witnesses. Away from rescue.

My insides twisted into a tangle of knots. What the hell were we going to do! Running wasn't an option. If either of us tried to make a mad dash for it, the other would be killed on the spot. Yet we had to do something. It was an impossible choice.

Jeff looked over his shoulder. "You don't have to do this!"

"You don't give me much choice." Almquist sounded put out, as if we'd done him a great injury.

"Killing us will only make things worse for you."

"You two got any idea where you are? It's the middle of nowhere. Who'll know?"

I turned around and stopped. "People know we're here! We're due back in Wolf Lake in an hour. They'll come looking for us."

Skepticism flashed in Almquist's face. "I think you're makin' that up."

"It's not too late. Just let us go."

"So you can go straight to the police?"

"We won't!"

"Yes, you will."

I didn't turn away from his cold stare, trying to seem as trustworthy as possible. But he was right; I would have gone straight to the police.

Almquist motioned for me to keep walking. "Two more dead people ain't gonna make a difference to a judge."

Maybe not. All I knew was it would make a hell of a lot of difference to us.

The last threads of daylight faded, the darkness impeding our progress. Jeff and I deliberately slowed down over the uneven ground, not wishing to get to our final destination any sooner than necessary. Twice our captor ordered us to move faster. My nerves, already on a hair trigger to bolt, needed reminding of the folly of running. The man was a crack shot.

"This way," he said after several minutes. We veered off toward a thinning stand of white pine and aspens. Eventually the trees thinned out to a clearing. The ground was rugged and seemed unusually dark ahead. In fact, it turned out to be a hole some fifteen feet wide. Almquist marched us right to the edge. Loose earth fell beneath my boot where it touched the crumbling lip.

A low bestial growl rose up from the darkness.

"What the—?" My eyes strained to see what was at the bottom of the pit.

"It's a sink hole." Almquist, immediately behind Jeff, dug the rifle muzzle into the small of his back. "I discovered our friend this morning. Guess he got too close to the edge sniffing out food or the scent of one of his litter mates before the ground gave way. He'll come in handy now."

Now I could make out what Almquist was talking about. A gray wolf. About ninety pounds and on full alert stared at us from the shadows. A survivor of the Red Iron pack? I glimpsed the gray lips curled back, revealing jagged canid incisors. A warning.

"Handy?" I repeated with trepidation.

Just as I spoke the word, Almquist shoved Jeff in the back. I gasped as he tumbled into the pit.

"Jeff!"

The wolf snarled, baring its fangs, crouching low. Jeff landed hard. He scrambled away, though there was no place to go. A scant ten feet separated them. Squatting, Jeff jammed back against the earthen wall. All the while his gaze locked onto the fierce yellow eyes trained on him.

Almquist chuckled. "You were right, y'know. I can't shoot you. That'd tie me to your deaths. However, there are other ways of getting rid of you. This wolf will do nicely. He's wild, scared and hungry. We'll let him deal with your husband, so it'll look like an accident."

"No! You can't do that!"

"Shut up and walk." The rifle threatened my abdomen.

I surveyed the pit with the idea of jumping in. Except Almquist must have guessed my intention, because he slammed the butt of the gun into my left shoulder. I yelped and dropped to my knees, writhing in pain. Bright lights sparkled across my vision.

Jeff cried out my name.

"Bad idea, lady. Two of you in there might have a chance

against that wolf. You might figure a way out. I won't take that chance. No, your hubby's on his own. You're coming with me."

The thought of Jeff trapped with a wild predator with ripsaw teeth, used to taking down prey larger than itself, struck fear into my heart. "No—wait. Let me stay," I pleaded, crawling back toward the edge.

This time a kick in the ribs stopped me.

"Get on your feet! Move or I'll shoot him and be done with it."

Reluctantly, I gathered my feet beneath me and shuffled a few steps. I turned, straining to see inside the sink hole. "Jeff—" I managed before my next words were choked off by a light jab from the rifle.

"Snake!" Jeff's anguished voice rose from the pit.

When I tried to answer, hardened metal cut me off. It was torture to leave Jeff. I desperately wanted to help. But the cruel reality was I'd be gunned down before I even took two steps. Tears of frustration blurred my vision. Oh God! What was I going to do?

"Get a move on. And don't look back."

Think! Almquist was leading me off into these dark woods to my death. Fear, anger, hopelessness flushed through me. The farther we got away from the sink hole, the more despair I felt. Even so, I knew I had to do something.

"You're pretty good with that rifle, aren't you?" I said, summoning up my courage.

"Damn right, lady. So don't try anything."

Good advice. Except I had nothing to lose. I was also getting tired of him poking me in the back every ten seconds, so I started walking a little faster, which put a little distance between us.

"You shot those four wolves by yourself," I said, as though admiring his skill.

"Yeah. Didn't want to do it. They weren't bothering me. But when I saw them radio collars, I knew one day folks'd come looking for 'em."

"And would find your dump. That's what you were afraid of."

"A guy tries to make an honest living and people gotta mess with him. I spent seventeen years underground, lady. Seventeen years at the bottom of an iron ore mine, then another ten at the taconite plant until that closed. Now I try to get by with my leather goods. My hides are the softest ever. That's what sells jackets. Except it costs too much to get rid of the few chemicals I use. I do what I have to."

Damn the world and everyone in it; that's what I got from that speech. Following the law didn't seem to be a particular concern for Lyle Almquist.

The ground began to slope upward. The footing got trickier. Exposed roots from large trees stretched across the path, in parts acting like organic stair treads. I turned slightly. Almquist grimaced as he took the slope one step at a time. I was six feet in front of him now. His crack about "a few chemicals" annoyed me. It also occurred to me if I could raise his hackles a little, he might get reckless.

"Your dump is toxic," I said pointedly. "It's poisoning the water."

"So I figured," he said with a labored grunt as he struggled with a step. His bad hip, I assumed.

"Is that why you killed Bjorklund and Hansen? They'd figured it out and were threatening you."

"If Ivar wasn't such a cranky old cuss, he'd still be alive."

I dared not look back. I nearly stumbled over a buried rock. I tried to widen the distance between us without Almquist catching on. Ahead, at the crest of the hill, a couple of stars winked in the cloudless sky. Behind the trees a sliver of the waxing moon was rising.

"Still alive?" I huffed a little from the uphill climb. "Oh!" I turned halfway around, wide eyed, feeling like a total doofus for not having put it together earlier. "Bjorklund confronted you in Zup's parking lot, didn't he? He was waving the water quality report from the health department under your nose. He somehow figured you'd contaminated his well."

"How the frickin' hell did you know that?"

I ignored his question, wanting him irate.

"Bjorklund figured it had to be you. He knew or figured out you use chromium six in your tanning process. How long have you been dumping chemicals here? Years? The toxins must've leached into the aquifer and traveled downstream to the Bjorklunds' well. He blamed you for killing Lily, didn't he? That's why he was so angry with you."

"Yeah, all my fault. Said I killed Lily. My fault he got sick. Everything was my fault. He said he was gonna get back at me. Report me to the EPA or some other frickin' government agency!"

"You did make him sick. You did give his wife cancer. You poisoned his well and how many other wells in the area?" I thought of the Vangs who lived across the road from Bjorklund. Moua Vang's yellow teeth, the same shade as Bjorklund's.

Almquist was unmoved. "Ivar was sick, all right. Sick in the head! Couple of days ago he comes over and threatens me with a gun. The guy was freakin' out of his mind! After getting that water report he kept thinking about me and the chemicals I use. He spied on me one night. Saw me loading up one of the barrels on my truck. He tried to follow me, he said, but lost me. So a few days later he's snooping around in my house while I was in my workshop. He comes out with my rifle and orders me to take him to the site."

"And you killed him. How? He had a gun on you."

273

I was open to pointers on the subject.

"Damned fool had that school bus. He had me get in and drive while he kept a gun on me. Well, I didn't take him here. I'm not that stupid. I took him along a stretch of Black Fir Road that's filled with potholes. I floored that damned bus like a hotrod. It popped up and down like a prairie dog." Almquist chuckled at the memory. "Ivar hit his head on the ceiling, and I slammed on the brakes and grabbed the gun from him. I stopped the bus and we changed places. I had the old coot drive to a deserted old driveway in the woods. And that's where I left him and the bus."

Carefully, I stepped around some loose boulders. "You shot him in the chest and left him to die. But"—an odd thought suddenly struck me—"how did you get home?"

"I walked," he answered with pride.

"That's four to five miles."

"You think 'cause my hip keeps me from moving fast that I can't walk? You must be a city girl! I grew up here. I used to walk in the woods all the time when I was a kid. I might be slower nowadays, but I'm not crippled!"

I could feel Almquist's indignation directed at me. "Black Fir Road ain't got a lot of traffic on it most of the day. I just kept to the shoulder. The one or two times a car was coming I'd slip into the forest. You may not know this, but a section of the road loops around a marsh. Well, there's a path through that marsh you can walk across. A shortcut. I took it. Yeah, it took me a couple hours to get home, but it was better'n being shot by Ivar or hauled off by the police."

The hill grew steeper. We'd be at the crest in a minute. Is this where I'd meet my end? My throat went dry as I tried to find my voice. "So why did you kill Forrest Hansen?"

"The damned fool found me when I was at Ivar's place. I was trying to find that letter from the health department when he drove up. I had to shoot him."

The toe of my boot struck a fat tree root, nearly tripping me. A high step. Too high for Almquist's hip to take easily, I was willing to bet. If I was going to make any kind of move to escape it had to be here. I was running out of hill. Plenty of tree cover loomed in every direction. The trick was getting behind something before my butt got riddled with lead.

This abrupt step would be it, I knew. My launch point. Almquist was six steps behind me. I wet my lips and tried to calm the riot inside my belly, which wanted to stop the madwoman from acting on her insanity. Almquist's breath was labored as he trod up the slope.

He stepped and wheezed. Stepped and wheezed. Then an extended grunt as his hip joint labored to hoist his beefy leg up just a tad higher. For a split second, his attention wasn't on me but on his hip and the ground. The tip of the rifle barrel lowered several inches.

Now!

Almquist was in mid-step when I launched myself to the right in a frantic swan dive. I landed with a heavy thud, nearly knocking the wind from my lungs. I rolled down the slope toward the base of a white pine. Its needled skirt screened me just as two explosive rifle bursts ripped the air. Splinters of wood and pine needles showered my head. I worked my legs under me, sprang up, and ran like hell for ten more feet before I dove for the ground and landed hard on my abdomen.

I hardly felt my injured shoulder, adrenalin being the perfect pain killer. More shots shadowed me. A clot of dirt flew up and bounced off my thigh.

Shit! Too close!

# CHAPTER 27

Another shot zinged near my head and I was out of there! I slipped my arm from its sling and crawled, painfully, across the ground combat Marine–style. I slithered into a nearby group of young maples for cover. My pulse pounded so loudly and feverishly in my ears I was half convinced I'd die of heart failure before a bullet ever found me.

I scanned the darkness, expecting peril. There was nothing. Almquist hadn't followed me. But he was out there, close by, waiting with the patience of a deer hunter for me to make a move so he could draw a bead. For that reason, I couldn't afford to be reckless. Only thirty or forty paces separated me from my killer. In daylight that would be nothing. Yet in the gloom of twilight, shapes and shadows converged into a jumble of uncertainty. Trees and shrubs were my allies, the darkness my savior.

With my chin buried in the wild grass, I lay motionless, feeling the cool earth press against my skin. The smell of pine strong. I flattened myself into a shapeless form in the darkness.

Or so I prayed.

Almquist swore. And not far away, though I couldn't see him clearly. From the hesitation in his steps, I knew he'd lost me. He moved tentatively in my direction then paused. Turning. Listening. I was terrified he could hear my rapid breathing. I pressed my face against the ground and forced myself to take shallow, quiet breaths.

After a time of hearing nothing, I lifted my head, fearful Almquist might be sneaking up on me. I had to look.

There was nothing.

No movement. No sound. Nothing apart from a distant cricket rubbing its legs together. I dared to rise up on all fours, staying alert, and edged backward soundlessly. Since I hadn't yet been riddled with bullets, I decided to get into a low crouch. I turned around and picked my way between the trees and brush, hoping to put distance between me and Almquist.

I stopped by a sturdy oak for shelter, sliding behind it. I braced my back against its wide trunk for concealment. I peered around, all senses primed, absorbing every moment, soaking in every sound. No Almquist. I wanted to take off like a wild hare, but I knew he was waiting for me to do just that.

No, I needed a plan.

Then an idea.

I wiggled out the cell phone from my pocket, hoping it would work in this isolated place, perhaps miles from any relay tower. I flipped open the clamshell and—

Oh shit!

A bright blue glow exploded into the night sky like a search light screaming: Here she is! I snapped shut the case and gulped in an anxious breath at the sound of footsteps. They hesitated. He must've seen the glow in the trees and now knew my general location.

I finally exhaled the breath I'd been hoarding, my fingers clenched so tightly on the cell phone I could feel my pulse. Lips dry as a mummy's wrapping pressed together as I weighed my options. The cell was my only link to the outside world. If I could get through to Gina or the Wolf Lake police, I might stand a chance. Slipping off my jacket, I pulled it over my head as a makeshift tent. Curled up like an armadillo, I'd use my body and jacket to dampen the light. I cracked open the phone and pressed it against my chest to smother any errant shine. I cupped both hands around the phone and brought it to my face.

The display said: No Signal.

No signal!

Arrrrgh! I jammed shut the case and smacked my fist against the ground. I promised myself if I got out of this mess I'd switch phone plans! Wolf Lake, Minnesota, was not the end of the earth. Other people's cell phones got signals. I couldn't blame a few million acres of boreal forest. Nor did it really matter. Whatever the reason, I was screwed.

Big time.

Crunch.

The sound clutched at my heart. Almquist was moving again. Then stopped. I peered into the trees.

Five seconds . . .

Ten.

Movement again twelve yards out. Right toward me.

Damn. The light had given me away. Useless piece of junk! I wanted to chuck the stupid cell phone away—

A new plan came to me, but I had to act quickly because Almquist was zeroing in on my location. The same luminance that betrayed me, I realized, might save me. A quick appraisal of his cautious, lumbering gait told me where he was. With my back pressed against the rugged oak bark, I got my legs under me and steeled my nerves. Quivering fingers flipped open the cell phone and I tossed it as far away from me as I could.

Then ran like hell in the opposite direction.

*Blam! Blam! Blam!*

The shots ripped the air. Raw fear lit a fire inside me and I ran for all I was worth, regardless of the consequences. I was gone! This was my last chance to break away, so I bolted full out like the frightened hare I was. Tree branches snagged my shirt and spruce needles scratched my face. I didn't care. I ran. I ran down the slope of the hill and to the side, weaving between shrubs and trees, using landscape as a screen. The light from my cell phone would go out in ten seconds. Long before then Almquist would know what I'd done. My legs drove for a full minute before I came to rest against the trunk of a white birch, holding the papyrus-like bark between my sweaty palms as I sucked in air.

My ears strained for the sounds of pursuit, hearing nothing but my own labored breaths.

I'd lost him!

Now to get back to Jeff. Which wasn't so easy, for the sameness of the wooded nightscape offered no quick landmarks. I jogged, desperate for a guidepost that would take me back to him. Whether or not I'd be in time to help Jeff was too horrible a thought to consider.

I stopped several times to get my bearings, frustrated by my lack of progress. Time was running out. Dark as it was, full darkness had yet to descend. If I wasn't careful, I could wander miles into the heart of the forest or worse, right into the arms of a killer.

A critter scampered in the brush near me. I wheeled around to make sure it wasn't a bear or Lyle Almquist. My eyes drifted up. A few stars winked in the indigo sky by a sliver of moon too small to cast much light.

My hand rubbed my shoulder, which I'd banged up with that first dive to the ground. Till now I'd been too pumped up to notice it. Now it complained.

I glanced around for a marker with no luck. Then inspiration. The moon! When I was being marched up the slope earlier, I'd seen the same moon rising in front of me. It was now behind me.

I turned about, keeping the shining crescent on my left as I navigated to a hard-packed trail. Parts of it looked familiar. The sight of exposed tree roots by earthen steps made my pulse race ahead. I'd walked up this way before, which meant the steps led back to Jeff. With a prayer to all gods everywhere, I turned my back to the moon and hurried down the path.

The moon kept me in the right direction. I ran quickly but not at full speed. Tripping and breaking an ankle wouldn't help Jeff any. Soon the path leveled out and I came upon a dark wound in the forest floor. The sinkhole!

A sudden dread brought me up short within a few yards of the edge. "Jeff?" I called tentatively. I was afraid at what I'd find.

There was no reply.

"Jeff?" I tried again, this time louder. I angled closer to the hole, willing myself forward in spite of the horror I might find waiting.

Still no answer.

A scuffling noise rose up from the depths of the pit, animalistic, like claws clicking against stone, bringing despair.

"Jeff, are you there?"

No, he wasn't.

I fought the urge to sink to my knees and wail. The wolf had gotten him. I didn't dare see what remained. But I had to! What if he wasn't dead? What if he was badly hurt and needed help? That shred of hope trumped my misgivings and propelled my legs to the sink hole.

Just as I moved, the rasp of metal against metal registered in my awareness. A rifle bolt! I twisted my body and dove for the ground as a gunshot detonated. A clump of dirt spewed into my face. I barely noticed. I'd landed on my bum arm and felt a thousand stinging needles explode in my shoulder. Writhing, I rolled onto my back and cradled my elbow.

Heavy footsteps tramped louder. I mustered enough strength

to sit up just in time to see a heavily breathing Lyle Almquist level the muzzle of his rifle at my chest. His bearded face contorted with rage. "Don't move! I got you covered." He huffed out several breaths. "Enough of this running-around shit. I'm just gonna have to kill you here."

I worked through the pain, speaking through breathy gasps. "Kill me here and it won't look like an accident."

"Don't matter. No one will ever find your body. So who'll know? Just means a little more work for me. Done that before."

He brought up the rifle, not even bothering to aim, we were so close.

"No, Lyle!"

His eyes narrowed.

*"Kia Kaha E!"*

The shriek erupted from the forest and startled us both. We turned as a bat—or other swooping night creature—flew out of the darkness and smacked Almquist in the head. He cried out, a hand springing to his temple. The rifle lowered.

As I cringed back instinctively, a voice screamed inside my head telling me to get a move on! Without a thought, I flung myself at Almquist's legs, cutting him down below the knees. He tumbled hard to the ground inches away from my face. I scrambled to a sitting position while the big man surged to his legs. Before he could do anything, I rolled over and swung out my leg, kicking his knee out from under him. He grunted and crashed forward. Without missing a beat, I jumped over and dug my knee into his back and put him into a ferocious head-lock. I pulled back with every bit of strength left in me, hoping I had enough to get the job done. Having a brother on the wrestling team can sometimes work in a girl's favor. Not to mention lessons learned from jumping on the backs of a few ferocious crocodiles, thanks to Jeff's relocation methods.

I held on for dear life. I swear I was going to kill him. Him or me. Those were my choices. I didn't think I had the strength or leverage on him to do it. But if the big man managed to roll on top of me, I was doomed.

I tightened the choke hold before my battered muscles gave out.

"Now there's a wife a bloke can be proud of!" mused an approaching voice. "Better ease off a bit, luv. His lips are turning blue, though it's hard to tell in the dark."

*Jeff!*

I couldn't believe my eyes! I wanted to spring into his arms but had my hands full. Fortunately, Jeff had come prepared. "Try these."

Bungee cords from the Jeep landed near me. Together Jeff and I bound Almquist's arms behind his back and secured his legs. Panting from exhaustion, I struggled to get back up on my feet.

I stared at Jeff. "I thought you were—" I rushed to him, burying my face into his chest as his powerful arms crushed me to him.

"My shoulder," I winced painfully.

He backed off.

"No . . ." I protested in a small voice. My shoulder could deal with a little more pain. My soul, however, couldn't do without his embrace. Jeff drew me in closer, gingerly, as though I were made of papier-mâché. The torment and joy of the last thirty minutes flooded from my depths and I began to cry. The wetness on my cheeks stained Jeff's shirt.

"Snake?"

He lifted my chin. His eyes locked onto mine. They pierced through me with an overwhelming sense of relief. And something else, an anguish I'd never seen in them before.

"I thought I'd lost you." He barely got the words out.

I raised my head and kissed him with everything I had. Only

after that tender moment, when I came up for air, did I fully notice his appearance. Jeff was a total mess. His face, arms and bare legs were streaked with dirt. His clothes filthy. Dried blood caked dirt-stained hands.

"Cripes! What happened to you?" I blinked.

"It wasn't easy getting out of that sink hole."

"That's right! How—?" was all I could manage, distressed at the filthy, bloody state of his fingers.

"Wait a tick, sweetheart." He was gazing behind me. "We've got company."

My heart jumped. The rest of me tensed for action.

"No—it's all right. These should be mates."

Jeff pointed in the distance where all things merged into shapeless black. Splinters of light flickered between the trees. Flashlights.

Jeff bent down to check out our prisoner, who struggled to get free of his bonds. "I wouldn't bother, mate. We've tied down meaner critters than you. You won't be getting loose. Ah! Here it is." Jeff, who'd been searching the ground, now stood holding his prize, a heavy duty flashlight.

I laughed. "Was that what you threw? Heck, I thought it was a rabid bat lunging at us."

"No. Just me torch. Only thing I had to throw."

"Ah, all that time spent tossing boomerangs in your youth finally paid off."

His brow furrowed. "What d'you mean? I've only thrown a boomerang three times in me entire life."

"Sounds better my way. How am I supposed to create a larger than life legend about Jeff Jones, the Crocodile Wrangler, if you don't let me embellish the stories a little?"

He shrugged with a dismissive laugh while adjusting the aluminum alloy tube. The flashlight hadn't appreciated being thrown and didn't want to work. However, after a turn of the tail cap, a harsh white beam flooded the night sky like the Bat Signal.

"There we go." Jeff waved the light toward our rescue party. "Oy! Over here!"

Minutes later, three human shapes formed out of the darkness: first came Gina Brown's petite frame, which was followed by Peter Bunyan, who was flanked by Officer Lomax from the Wolf Lake police. The two men carried firearms in addition to their flashlights.

Gina raced over and threw her arms around me. "Thank God you guys are alive!"

Her relief was almost palpable, grinning at Peter and Lomax. When she saw the state of Jeff's appearance, her eyes got big. "Holy freakin' shit, Jeff! You look like you just crawled out of a grave."

"I nearly did."

The somberness of his tone gave her pause. She went over and wrapped her arms around him.

Peter, moving a bit stiffly from his injuries, inspected our prisoner. "Seems you did all right on your own. Guess you didn't really need us."

"Oh," I countered, "we're damned happy you're here."

Officer Lomax took hold of Almquist. "Quit squirming. Even if you got loose, Lyle, where d'you think you're gonna get to? With that hip of yours, you'll never outrun me. So give up peacefully and make it easy on both of us."

Almquist spewed out obscenities while Lomax worked loose the bungee cords and snapped on a shiny pair of handcuffs. Peter helped the heavyset man to his feet, unable to contain his disgust. "I hope they throw the book at you, Lyle. The killing. The chemicals. All the damaged you've caused just to save a few bucks. I could've helped you find a proper facility for your chemicals."

All that got him from the tanner was a disinterested sneer.

I was burning to know one thing.

"How'd you know where to find us?" I looked from Peter to Gina.

"Thank Jeff," Peter acknowledged. "He phoned Gina for help."

"Your phone worked?" I eyed Jeff with mixed amazement and annoyance. "Guess I'm switching over to your plan."

Peter went on. "Jeff told Gina where he was and to bring help. I was in the middle of dinner when she called and said you two were in trouble. I thought she was freaking out." The conservation officer suppressed a smile. "She blurted out the whole story about Jeff trapped in a pit with a starving wolf and you being led off by gunpoint by Lyle Almquist in, like, four seconds. I had to get her to slow down."

Gina removed her jacket and slipped it over my shoulders. "Yeah, I had the GPS coordinates. I knew where you guys were in general. Finding your Jeep was easy. Finding you wasn't."

"That's for sure." Peter agreed. "But Jeff, I'm really curious. How did you get out of that sink hole without getting ripped to shreds?"

"Later, mate. Something's more important. I need you to take a gander at this." Jeff led us to the open pit. "Careful you don't get too close to the edge." He trained the Maglite beam into the blackness below where it lit up a gray wolf. Underfed, fur bristling, with flattened ears and tail straight out, his lips curled back into a snarl, watching us with intensely distrustful yellow eyes.

"Rufus?" I blurted, hopeful we'd found our wayward lupine. How else could Jeff have escaped those crushing jaws in one piece unless the creature had been hand raised by humans?

"I wish!" Gina sighed. "I think he's one of the junior members of the Red Iron pack. I've seen those facial markings.

God, he's thin. Bet he hasn't eaten in a couple weeks." She studied the face of this frightened wild creature and considered Jeff. "You were in there with this guy? Really? How the hell did you get out without getting eaten?"

"Time for that later. Let's get this poor blighter out first, shall we?" Jeff turned out his light and pulled away from the pit. The rest of us followed and rejoined Officer Lomax.

Peter Bunyan drew in a thoughtful breath. "That might have to wait till daylight. We can get some planks and lower them in. Meantime, we can feed him. Gina, don't you have some leftover road-kill beaver at the institute?"

"Sure do! And ten pounds of venison. I'll fetch those and come back. Give him a hearty meal before we return in the morning."

If only he'd been Rufus. I tried not showing my disappointment. Jeff reached for my hand. I clung to his dirty, calloused fingers, finding comfort in the touch of his skin. Tangible proof he was still part of my world.

## CHAPTER 28

"I hope you brought good news," Signe greeted affably, as Gina stepped on to the well-worn floorboards of Last Chance Outfitters.

"Depends. On what subject?"

"Why, your wild wolf from last night!" the other teased, hands on hips. "The one at the bottom of that sink hole."

"Oh, him."

"That is where you've been this morning, isn't it? Well, did you get him out?"

"All's good. He snarfed up all the food I left last night. This morning Peter and I sedated him, got him out of the sink hole, attached a radio collar and waited for him to come to and trot off into the forest. I just got back." A fact affirmed by the dirt smudges on her jeans and jacket. "I wanted to make sure I got back in time to say goodbye to Snake and Jeff—Oh, hey boy!"

Gina knelt to pet the border collie, which had padded out to greet her. She got a face full of dog slobber.

"Down, Oskar," Signe commanded.

"Are you taking care of Ivar's dog?"

"No, Gina. He's my dog now."

"Way cool, Signe. I'm glad he found a good home." Gina stroked the collie's head.

"He'll still get to the farm to take care of the sheep. That's his job, and you can't keep a dog like that cooped up. He needs to run and work. Though I think from now on he'll be sort of semi-retired."

"Tell that to Oskar!" I chortled, falling back into my chair as he jogged over, having seen me stand. I was unable to deter the sheepdog's attempt to corral me into his impromptu flock. Half an hour earlier, when there'd been four customers in the store, Oskar managed to nudge and bump them into a neat little group near Gus and Mooney's table at the coffee bar. Only Signe's ministrations had convinced the border collie to reluctantly give up her clientele. Now he was at it again, trying to add Gina to his flock. Oskar sat nearby, relaxed and contented, his eyes flicking toward Gina every so often. I suspected he wouldn't be happy until he had us all in one tidy bundle, which he could watch over.

"Good dog." Gina scratched under his chin, after which she joined us at the tight cluster of tables. Oskar barked approvingly. She pulled up a chair, gave Gus and Mooney a flirtatious wink, then flipped her auburn hair behind her back. With her elbows resting on the small table, she peered expectantly into Jeff's face. "I'm waiting. You promised me you'd tell me this morning how you got out of that sink hole."

When Jeff and I had emerged from the forest, all we wanted to do was take a shower and crash for the night. I also had to let Cricket know we'd be home later than planned. We owed her big time for sticking around our place an extra day. More so after explaining why. She freaked out when I explained we'd almost been murdered. I swore my sister to secrecy. Mother was to be kept in the dark about certain events during the past week; the woman disliked what I did as it was, and I sure didn't want to give her any more fodder.

By morning, my shoulder grumpy at being slammed against the ground, Jeff and I opted for a hearty and relaxing breakfast at the Northern Grounds Café rather than help Gina and Peter extricate the wolf. For once, I was happy to stay out of it and let the wolf biologist and the conservation officer do their jobs.

"Well, Jeff, I'm listening," Gina wheedled, signaling to Dimitry for a coffee.

Jeff inched forward in his chair and sat up. His expressive blue eyes took in each and every person in our little conclave before he began. "After I fell into that sink hole I thought I was a goner. That wolf arched its back, snarled and growled like he'd had quite enough of me. When he lowered his head and glared at me, I thought for sure he was going to pounce." Jeff exhaled sharply. "I can read a croc's body language like a book. But I don't know wolves as well. I could see he was as afraid of me as I was of him. The difference being I knew I wasn't going to hurt him. I didn't know if he felt the same way. The space was so small. I kept waiting for the attack."

"Oh my!" Signe blurted as she set down a water dish for Oskar. "That sounds frightening."

"It was!"

Jeff could not talk without using his hands. Or his entire body. He put his arms out in front of him in a warding-off posture. "I backed as far away from that blighter as possible. Which wasn't far. Perhaps three yards. I couldn't tell which of us was more scared. But it was important for him to understand I meant no harm."

Mooney's wizened face looked back with confusion. "The wolf never attacked you?"

"Had two things in my favor, mate. I knew wolves don't see people as food. They're afraid of humans and don't want anything to do with us—unless they've been raised by people. And I read that a wolf will accept a human being as a pack leader."

Mooney was spellbound. "What's the other thing?"

Jeff smiled confidently. "That I've dealt with cornered, frightened animals for most of my life. I continuously spoke to him in a soothing, quiet voice. Tried not to make any movements he'd find threatening. First I needed to calm him."

Skepticism creased the lines in Gus's face. "How d'you calm a wolf?"

"I sang to him."

Signe clapped her hands with delight. "Oh, I wish I could've seen that! What did you sing?"

"An Australian lullaby. I sang for a minute or so, then slowly got to my feet and started to feel the walls of the pit." Jeff acted out each minute of his ordeal as if he were reliving it. I might have been the person who'd been marched away at gunpoint to my demise, but he was the man with the more thrilling story. "Every so often I peeked over my shoulder to see what he was up to. I slowly moved along the walls, singing, stopping once in a while to tell him he was a good old wolf and I wasn't going to harm him."

"How did he react?" Gina wondered with professional interest.

"Anxious. After a while, I could see his body language change. He still didn't trust me, but he calmed down. He didn't snarl anymore. Just growled. And me yabbering like he's me best mate in the whole blessed world. I'd turned my back on him again to search the wall."

Gina shook her head. "It sounds so . . . wrong."

"It was a risk. Turning my back showed him I wasn't a threat. I also didn't have time to spare. I was desperate to get out. Worried sick about Snake." He reached out and took my hand. My fingers squeezed back.

"I don't believe it." Gus protested, eyebrows bristling. "That varmint should've ripped you to shreds."

"It's a myth wolves are bloodthirsty killers," Gina came back, primed to defend her animals. "They've had bad press since Biblical times. All unfair, I'll have you know. In fact, Jeff, what you're describing has happened before."

Jeff was intrigued. "Oh?"

"Absolutely. A year ago I was reading a history on the wolf in North America. In Colonial times wolves were abundant. Too abundant for the settlers. According to one story, these two farmers dug a trap in hopes of catching and killing some wolves. One morning they visit their big hole in the ground and, to their surprise, discover they've caught two things. At one end of the trap was a wolf. At the other end a local Native American! They'd both fallen into the pit the night before and had sat there the whole time, terrified of each other. And yet, the wolf never attacked the Indian."

"For real?" Gus asked. "That really happened?"

"Well, it was recorded in someone's diary, for what it's worth. And I've read about incidents like this elsewhere, in which humans and wolves encounter each other unexpectedly in the woods. In every case the wolf turns and runs off, unless there are extenuating circumstances."

Delighted, Jeff clapped his hands. "Wished I'd known that! I would've felt a whole lot more confident at the bottom of that hole." He slid his chair back a few feet away into the open floor, pantomiming his next actions. "I'm patting the earth hoping to find a section solid enough to climb. The wall crumbles every time I dig into it. Finally, I find a firm section. Solid. So I dig. And dig. Using me fingers with mixed results. Then—blimey!—I remember I have me mobile. I whip it out and call Gina. I tell her where we are, what's happened, and to bring help."

Jeff set his battered cell phone on the table.

Mooney's gazed narrowed. "I hope your warranty isn't up on that thing. I'm surprised it even worked."

"It didn't look this way when I called. That came later." Jeff shifted his weight, slicing the air with a broad gesture. "The call to Gina was always a backup plan, to let her know about Almquist and what he'd done. I knew it would take time to get to us. Snake didn't have that time. So I dug. I used my hands and the nubby antenna on me mobile phone to cut out hand holds."

Signe, her hands to her face, chuckled. "And what did the wolf think of all this?"

Jeff shrugged. "I think he was curious what this human was up to. He stopped growling completely. I was still telling him I'd get him out. Only eight feet up, I reckoned. I could do it. I told him that, too." Jeff's chin tilted up, as did his eyes, seeing the earthen wall again in his mind. "Ten times I climbed. And ten times I fell on my arse. After each attempt I'd refine the hand holds, nearly ripping the skin off me fingers until I figured out to use my pocket comb. What saved me were the roots."

"Roots?" Signe repeated.

"As I got near the top I found tree roots. Some thick as a wallaby's tail! I brushed them off and pulled myself up the last few feet to the top. Getting over the edge was the tough part."

The others gaped at him in various stages of disbelief. I whispered a prayer of thanks that the teenaged Jeff Jones had spent summers scrambling over the basalt cliffs at Toowoomba. I still shudder whenever he tells me of his bare-handed climb on Point Perpendicular near Sydney, dangling over the raging waters of Jervis Bay.

Gina leaned against her chair back with a wide grin. "Jeff, you are good."

"And lucky." He scooched his chair back to the table, never removing his gaze from me. "Once I made it topside, I saw it wouldn't be easy finding Snake. It was too dark and I was too tired to find the trail. So I ran back to the Jeep, got the torch, the bungee cords, and the night vision binoculars."

"We keep them in the glove box," I interjected, "in case we want to watch deer or other wildlife at night."

"Yes, those night vision glasses came in handy. With them I

could see heat signatures in the dark. I got back to the sink hole and went off in the direction where I'd heard Snake and Almquist go earlier. At first the only things I saw were small mammals. Then a moving ghostly outline: Almquist. I followed. And the rest you know."

In the silence to follow, Mooney elbowed Gus in the arm. "This is better than TV!"

The other nodded vigorously.

Jeff sat back and scratched a blond eyebrow. While the others barraged him with more questions, I took the opportunity to pull Signe aside.

"You knew it was Lyle Almquist who was polluting the Bjorklund's well water," I said, my voice low, trying to keep the accusation out of my voice. "You lied to me when I asked you about it."

Signe's eyes were startled. "I did no such thing."

I was disappointed in her. Disappointed that she was still lying when I had caught her red-handed. "Mooney and Gus told me Mr. Bjorklund had been in here a couple of weeks ago. He was angry. He said he was going to make Almquist pay. What was that about if not the well water?"

She was silent, bent over the counter, avoiding my eyes. I waited for her to gather her thoughts. When she spoke, there was no apology in her voice. "I'm not one to toss around accusations, Snake. Ivar had no proof. I was afraid someone had put a bug in his ear about Lyle." She raised her eyes to mine. "The Lyle I knew was a good man, an artist. He was no different than Ivar, just an old man trying to get by. I wasn't about to make his life any harder than it already was."

"He could have come after you, too, if he had known you knew about his polluting Bjorklund's water," I pointed out to her.

"If he did, I would have been ready for him. I keep a gun

under the counter and a rifle in the storage closet. No one is sneaking up on me, I assure you."

"If you had told someone, you might have saved Jeff and me a harrowing evening with the man."

Dimitry took the opportunity to duck past us to the coffee bar and brew up a mocha latte for Gina, forcing me to give up my conversation with Signe as Gina meandered over.

"Snake," Gina said, "I still don't understand one or two things. Like the v-gouge I found." She slurped up the whipped cream, swiping her upper lip with her tongue to remove the foamy mustache.

"That was Almquist's gouge." I replied with a blasé flip of my hand, still keeping an uncertain eye on Signe. "He must've had it in his pocket when he shot Mr. Bjorklund. During the squabble, his pocket probably ripped. The man was a really messy person. His pickup truck was a mess. His workshop not much better."

Gina frowned. "Yeah, but Peter said it was a woodworker's tool."

"It's also used by leather crafters for fine detail work, like the kind of thing done on fine leather jackets." The front window offered no illustration. The expertly crafted leather jackets of Lyle Almquist were gone. They'd been removed, as had the finely tooled mouse pads usually up front on the well-worn pine counter.

"Really? When d'you figure this out?"

"Like ten minutes ago."

"I told her," Mooney clarified, smiling like the cat that ate the canary. "Heck, I coulda told the police what that v-gouge was for in the first place. 'Cept nobody asked!"

"Mooney, I'm impressed," Gina said in a suggestive manner that warmed the old man's heart. "How do you know about this stuff?"

Mooney cleared his throat. "Who do you think taught Lyle Almquist how to work with leather? He was an iron ore miner for most of his life. I'm the guy who taught him the craft. Heck, that was more'n eighteen years ago."

"You betcha." Gus leaned in. "Ol' Moonface used to have an outfitter and craft store right here on this very spot before Signe bought the place. Why d'you think we hang out here?"

"Ah." Gina sat back, enlightened. Then turned to me. "What about the rifle? Didn't the police say Lyle's rifle wasn't the murder weapon? And it wasn't used to kill the wolves. What gives?"

"Easy enough to explain. Almquist had two rifles. When Chief Manske asked to see his rifle, Almquist dug out the other one. There wasn't a search warrant. It was a simple request. Officer Lomax told us that this morning when Jeff and I were at the station giving our statements."

Gina's mouth formed a perfect O.

It's not every day I can completely silence Gina Brown. I reached down and patted Oskar on his head, redirecting my smile toward him. "Lomax said they found a bolt cutter behind the seat in Almquist's pickup. He's fairly sure they can prove it was used to cut the fence at the wolf institute."

"But why?"

"To rattle you. You and Debbie. The MWI was collecting and processing radio collar data from the DNR and USGS. Eventually someone would go out to check on the Red Iron wolves. Almquist was afraid they'd find his toxic dump." I pressed my palms together and gestured for emphasis. "I think he panicked after he killed Mr. Bjorklund. That's why he lured us out of town to shoot the three of us—right after we'd visited his workshop. I wonder if he overheard me talking to the chief and Peter about doing a DNA analysis on the fur in the back of his pickup. If he did, he figured he had to do something to stop us."

No one spoke. Even the espresso machine was quiet.

Then Gus angled his head toward me. "So all the killings had nothing to do with crazy environmentalists or revved-up wolf haters or wolf lovers. It was all about a guy trying to cover up a secret."

Gina was taken aback. "Wow, Gus . . . I hadn't thought of it like that."

Signe bowed her head. Several white strands of her tumbleweed hair dangled before her face. When she looked up, it was with a pained expression. "Ivar's funeral is tomorrow."

I put my hand over hers, a conciliatory gesture. I couldn't blame her for not being a gossip. Under other circumstances, I would have applauded her for her silence. "That's gotta be tough. You knew him almost your entire life."

"Yeah," was all she managed to say. She seemed to have aged ten years since the death of the old Swede.

"You'll be there to tell the good stories about him."

"I will. I wish you could come." Her steady gaze met mine.

"Me, too. But we're overdue as it is. The zoo staff have filled in for our shifts this past week. We couldn't ask them to do it another day."

She nodded with mixed sadness and understanding. Lyle Almquist had been a friend of hers as well. His arrest and the realization of his crimes must have added weight to her already sizable burden.

It was a disappointing way to leave Signe and the others. But I'd reached a dead end in search of something more positive.

That's when Gina's cell phone chirped like a chickadee. She stared down at the screen. "It's the wolf institute. Hang on." She stood up and walked away a few paces. "What? Holy crap! Okay, I'll be right over."

She put away her phone and actually did a little dance in front of us. "That was Debbie. Guess who just showed up at the back fence?"

"Rufus?" I dared to guess.

"Yes!" Gina let out a loud whoop that set Oskar to barking. "I guess our wanderer finally got tired of the free world. He missed his family and the free meals."

"Is he okay?"

"Debbie says he may have had an encounter with some other critter. He's got scratches on his muzzle. Otherwise he's his usual handsome self."

The news even brought a smile to Signe.

"Jeff." I wheeled around with puppy eyes. "Can we spare thirty minutes to see Rufus?"

"I don't see why not. I've been dying to meet this bloke everyone's been talking about."

I reached over and kissed him. "Oh shit!" I jammed my eyes shut. "We don't have a camera. Billie's gonna kill me when she finds out."

# ABOUT THE AUTHORS

An animal lover since she could walk, **Marilyn Victor** was a volunteer at the Minnesota Zoo for many years and fosters small pets for a local animal rescue group. At the moment she shares her home with an overindulged bichon frise. She enjoys reading all elements of the mystery genre and is the current president of the Twin Cities chapter of Sisters in Crime.

**Michael Allan Mallory** works with computers in the information technology field, which allows him to support his cats in the lavish lifestyle to which they have grown accustomed. An avid animal lover, he is interested in the welfare of wildlife and the conservation of nature. Michael is a member of Mystery Writers of America and the American Association of Zoo Keepers.